Unmasking

A Journey of Awakening

PHILIP PERRY PhD

FriesenPress

One Printers Way
Altona, MB R0G0B0,
Canada

www.friesenpress.com

Copyright © 2022 by Philip Perry Phd
First Edition — 2022

All rights reserved.

ISBN
978-1-03-912163-8 (Hardcover)
978-1-03-912162-1 (Paperback)
978-1-03-912164-5 (eBook)

1. FICTION, PSYCHOLOGICAL

Distributed to the trade by The Ingram Book Company

Table of Contents

Dedication

Awakening can be an amazing continuous journey for those who chose to make it so. This book is dedicated to those who seek to uncover their own wisdom as their journey in living unfolds.

Chapter One

❖❖ Confused Beginnings ❖❖

S URROUNDED BY THREE BULLIES in the school play yard, Mason Walkway was shoved and pushed to the ground, then kicked repeatedly in the body and head. All he could hear them say while laughing at him was, "you're nothing but a stupid dirty Indian."

With bruised ribs and a bloodied nose, Mason got up from the ground, brushed off the dirt, and slowly walked home with his head down and tears streaming from his eyes. Over and over again his thoughts were fixed on *Why did they call me a stupid Indian? What was dirty about me? What did I do wrong?*

At nine years of age, Mason felt he was different from other kids. Most of his classmates seemed to be happier, and

1

they easily engaged with one another in playful ways. They wore more colourful clothing than he did, and they often bragged about their possessions. All his clothing seemed too big for him and, not having much clothing to choose from, he often wore the same thing for several days in a row. Mason preferred to watch other kids play at school, choosing to get involved only when he felt he could blend into the background.

Being the youngest in his grade five class, since his birthday was in December, he was smaller than almost all his other classmates, with the exception of a few girls. Wearing his baggy clothing made him feel insecure and unaccepted, yet something inside him told him there was more to him than his clothing.

Arriving home, his mother, shocked at seeing him bloodied, blurted out, "What happened to you?"

Mason was without words. His trembling mother tried to console him, hugging him and crying at the same time. Mason went limp as he stared into the wall in front of him.

Mason sensed she was doing her best, yet he felt that she was somehow more of a victim than he was, given the many times he had seen her battered about by his father. He felt the urge to hug her back, but he remained motionless. Etched in his memory, he recalled his mother saying, "Bad things happen to good people. You are just unlucky."

Deeply confused, but coming out of his stupor, he asked, "Is something wrong with me? Why was I called a 'stupid Indian'?"

She remained speechless, dropped her head, and slumped in her chair. A voice in his head told him that she was not going to give him any answers, so he trudged off to the washroom to wash the blood off his face.

At first, he found himself gazing in the cracked mirror, looking to see what might be "Indian" about him. His hair was black like the few other Indians at school, and his skin tone was light brown—not as dark as most Indians he had encountered, including his father's.

Continuing to look wide-eyed, staring at himself in the mirror, what he saw began to get hazy. The image faded in and out, almost as if he was a shadow. His face appeared to be empty of any energy. The meore he gazed, the more he seemed to fade away until he could not see himself. *Who am I?* He thought.

This reminded him of what his mother once said when he discovered his shadow. "Your shadow is a reflection. It is not you, yet it always is around. Hiding in your shadow can protect you from having to experience bad feelings."

He hadn't understood what she was saying to him, so he had just ignored it. Yet, something about having a shadow was comforting.

Shifting his focus to his hands, which clasped a facecloth, he slowly began to wash the blood off his face. Returning his gaze to the mirror, he saw the dried blood. In a curious way, he wondered if his blood was Indian blood—if there was such a thing. *What part of him, exactly, was Indian? Were Indians bad people?*

His thoughts began to wander as he reflected on the habit he had developed—a habit of speaking only when spoken to. This is what worked for him with his father.

Mason's father, also called Mason, didn't seem to care that his son was named after him. For the most part, Mason's father ignored him and always seemed to be unhappy that Mason was his son. Seldom did he speak directly to Mason, unless it had to do with doing chores that had been laid out for him. They never spoke about being Indian. His father always looked at him as if something was wrong about him, but he never spoke about it.

He recalled his most unsettling experience with his father, occurring when he had timidly come up alongside of his father while he was working on his truck engine and asked, "What are you doing?"

He remembered his father looking up with a scowl on his face and a stern voice saying, "Go play in your room." From that time forward, Mason steered clear of his father. It was easy for Mason to simply disappear, either by absenting himself when his father was around or by melting into the background, as if he was not really there. It seemed that his father also seldom noticed that he was there at all. Secretly, Mason would harbour the thought he did not really have a father.

The mirror did not give him any clues about how Indian he might be or the ways in which he was stupid. *What is stupid about me?* He thought. Schoolwork seemed not to be a problem. Oddly enough, when teachers would ask the class questions, he often would know most of the answers.

Some of his classmates would automatically turn to him for the answers, given that he usually knew what they were. His teachers seemed puzzled about him, and they allowed him to sit at the back of the room.

Was he being branded as stupid just because he was an Indian? He did not know. His thoughts told him that he was not stupid; there was more to him than people thought.

Getting called a "dirty Indian" did something inside to him that made him want to just hide out in his shadow. He did not want to return to school the next day but knew he had to please his mother's wishes that he remain in school. *Thankfully*, he thought, *the last day of school is almost here. Then I'll be free to spend time with the wind.*

His thoughts wandered as he continued to gaze into the mirror. He was curious about why kids became so attached to one another and their belongings. One minute they could be full of laughter, and the next they could be angry or sad, especially if they didn't get their way. He felt different from them. Sadness was uncommon for him, as he chose to maintain a distance from people when they got emotional, and he did not feel the need to possess anything.

Mason was reminded that he preferred to spend his time watching and listening to the world around him, while remaining at a distance from the action. He was awestruck at how birds flew and how the weather was constantly changing. He was also fascinated by sounds the wind made through the trees, and by how clouds would be constantly changing, coming and going, driven by the wind. He wondered where the wind came from and where it went when it stopped.

Crossing his mind were how taking long walk were comforting, especially on windy days. He recalled how he felt when the wind would swirl around him, and he would imagine that it was a blanket taking care of him. He felt protected by it. He would even imagine it to be a special friend—one that nobody else had.

It occurred to him how possessing anything was unimportant for him. He possessed only a handful of toys. Actually, not much was important to him including social activities or school events except the one time he remembered when his class visited the local airport. Once at the airport he remembered staring in awe as the airplanes took off and landed. Now he would from time to time imagine flying off to some faraway place just to get away from everything. Whenever he came across any books or magazines on airplanes, he would spend any spare time he had reading about airplanes and the history of flying. On his walks along the nearby river, he would try to find driftwood that he could carve into a model airplane.

He did not feel any interest in spending any time at home, as his mother was sick with polio and his father was unapproachable. When he was not in school, he was almost always by himself.

When his father was not around, Mason's mother would say that he was working in the logging industry as a tree faller. He did not know what a "faller" was. This was never explained to him. He knew his mother to be always soft-spoken and quite timid, with few friends. They had no relatives in BC, as far as he knew, and he was unaware of any relatives anywhere else. Mason wondered about his mother and father's relatives, and when he asked about them, his mother said that his father came from a family that lived on an Indian Reserve in Southern Alberta. But his father was not close to his family and never mentioned them.

He remembered his mother had told him that his father was born in 1930 on a Blackfoot Reserve that was about six hundred miles away. She also told him on several occasions that she was not native. She met his father while they were both attending the same school near the reserve, and they got married when she was seventeen years old. She mentioned that Mason was born shortly after they married, and they then relocated to BC as there was no work for his father in Alberta. Once in BC, his father got a job at a Vancouver Island logging camp, as logging was booming in the late sixties, and there were many jobs to be had.

On one occasion she spoke of a younger sister, Debbie, who was still living in Alberta in the town where they both grew up. Mason recalled asking his mother about her parents, and she hesitantly responded that both of them had died in an auto accident when she was eleven years old.

Then what crossed his mind was a vision of his father returning home from the logging camp drunk and getting very angry at his mother. He cringed memorably seeing his father throwing things around yelling at his mother and violently hitting her repeatedly with his hands yelling at her saying nasty things like how useless she was. His mother would just say nothing become very quiet and shrink in her wheel chair. *What made his father so mean? Was he in some way the reason for his father beating his mother? Was he also unwanted?* Confused all he could do was slink away to his room and cry.

He remembered from time to time, when his father was away at camp, his mother would ask Mason how he was doing in school. He recalled always finding something positive to say about school, even if it was untrue. He steered away from telling her anything that might worry her or make her get upset and cry. It hurt him to see her cry; he found it unbearable.

When she would ask him about his friends, he mentioned playing basketball at school, fishing off a bridge, or hiking with other kids in the neighbourhood, even though he did not like fishing and seldom played with anyone except when he had to as part of school activities.

It bothered him that he felt compelled to lie to his mother. She never questioned him for more information even though he sensed that she might silently know that he was lying by the way she looked at him with sad eyes.

Interrupting his thoughts and visions he became aware that the tension in his whole body was releasing and a strong urge to go lie down overcame him. His fixation on the mirror ended and he then slept for twelve hours. The next day arrived, his mother asleep and his father not there, he felt fearful about returning to school so he decided to discontinue going altogether. Fortunately there was only one week left before school was out for the summer. All alone and unsupervised what was next for him   he could not imagine.

The summer upon him, Mason spent most of his time building a fort in the woods nearby. He had come across a pile of broken wooden pallets that were left at the back-end construction yard bordering the woods. Approaching a construction worker in the yard one day, he asked about them and was told that they were his if he wanted them.

Mason hauled them into the woods and, over the summer, built a fort by scavenging whatever discarded materials he could find in his neighbourhood. He was able to acquire a small table, a couple of broken chairs, an old rug he used for a floor, and a torn tarp that he patched up with duct tape to use as a roof. He made a door out of a blanket and set up a small piece of plywood as a drawing board. When he wasn't drawing or playing in his fort during the summer, he would work on crossword puzzles that his mother had long abandoned.

Sometimes he would wander through the neighbourhood, people-watching, taking care to keep his distance and to blend into the background. He was curious why most people seemed to be worried about something. Often, he would stop at the local playground and watch the kids play. It never occurred to him to join in with them.

The summer having passed, Mason returned to school anxious about what he would experience given what happened near the end of the last school year. He was happy to find out that the bullies were no longer at his school, as they had been moved to a middle school. But while things got more stable at school, Mason's home life became bleaker.

His mother was having more difficulty getting around and now required a walker. She seldom left the house.

Chapter Two

❦ Abandoned ❦

ARRIVING HOME FROM SCHOOL a week before his tenth birthday, he discovered his mother sitting on the couch looking very sad but with no tears showing. She abruptly blurted out that his father had been killed in an accident at the logging camp. A falling tree had crushed him. This was Mason's first experience with death.

As best he could remember, it did not make him feel anything; no emotions surfaced. He really did not have any strong feelings for his father, as his father seldom spent any time with him. What stuck in Mason's mind, however, was how his father did not show any affection toward either him or his mother. He could not remember seeing him ever hug or kiss her or anything of the sort with him.

Without any income, Mason and his mother were forced to relocate to a one-bedroom, low-cost rental unit in the local town at a place known as "the projects." This subsidized welfare housing was set up in a square with four two-storey buildings and a playground area in the middle. In their complex, there were people from many different countries. Different languages were spoken, but most residents generally spoke English. Violence was common and occurred almost on a weekly basis. Drugs seemed to be everywhere. Youth gangs were also common. Mason did whatever he could to stay clear of the gangs.

Mason was given the bedroom, as his mother found it easier to sleep in the living room given her need to use a walker to get around the apartment. Mostly, she would remain in her recliner throughout the day and sleep in it as well due to her limited mobility. Mason was responsible for cooking and cleaning. A home care nurse would come by twice a week to attend to his mother's health care and basic needs.

With no source of income, they lived on welfare and very little else. Mason felt fortunate to be given a bike from Social Services, which allowed him the freedom to wander about the community. On one of his rides, he discovered the Salvation Army food bank and resorted to going there about once a week to obtain food. The Army also had a second-hand store for clothing, which he also frequented. Both the food and clothing were free.

He became a regular, and he quickly learned that the people at The Salvation Army were kind and very supportive toward him. They always asked how his mother was doing. He usually said that she was "okay," adding little else.

When he did on one occasion share that her health was getting worse, they asked for his home address; thereafter, a food hamper was dropped off once a week. On special holidays and birthdays, he would often receive gifts from the Army. These caring gestures were hard to respond to, and mostly he offered timid thanks. He wished that he could express his thankfulness in more meaningful ways, but it just didn't seem to be something he could do. Later, he would feel bad about being so withdrawn.

Mason watched very little television, as his mother was glued to it almost every waking moment. She seemed addicted to watching the game shows such as The Price is Right or the Wheel of Fortune. As well, she watched the Beachcombers or the MASH series over and over again.

While at home, he drifted around the apartment, and when he was not doing chores, he tried not to bother his mother. He spent most of his time in his small bedroom. He either played with a donated Salvation Army Lego set or, when he could, stared out his window and imagined that he was taking a journey to a far-off land where magical things happened. He would imagine that in this land, there was no talking, yet everything in this land was connected. Trees, plants, animals, and humans used sign language to communicate with one another. It was always peaceful and amazingly colourful.

Sometimes at night, he took to gazing at the stars and planets, especially the moon when visible. The stars were like his silent friends, as was the wind. Over time, he became more and more interested in the stars. They looked so quiet and peaceful. On the other hand, the power of the wind was unpredictable and magical at times, especially when he watched eagles soar and airplanes fly by.

When he showed up at the Salvation Army one week, he asked if they had any books on stars and planets. Frank, one of the volunteers, said they didn't, but the Salvation Army had an astronomy club that met every Thursday night, as long as the weather cooperated. Frank suggested that Mason come by next Thursday.

At the first meeting, Frank introduced Mason to the other club members and invited him to look through a telescope that had already been set up; it was focused on the planet Mars. Mason was spellbound by what he saw. Frank described the difference between planets and stars, and how there were more stars than people on earth. He took to naming some stars that were easier to see, and then he would draw a map of the night sky, showing how their positions remained the same, which was not so for planets that moved, like Earth and Mars.

This experience prompted Mason to come by the astronomy club whenever he could. After a month, Frank approached Mason and offered to loan him a book on star mapping, another on galaxies, and yet another on the Milky Way Galaxy.

Mason dove into these books, reading them over and over, cover to cover. Eventually, his thirst for knowing more took him to the school library, where he found more books on Astronomy. *Why have school friends,* he thought, *when the stars are always there for me and never bug me?*

This preoccupation was further enhanced by reading National Geographic Magazine editions that focused on the different galaxies, the solar system, and black holes. He hunted down every edition of the National Geographic that had anything to do with astronomy.

One day, while flipping through the magazines, Mason came across an article on dolphins. The amazing colours and variety of sea life under the ocean fascinated him, much like the pictures of galaxies did. This article mentioned how smart dolphins were and how they loved to play with one another. What really struck home were the pictures of dolphins swimming in unison and seemingly always smiling. In contrast, people seemed quite different when Mason watched them interact. People were always worried, angry, or sad about something going wrong; they were only happy once in a while.

The undersea universe was now drawing him in. Mason found himself dreaming of swimming with the dolphins and imagining that he was one of them. There was nothing interfering with his imagination. Life as he was experiencing it was slowly becoming more and more interesting. He took to drawing pictures of dolphins and sea creatures like sea urchins and starfish. At first, he did his best to copy what he saw in the magazines, but as he got more into it, he would draw them freely. He felt that he needed to learn how to swim, so he could see and feel the wonders of the ocean for himself.

Then, a few months after his uneventful eleventh birthday, on the last day of school before the Christmas holidays, he returned home to find his mother slumped over in a chair with the television on. At first, he thought she was sleeping, as this was often the case when he returned home from school.

Out of habit, he went off to his room so he wouldn't bother her. In his room, he noticed a note written on a piece of paper, which was unusual as it was not something he had left there. He picked it up and realized that it was a note from his mother. As he read the note, he suddenly felt a chill run through his body. The note read:

Dearest Mason,

It is time for me to move on from my world of pain. There is no point in continuing, as I am a burden on everyone. You have always been the best thing that has ever happened to me. Every day, it saddens me deeply that I cannot find the energy to be a good mother to you. There is something special about you that I cannot put into words. You have gifts that need to be appreciated, and I am sure the road ahead for you will show your specialness.

Saying goodbye to you breaks my heart. I only know that you will always be in my heart. Goodbye to you, my son. Stay safe and follow your dreams.

I have always loved you.

Mom

What does this mean? He felt an urge to go check on his mom. Approaching her slumped body, he noticed his father's old eagle feather clutched in her hands and several pill bottles open on the floor, which he did not see when he first entered the apartment.

His heart started to pound. He had the urge to run but froze on the spot. Something had gone terribly wrong. He thought of trying to wake her, but he was stuck, unable to move toward her. All he could remember next was falling to the carpet.

The next thing he knew, he was being shaken by the next-door neighbour, a black single parent named Margery. Startled, Mason realized that he was lying on the carpet with Margery kneeling beside him holding his hand. Margery, with tears in her eyes, was telling him that an ambulance and the police were on their way, and that he should stay where he was for now.

After a few moments, Mason felt the urge to get up. Realizing that he had likely fainted, he started to tremble again. Margery grabbed him by the arm, and in a soft but purposeful way, said, "Let's go for a walk."

They exited out the front door without looking back. Mason vaguely remembered walking with Margery around and around the tenement buildings for what seemed like a very long time. Not a word was spoken between them. Everything slowed down. His thoughts were scattered and seemed meaningless. All he seemed to be able to do was watch his shadow as he moved. His shadow seemed like the only friend he had.

He remembered hearing sirens, as he often did in the neighbourhood, but only vaguely. After several more passes around the building, a policeman approached them and asked if he could accompany them back to Mason's apartment.

Still dazed, Mason was asked by the policeman if this was his mother. Mason nodded and then heard the policeman say he was sorry about his mother dying. He went on to say that she must have been in a lot of pain, and that he was sure she had gone to a better place. The policeman then asked Margery if she could take him home to her apartment for a while until social services could be contacted.

What he remembered next was sitting at Margery's kitchen table staring at the light switch on the wall. Thoughts stopped coming, and even though he could hear Margery speaking to him, her words did not register. They were just sounds with no meaning. After a while, she left him to tend to her two daughters.

Margery returned to the kitchen table and in a soft voice encouraged Mason to come with her to the bedroom where her two daughters slept. She gave Mason a blanket and a pillow, pointed to a foamy carpet on the floor, and told him that it would be best if he slept in her house for the night.

Margery said that she was cooking a casserole, and he was welcome to come share it with her family. Mason followed her back into the kitchen and sat there, unable to eat, and just watched her two children eat and stare at him from time to time. When they were finished, they all went off to watch television while Mason continued to sit at the kitchen table, numb and speechless.

When it was time for the two girls to go to bed, Mason took the foamy, blanket, and pillow into the kitchen, placed them on the floor, and stared at the ceiling for what seemed like the entire night.

Many different thoughts crossed his mind during his sleepless night. Most of them didn't make any sense. At first, he was afraid to try and make sense of them for fear that he would break down and uncontrollably cry. His mother dying and his father having died the year before, now meant he had no parents. Now, he was totally alone.

She had died from taking too many pills. *Why did she do that?* Other questions occurred to him. *Why did she leave me without talking to me first? Why did she have an eagle feather in her hands? What did that mean?*

At first, it struck him that he was totally blinded to how bad her health was and how much suffering she had experienced. She had polio, he knew, and she needed a walker to get around, but why was he not paying any attention to how sick she was? She never, ever talked about her pain or how it interfered with her getting out and about.

I should have known how much she was suffering, he thought. *I seldom asked how she was feeling, and when I did, she would almost always say that she was doing okay. How blind could I be?*

Etched into his mind was how she was so kind-hearted and supportive of others. He never heard her say an unkind word or pass judgements on others. His mother, he felt deep down, cared for him with no reservations, and she never lectured him, even when he felt that he deserved to be lectured. All he could remember her saying, time and time again, was that she wanted him to do well in school and be kind to others, even if they were not kind to him. And she would always add, "Never give up on who you are." Being a loner with only few acquaintances and no boyfriends following his father's death, her life was uneventful.

What support did he have now with his mother gone, taken away, never to return? What was going to happen next? Could he take care of himself like he thought he was doing when he lived with his mother? He felt that his small world had shrunk even smaller. Nothing mattered anymore—not astronomy, the stars, the planets, the creatures in the ocean, or even his imagined friend, the wind. It was like he didn't exist. The past was gone, and the future didn't matter. Time seemed to have stopped. There was no place to go and nothing to look forward to.

The next day, a child welfare social worker stopped by and informed Margery that she had made arrangements to have Mason placed at an emergency foster home until they could decide what to do next. Sharon, the social worker, and Margery talked for a while, but what they were saying went right over Mason's head, as if he was not even there.

Then, Sharon took Mason by the hand and took him out to her car, and they drove off together. Mason didn't care where they might be going. Nothing mattered right now. He had no home, no possessions, and nothing to lose.

Arriving at the emergency foster care home, they were greeted by Barbara, a woman who had a soft, kind presence. Barbara asked Mason to follow her into the house, where she directed him to a bedroom. She asked him if he wanted anything to eat or drink, and Mason declined. He was then offered the opportunity to talk about what happened or to take some time to himself in the bedroom. He asked if he could go to the bedroom.

Sitting on the bed, he eventually fell asleep. The following morning, he heard Barbara knock on his door, inviting him to come out to the kitchen for something to eat. Mason did not want anything to eat but decided to come out anyway.

That afternoon, the police came by and asked him questions about his mother's health and her relatives. The questions again triggered feelings of guilt and a sense of helplessness about not doing anything to help his mother. He started to well up again, but the tears did not come this time; his eyes seemed to be flooded, as if he was drowning inside. Mason was unable to give them any information about either his mother's or his father's relatives even though he knew his mother had a sister living in Alberta.

Two weeks went by, one day after the next. Mason found himself staring off into space most of the time, as if he was not there. It was like he had disappeared. Nothing bothered him and nothing really interested him. It was as if he was dead, yet still alive and living outside of himself.

At the end of the second week at the emergency foster home, Mason was taken to a cremation ceremony for his mother, as arranged by Social Services. Learning from Mason that his mother had a sister residing in the next province, Social Services contacted her and arranged for her to travel out to BC in order to receive the ashes as the only known survivor. Sharon, the social worker who had placed

Mason in the emergency foster home, took Mason aside and mentioned that his Aunt Debbie would not be able to take him in due to serious health concerns. This meant that he would be sent to a foster home once they could find one that was suitable for him.

At first, this did not register with Mason at all. No detectable feelings surfaced. No anger, no sadness, and no anxiety, no sense of anything being important. The overriding sensation was one of being frozen in time and place. He could see and hear what was going on around him, but nothing mattered.

When he was introduced to his Aunt Debbie, it struck him how alike she was to his mother. She kept her head down and only made eye contact with him briefly. She walked with a limp like his mother, making him wonder if she had polio as well. When she spoke, she stuttered and repeated the phrase, "I don't know what to say."

After the ceremony, she sat with him for about an hour, sharing history, as well as his mother's. Mason could not make sense of most of what she shared, as Aunt Debbie spoke in a low muffled voice. Sometimes, she would look up and smile with her eyes looking off in space. It was as though she wasn't there and could not see him. He wasn't even sure he was there.

What he picked up in bits in pieces was that she and his mother had both been born on a farm, and both their parents had died in an auto accident. They were both raised in separate foster homes. Debbie was nine at the time, and his mother was eleven. *How coincidental,* he thought. He was also eleven, and now he was being sent to the emergency foster home.

Debbie mentioned that his mother liked to read a lot, and she was a very good student at school. She mentioned that his mother had left the foster home when she was seventeen, before she finished high school. Aunt Debbie went on to say that his mother and father met at a powwow on his father's reserve. She then moved to British Columbia with his father. At that point, she lost contact with her sister, only discovering that she had passed away when social services contacted her about taking possession of the remains.

Later that afternoon, Aunt Debbie departed on a Greyhound bus to return to Alberta. Back at the foster home, Mason retreated to his bedroom and stared out the window overlooking a large oak tree. Suddenly, a strong undercurrent of unsettledness washed over him. It was now evident that he didn't belong anywhere. There was no one that was important to him, and he was important to no one. He also had mixed feelings and thoughts about who he was. Was he white like his mother—warm hearted, kind, and soft-spoken? Or was he Indian, like his father—moody, gruff, and angry toward the world? Or was he simply a "nobody", unnoticeable and without any real value? Time will tell.

It was spring break, so school was out. Mason spent most of his time walking in the woods behind the foster home, imagining that he was in a far-off land looking for a lost civilization. He could not remember one day from the next, and it felt like he had no feet—or if he did, they were not making contact with the ground. It did not matter where he was going at first, but he eventually wandered off to the local beach, where he stopped to collect seashells and make designs in the sand. Sand dollars were his favourite. The smell of the sea air and wide-open spaces started to awaken him. He imagined the sand dollars to be stars in the universe. The universe was quiet, calm, and inviting. He would often imagine that he could travel from one star to another by taking a clam shell and carving pathways from one planet to another. He felt secure and accepted in this imagined universe.

From time to time, his thoughts would take him back to his past. He remembered that living with his mother and father had been very uncomfortable. Parenting, such as what was offered by his current foster parents, did not occur with his parents. There really was no guidance. Still, Mason was not sure he really wanted any guidance, and he tended to ignore any offered by his current foster parents.

When he lived with his mother after his father had died, he felt more like he was his mother's caretaker. Even though his mother was always there, he felt alone most of the time. Being alone was like not even being there, almost as if he was just a shadow. This reminded him once again of what his mother once said: "Your shadow is a reflection. It is not you, yet it is always around. Hiding in your shadow can protect you from having to experience bad feelings." Mason did not like being a shadow as it seemed so lifeless and unimportant. Yet he took sanctuary there. What did not make sense to him was how he actually wanted, at times, to hide out in his shadow space even though it was an empty place to be. If he was not his shadow, then who was he?

Mason had a passing thought about missing his mother—her softness, her smells, and her kindness. When she laughed, it was always about something she had forgotten to do or remember. She didn't have a mean bone in her body. She loved to knit when she could; she was always working on something for him, like a sweater or a toque. He felt that she had tried her best to be there for him, but her pain must have been so bad that it was time for her to say goodbye. Mason loved his mother—at least he thought he did, whatever love was—and he knew without question that she deeply cared for him.

When his mother did speak to him, she would almost always apologize for not being able to do anything for him. She would often have tears running down her cheeks as she was speaking to him. He could remember her pleading to him over and over that he should do his best to be kind to others, to do his best in school, and to never give up on his dreams. He, in turn, asked very little from her and did all he could to help her with chores around the house and avoid making any problems for her.

He reflected on the many occasions he found his sleeping mother slumped over in her walker, and how he would take a blanket and wrap it around her. He sensed that she experienced a lot of pain, but how much he really did not know at the time. There was little that happened to brighten up her day-to-day life. Mason thought how sad this must be for her, but she never complained.

At the end of spring break, Sharon the social worker made arrangements for him to be moved to a long-term foster home. At first, Mason was disappointed even though he knew that his current placement was only temporary. The foster parents treated him quite well and did not pressure him in any way. They gave him the freedom to regain his balance after the loss of his mother and his way of life. While he still felt the need to live in his own bubble, he sensed that he was starting to feel more and more alive.

Arriving at the new foster home with a backpack filled with all his clothes and the few books that he possessed, Mason was very tense. He wanted to bolt and take off somewhere but did not know where to go. So, with head down, he was introduced to his new foster parents, who greeted him by saying that they were pleased to offer him a place in their home of faith. Looking at them out of the corner of his eye, he guessed that they were older than his last foster parents and much more rigid. Mason did not respond. With some awkwardness, Mason was given a tour of the home, which was much bigger than the emergency foster home and much less inviting. Everything was orderly, and he could not help noticing religious symbols everywhere. When he was shown to his room, Mason felt uncomfortable, as the bedroom was colourless and uninviting. There was a cross above the bed and one picture over a small desk of Jesus with a halo over his head.

Then Mason was given a Bible and told that it would be proper for him to read selected passages before a prayer meeting that would occur every day before dinner. Since he was entirely unfamiliar with prayer, Mason was confused about how this was important, but he could not bring himself to ask the question.

At first, he attended the sessions and quickly discovered that they were designed to control his thinking and behaviour. His foster parents would tell him that God was looking over him to protect him and remind him that lying, stealing, and swearing were sinful and would not be allowed in their home. Then they would cite passages out of the Bible that did not make any sense to him. Often, they would repeat the same religious statements from one session to the next. He found himself biting his lower lip and cringing when they asked him to hold hands with them. He desperately wanted to go hide out in his shadow. Overall, these sessions were boring, he hated them.

Mason resisted participating as best he could, but for the most part, he had to endure these prayer sessions. It felt like he had no choice. He found every excuse he could to get home late from school, beyond the rigidly scheduled time for the prayer sessions. When they confronted him about not participating, Mason found himself walking away and either going to his room or going outside. Mason also felt that in addition to his non-compliance, they were uncomfortable with his "nativeness." They pressured him daily to speak up, and it was clear that they were unhappy with his non-responsiveness.

The last straw for them occurred when he refused to go to their church on Sundays by barricading himself in his bedroom. After six months of this stand-off, the foster parents decided that he was not a good fit in their home and requested that he be sent to another foster home.

The second foster home was totally different. The foster parents, Bob and Judy, were younger than the last foster parents, and they had two young children of their own, which occupied most of their time. Bob was a high school teacher and Judy was a stay at home mom. They joked a lot and were very playful with their two girls, who were four and five years of age. The two girls, Jennifer and Karen, tried to be friendly with him at first, but soon tended to ignore him, as Mason was not receptive to playing with them. Mason liked the two girls, but he could not find the desire within himself to play. He instead resorted to his usual behaviour: he faded into the background and stayed within himself. Overall, they were kind and respected his need to be alone, but they often mentioned that they worried about his health. He liked them, but that was not enough for him to want to spend any time with them and their family. Despite his resistance, the foster parents never stopped encouraging him to participate in their family life.

Every once in a while, the social worker would stop by and have long private discussions with the foster parents. He felt certain that they were talking about him being sad, uncooperative, and maybe even mentally unwell. This awakened him a little, as he began to feel some discomfort at being judged. At one point, it occurred to him that he might just leave or run away, but this did not persist, as he really wasn't motivated to go anywhere. So, he covered his discomfort up as best he could.

Then, after one of their meetings, the social worker took him aside and said that she wanted him to get a medical check-up to make sure that he was developing normally. After his visit to a ministry-appointed physician, he was told that his physical health was normal, but that being quiet and withdrawn was not. This prompted an arrangement for Mason to see a child psychologist. The social worker told Mason that the psychologist was someone who could help him learn to participate more with others, both at the foster home and at school.

Confused at first, Mason didn't understand why others thought there was something wrong with him. His school-work proved that he was capable. He also knew that he could talk and make friends if he really thought it was important. The problem was that he just didn't want to. He liked being quiet and by himself. It gave him a sense of control over himself.

He felt like being quiet also allowed him to stay focused on his schoolwork, which is what his mother had always asked him to do. Mason was also reminded of what his father repeatedly told him: "Speak only when spoken to." *Most people talk too much,* he thought.

Then, his own thoughts started to turn on him, sowing doubt that maybe something was wrong with him, and he didn't know it. On second thought, he pushed these thoughts aside. With a budding stubborn streak, he thought, *No, there is nothing wrong with me. There is nothing wrong with being quiet. They are making a mistake. I will show them.*

Chapter Three

 Masks

THE DAY THE APPOINTMENT was arranged the social worker picked him up and drove him to the meeting. On the way there no words were spoken for the longest time, until suddenly Mason blurted out, "I don't want to see a psychologist. There is nothing wrong with me! "The social worker replied, "You just have to go once, and if you don't like it, you don't have to go again."

Arriving at a strip mall on the edge of town, they approached a door at the end of the building with a sign saying, "Next Generation Youth and Family Counselling Services." Upon entering a reception area, Sharon the social worker introduced him to a heavy-set man with a ponytail named Arnold Armstrong. Then she left.

Mason noticed that Arnold had a scarf hanging around his neck with the logo of a Bear and the letters "AA" printed under it. He wore a vest decorated with beads and walked in sandals. It startled Mason when Arnold turned towards him and with a softening smile and a gleam in his eyes invited Mason to follow him into the treatment room.

The room was quite large like the art room at his school. Along one wall, there were numerous musical instruments—several guitars, flutes, a keyboard, and a small table with several painted hand drums. He also noticed some big floor speakers and a cabinet with audio equipment.

On the other side, there were two paint easels and a table with clay on it. Off in the far corner, there was a large, approximately four-feet-wide floor drum surrounded by six chairs. Drum sticks with round, large onion-sized tips were placed around the drum.   In the middle of the room there was a large round woven rug crafted with many multi-coloured overlapping circles. Surrounding a small round table placed on the middle of the rug were several leather arm chairs. On the table was a small chest with indented carvings which were mysterious to him yet very appealing to look at. In addition, beside the chest was an attractively carved stick about twelve inches long.

Arnold started off by asking Mason if he liked to paint or listen to music. Mason just shrugged his shoulders. Arnold then asked Mason to come and sit with him around the big drum. Mason stood still, refusing to move, and watched as Arnold went over and sat down on the round stool in front of the big drum. He then picked up a drumstick and slowly started to beat the drum. Mason just stood where he was and watched. After a few minutes, Arnold again invited Mason to come over, only this time he said, "Don't come if you really don't want to. It's okay by me."

Arnold continued slowly drumming and talking at the same time, saying that drumming is not for everyone. It takes courage to be a drummer. Then, unexpectedly, he tossed a drum stick toward Mason. It landed at his feet. After several minutes, in a mesmerized way, Mason bent over, picked up the drumstick, and walked over to the drum. Without talking, Arnold motioned for Mason to sit next to him. Several more minutes went by. Mason had the urge to pound the drum as the rhythmic sounds Arnold was making were quite appealing to his ears, but he resisted.

Arnold handed him a second drumstick and invited him to use both. Without thinking, Mason started to pound the drum in unison with Arnold. After a short while, Arnold encouraged Mason to pound harder while he began to chant, inviting Mason to do the same. Again, without thinking, he found himself pounding harder and harder and then, all of a sudden, sounds were coming out of his mouth. At first, they were muffled sounds that mimicked Arnold's, which sounded as if he was repetitively chanting "hi, yia". When Arnold's chanting got louder his voice also got louder and louder. It felt like he was on the verge of losing control.

Then, suddenly, Mason stopped drumming and froze. His mother's passing flashed through his mind. The pounding of the drum triggered the memory of the way his heart pounded like it was going to burst the moment he found his mother slumped over in her chair, dead.

Arnold immediately stopped as well and took the drum sticks from Mason. He then got up and returned with a blanket and placed it over Mason's shoulders. Several minutes passed before Arnold invited Mason to come and sit with him in the middle of the room. At first, Mason couldn't move, until Arnold touched him on the shoulder. This seemed to break the frozen state he was in, and he got up, walked over, and sat in one of the chairs across from Arnold.

Arnold asked Mason if any questions popped up while they were drumming. At first, he could not think of any questions, feeling like he had been put on the spot. Arnold then asked him what it was like to drum with him.

"Why do you drum?" Mason asked.

Arnold replied that drumming allows us to get connected to our body.

Unexpectedly, Mason asked, "Why did you become a psychologist?"

Arnold responded, "I felt it calling me…to be of service to others in a way that could allow them to understand their lives better and find ways to overcome problems in their lives." Arnold followed up by saying, "This is something we could explore further at a follow-up session, if you would like."

The meeting then came to an end, and Mason was asked if he wanted to return for another session. Mason nodded without thinking, and a follow-up time was set.

On his way back to the foster home, Mason thought this was nothing like what he had expected. *Psychologists don't play with you,* he thought. Puzzled yet curious, he wanted to know what was going to happen next.

The explanation the social worker gave him about what psychologists do did not come close to what he experienced in his first session with Arnold. The social worker had told him that the psychologist he would see was someone experienced in working with young people who were depressed or troubled by losses. The psychologist would sit with him and mostly just talk, asking personal questions about how he might be feeling and what might be troubling him. And, of course, she said, "We want him to find out more about why you are so quiet and don't spend time with other kids."

Mason found the next session with the psychologist even more unusual. Arnold started by inviting him to make clay models of whatever crossed his mind in the moment. Mason started by making a model of a dolphin, then a manta ray, and then a model of the planet Mars. These images came to mind as he recalled seeing pictures of them in the *National Geographic Magazine* when he was younger. When he had finished making these three clay models, Arnold asked him to set them aside and join him at the easel board.

Next, Arnold invited Mason to throw paint on an easel board. He suggested that Mason not think about what he was doing. Then, he told Mason to take his hands, place them on the easel board, and move the different colours of paint into whatever designs occurred to him. Mason first started painting rainbow-like circles. His next painting was of a whirlpool coloured in blue, and his last was of what he thought could be a black hole in the universe. On one of his aborted attempts, he tried to make all the types of clouds and galaxies he had seen in the *National Geographic Magazine*. But he ended up leaving it unfinished, throwing it into the wastepaper basket. When he was done his artwork and the clay models, they were placed on a table that had "MW," for "Mason Walkway," on it...

How could these experiences have any meaning? He thought. Perhaps Arnold was showing what psychology was in action instead of speaking about it.

The sessions went on for three months, involving drumming that got more rhythmic and surprisingly more enjoyable. It was a relief to him that no more troubling memories surfaced, as they had when he first started drumming. He vividly recalled how disturbed he felt and how he stopped drumming and froze.

In some later sessions, Mason moved toward drawing human figures—he drew his mother and several of his teachers at school. Arnold would sometimes draw with him. Arnold remarked several times that his drawing skills were amazing. He went on to say, "Every time I look at them, I see something different."

Mason felt the freedom to express himself without restrictions, and at no time did he feel judged or advised to follow any particular instructions Arnold might have had in mind. His drawings were later placed on the wall. Mason was encouraged to add to them at any time. Mason liked hearing Arnold offer him that freedom.

Another unusual session that stood out for Mason occurred when Arnold got him to make a papier-mâché mask of his face. Arnold also did the same, and then he placed a mirror next to the masks and asked Mason to look back and forth at the mask and the mirror to check out the differences. Strange as this seemed, Mason caught himself smiling, especially when what he saw shifted from the mirror to the mask. After shifting back and forth for several minutes, Mason began to chuckle. Laughing was rare for him, but this somehow stimulated his funny bone. Arnold also started to laugh with him, as he shifted back and forth from the mirror to his mask. Quickly, the laughter became more pronounced. They started to exchange glances at one another, which only triggered more laughter. Mason didn't know why he was laughing, but it certainly felt good. They were laughing so hard that they both doubled over and started rolling on the carpet. Exhausting as this was, Mason did not want it to stop. When they both finally settled down, Arnold, with a warm smile, said, "It is good that we can laugh at ourselves. Laughter is sometimes the best medicine."

At the next session, Arnold took down four large native masks hanging on the far back wall, each big enough to cover his face. They were mysterious-looking, but they also grabbed Mason's interest as he found them to be very attractive. They were most likely carved by someone who took great care in what he was doing.

Arnold explained that the first was a Raven, the second a Bear, the third an Eagle, and the last an Owl. Arnold encouraged Mason to examine these colourful masks and to ask any questions that came to mind.

"What are the masks for?" Mason asked.

Arnold replied, "They can be what you want them to be. In my First Nations culture, they often represent the Four Dignities. For example, some consider the Raven to be cunning or intelligent and very quick to learn. This mask represents the dignity of Energetic Boldness.

"The Bear symbolizes power, being self-contained or content with oneself, strong willed, and caring for family, yet having little need for fellowship. This mask represents the Dignity of Quiet Compassion and Caring.

"The Eagle is the messenger from the Creator. It represents the Dignity of Spirited Being. It is commonly viewed that possessing an eagle feather can connect you to the Creator and release one from suffering on earth.

"The Owl symbolizes the Dignity of Wisdom. It reminds us to take care with our actions, to not get ahead of ourselves, and not to seek to be noticed for what we do. The owl is known for its quietness and apparent calmness."

Arnold then asked Mason to place each mask over his face one at a time and imagine what it would feel like to be the Raven, the Bear, the Eagle, and the Owl. Mason very carefully picked up each mask and held it in front of his face for what seemed like several minutes. Having the mask on gave him a feeling of being protected from others and a sense that nobody could really see him, which he liked.

"What was that experience like?" Arnold asked.

Mason shared that he felt most comfortable with being the Owl, because he liked owls for their quietness. He also liked the Bear, because nobody would challenge a bear, and it could protect you. The Raven felt annoying. The Eagle felt non-caring. He liked the feeling of having these two around, but not too close.

Arnold then responded, "We all wear masks for the different situations we experience in our lives. It is good to know when you are wearing a mask that it is only a mask. You will wear many masks in your life. Treat them with respect. They are there to serve you when you need them. You do not serve them."

Overall, this mask experience felt almost magical. Mason did not want to forget any of it.

Following the mask experience, Arnold shared that he was asked by the social worker if he thought there was anything mentally or emotionally concerning about Mason. He looked at Mason for some time before saying this, "I told the social worker that as far as I am concerned, you are mentally healthy and a very capable young man. The only issue worth noting is your unusual upbringing. There is really nothing wrong with you, and there are many things about you that are admirable and worthy of praise."

Arnold said that he would write down his findings and all the things they did together and give this to the social worker. "But before sending the report, I will review it with you. It will not be sent without your full approval."

Finally, Arnold added that when Mason first came to see him, the social worker had concerns about Mason being depressed because of his mixed heritage coupled with the loss of both parents. He said, "As far as I am concerned, these background issues are important to explore further when you are ready. I will advise the social worker that you are the one who will decide when to explore these issues, and that depression should not be used to describe your unique way of taking charge of your life."

Buoyed by Arnold's remarkable honesty and forthrightness, Mason decided to ask, "Is depression a disease?"

Arnold responded, "Many professionals believe so, although they do not all agree with one another about the underlying causes."

Mason then asked, "Are all humans at risk of getting depression or being depressed?"

"That is very difficult to say. First, we need to be clear what depression means. For example, the word depression is used to describe a lot of things, from a minor sadness to a really bad feeling of hopelessness and unhappiness. Bad things do happen to all people, and each person handles these bad things differently. Sometimes, we can get so caught up with these bad things—thinking about them over and over again—that our energy for living drains away. When that happens, it can be a serious problem."

Mason then decided to ask the question that bugged him most. "Why are social workers and foster parents concerned about me being depressed? Why do they think that my quietness or the things I don't do are a problem?"

Arnold replied, "It is understandable that they would worry about you for having sadly and unfortunately lost both parents and having no other family to support you. And with you being so quiet, they worry even more about you. On the other hand, Mason, your determination to find your own way in life clearly means that you do not have any time for being depressed."

And then he said, "Sometimes, when one storm after another occurs, we find the need to retreat within ourselves. I think that in your situation, even with the loss of both your parents, living with a lot of disadvantages, and no clear way to move forward, you found a way to protect yourself from further loss. Hiding away for a while until your storm or storms pass is a good way to ride them out. It's like living in your shadow, which allows you to escape being noticed by others. Your shadow is important and useful, but you will find that it is not the real you. While your place of hiding can save you from falling apart and losing control, it could become a habit or a pattern that becomes difficult to let go of even when you no longer need or want it.

It takes courage and trust in yourself to come out of hiding. I am confident that you have the courage to come out from behind your shadow. One day, you will be ready to do so, and when that day comes, you will know what to do."

Mason's mind raced at the possibilities. Arnold's comments were relieving to hear and quite energizing. Releasing through his mind were the thoughts that he had a shadow but wasn't his shadow. He wasn't his mistakes. He could be whatever he wanted to be.

As they were finishing up their session, Arnold encouraged Mason to take his drawings with him, including the clay figures and the papier-mâché mask he had made. Arnold suggested that Mason take the mask with him and color or draw on it anytime he felt the urge to do so. He then added, "As you change, so will the masks you wear. The masks you wear or make are not to be thrown away or cast aside. In time, they will reveal the true nature of who you really are."

Arnold then asked Mason if he wanted to continue with more sessions. Taken aback by the question, Mason had never considered that the sessions would eventually come to an end. Arnold was the first adult he ever felt a strong connection with and deep down he wanted the relationship not to come to an end.

On the flip side, he wanted to reveal to Arnold he was ready to strike out on his own. He wanted to confirm to Arnold that the sessions had made him more confident about his future. In short, he wanted Arnold to be impressed with his capability to be self- sufficient. Arnold was the first adult he had met who thought that nothing was really wrong with him.

Mason replied, "I have learned a lot from these sessions. I think it would be good for me to take these experiences and see what I can do with them."

Arnold responded, "This makes good sense. Please feel free to contact me again if you want to just talk or have a follow up meeting."

When Mason left their final session, crossing his mind was the thought that he wanted to learn more about psychology. There was much more to psychology than he thought, given what he had been told.

Chapter Four

 Waking Up

AFTER HIS SESSIONS WITH Arnold, Mason felt different when he was at school and at the foster home. He felt awake and more alive than ever before. Mason discovered that he was talking more with the foster parents, and he actually found himself asking questions of his teachers. When anything to do with psychology came up in school, it immediately attracted his interest. He would ask one question after another, often appearing to frustrate his primary room teacher, as she did not have many answers for him. Once, she looked inquisitively at him and asked, "Where are all these questions coming from?" Another time, she rolled her eyes and just laughed, saying that she liked the new Mason.

Gradually, over the next two years, Mason started to participate more in his foster parents' family life, and the more he did it, the more he liked it. He began to connect with Bob and Judy, as they left him with the sense that he mattered and that he belonged in the foster home. Their two girls, Jennifer and Karen, approached him more often asking him to play with them, which he surprisingly enjoyed doing. They would play board games or draw and occasionally they would all go to the local park to play. Bob and Judy had given him a chess board on his last birthday, which he learned how to play as Bob would spend time every week teaching and playing with him. An even more meaningful experience was how they supported him in his interest in airplanes. Every couple of months, he would find a new model airplane kit in his room without any explanation. What amazed him beyond his wildest dreams was when Bob had arranged for them both to take a sightseeing flight in a small Cessna airplane. Once up in the sky, he knew that someday he wanted to be a pilot.

At school, he started to make a few friends who tended to be loners like him. He would play chess with them whenever he could. He also started to participate in after-school sports activities, such as soccer and basketball although he preferred to watch others play rather than playing with them.

His world had come alive for him and his shadow was no longer showing up. He felt no desire to hide out anymore.

What happened next abruptly shook him to the core. On an early Saturday morning the police showed up at the door, arrested Bob and took him to the station for questioning. Judy, with tears streaming down her face asked me to go play outside with Jennifer and Karen mentioning this was all a mistake and Bob would return home once they realized the mistake they were making. This did not happen. Two weeks went by and finally Judy took him to one side and again with tears in her eyes said that Bob would be away for a long time. Mason asked. "What did he do wrong?" Judy responded, "He has been accused of assaulting kids at the school but it is not true. I am sure they will find him innocent. Unfortunately though, child welfare will be removing you from our home in a few days. The plans are to take you to a group home."

Stunned at first all he could do was retreat to his room, curl up in a ball and sob. *Why was this happening?* Anger started to boil up inside. Not knowing what to do, he started hitting himself and banging his head against the headboard in his room. When that was not enough to get rid of his anguish, he took to breaking everything he could in his bedroom; his model airplanes, the chess set given to him by Judy and Bob, and the masks that he had made and collected. This made it worse until he finally started to tear up his cherished *National Geographic* magazines.

Exhausted from his tirade, he spent the next several days taking long walks to nowhere. An overwhelming sense of emptiness and his shadow had returned. He had the urge to go and drown himself. Nothing mattered anymore. Everything around him faded away in the background. The sense of being insignificant flooded over him like a dark black cloud. He wanted to bury himself in a deep hole.

The only thing he could think of doing was to try and get in touch with Arnold. Out of desperation he found himself at the strip mall in front of what once was Arnold's "Next Generation Youth and Family Services" but now unexpectedly was a bakery. *Where had Arnold and his counselling services gone?* Returning to the foster home, he once again felt the emptiness of abandonment as he had so indelibly experienced so many times in the past. *What happened to Arnold?*

The next day, he called the social worker and asked for Arnold's contact information, only to find out Arnold had passed away a year ago. The sadness that overtook him was overwhelming. It drove him deeper into his shadow. What was different this time was that he had carried his anguish in with him.

Two days later, the social worker came by to take him to a group home. On the way to the group home, in her car, he found himself yelling uncontrollably at her. The urge to lash out at her verbally and physically scared him to the point he withdrew, slumped down, and cocooned himself for the remaining trip. Arriving at the group home, he felt a strong urge to cause trouble and strike out at anyone who got in his way or disagreed with him.

At first, nobody paid any attention to him at the group home. As a fourteen-year-old, he was the youngest of six kids placed there. The group home was staffed by caregivers, and the home always had between six to eight male youths at any given time, but none were Indigenous.

When the other youth learned of his mixed-race background, they tried to bully him, pointed fingers at him, and belittled his appearance and interests. On numerous occasions, he was a target for aggression from the other male youths at the group home, but they soon learned to stay away from him. They found his unpredictable behaviour unsettling most of the time, and picking on him caused them more problems than it was worth. Mason did, however, feel the need to be especially alert and on guard with a safety plan when he was away from the home.

The home was constantly in chaos of one sort or another, as the other young people were into drugs or were generally very oppositional and non-compliant with the house rules. In an odd way, the negative behaviour around him served to settle down Mason's own negative energy. Instead, he actually felt that he did not have to be angry. There was enough of it around him. Getting angry just to be angry made no sense anymore.

Mason stayed focused on his schoolwork and easily distanced himself from the other youth at the home. For the most part, he went unnoticed by the caregivers. Mason learned to stay under the radar, never complaining, and he always did what was asked of him by the care staff. The group home was simply a place to pass through, and he did not take it too seriously.

Fortunately, school was a place where he found that he could blend in as long as he showed interest in learning and got involved peripherally in some intermural sports. Lurking in the back of his mind, however, was the sense that teachers did not think much of him, even though he did quite well in his schoolwork. His classmates also tended to exclude him in their social friendship circles. At best, they were indifferent toward him. It certainly didn't help that he was reserved and only talked when spoken to.

Mason developed a reputation for always being on the move, never hanging around to socialize. His classmates took to nicknaming him the "Roadrunner." Mason took advantage of this label, as it allowed him to avoid close encounters with others and gave him an excuse to do his own thing. On the other hand, it reinforced his sense of emptiness; that his life did not matter much.

While he was not totally a recluse, and he did participate in some social minimal interaction with his chess friends, he did not allow himself to get too close to any of them. He preferred to focus his energies on schooling and reading. Despite tearing up his *National Geographic Magazines,* he found his interest in the oceans had returned. He turned his attention towards learning as much as he could about ocean life and to find ways to engage more directly with it by taking frequent trips to the beach nearby. As in the past, he imagined he could swim like a dolphin, but the reality was he could not, so he asked if he could take swimming lessons.

The group home enrolled him in a swimming program, which he found both settling and energizing. For the most part, swimming was a solitary activity. Water attracted him like a magnet, and when he was swimming, he felt free from the never-ending questions his thoughts presented him. For him, this was a place to be at peace with his self.

He also avoided contact from others outside of the school environment, as he found most people were always worried or fretful about something, as if they didn't like their lot in life. They seemed to mostly fantasize about being somebody else. Oddly, it seemed like most people generally disliked themselves. Maybe he was just seeing himself in them.

Mason realized that, as he was getting older, he was also getting mentally and physically tougher and less concerned about what others thought of him. Interestingly, it didn't seem to matter too much if he was rejected or discounted by others. Any attempts to condemn him in any fashion were neutralized pre-emptively by his own self-condemning gatekeeping. In a mysterious way, he was able to let their rejection of him become their issue and not his.

He became increasingly aware that the world appeared to be preoccupied with money, territory, and violence. Lying and complaining was the norm, while sharing, genuine caring, and joy were secondary. Anxiety, fear, and frustration were about the main topics of conversation. Time was also a problem for most people, who either complained about there being too little or too much time on their hands. There was too much of it when they were bored with what they were doing, and there was too little of it when they worried about getting somewhere or having too much to do.

School was mostly boring, and it taught him what society wanted him to learn, not how to make use of the learning. He encountered very few students who were excited and joyful about school, except for the friendships it offered them.

Mason was most curious about learning why people got sad, mad, and glad. He found that running allowed him to clear his head of unwanted thoughts, and he started running whenever he could.

He would run to school, to the aquatic centre, and on the back roads when he was out by himself. When he was running, he felt that the elements were invigorating, and his mind was much quieter. It was like a meditative experience for him. He most enjoyed running with the wind at his back. The wind made him feel like he was floating when he was running away with it.

While at school, the track coach took notice of his habit of running everywhere and invited him to come out and run with the track team. The coach was also his physical education teacher, and Mason always felt respect for him and respected by him, so he decided to give it a try. At first, he discovered that his performance was applauded, which he actually did not like, so he started to back off, making sure that he did not win any races. For him, competing took the pleasure out of running.

However, over time, he felt the pressure mounting from the coach to always do better, to the point that he totally lost interest in running competitively. He did not like competition, as it made him fearful of being judged and worried that he would let other people down. Mason then dropped off the track team and returned to running for his own pleasure.

As he got older, Mason became more and more interested in mathematics. It struck him that mathematics was the core of all science. Recalling his early interest in astronomy, he discovered that mathematics was the cornerstone to understanding how the universe works. The origins of mathematical thinking fascinated him. Whenever he could, he read about historical mathematical breakthroughs; he was interested to find out what a difference they made. Einstein fascinated him—especially, of course, his theory of relativity and probing interest in black holes.

His math teacher, Mr. Baines, was a jovial, roly-poly man who seemingly smiled all the time, even when there seemed to be nothing to smile about. When he wasn't teaching math, Mr. Baines was the director of the school's drama club.

In Mr. Baines's math class, Mason took to sitting at the back of the room, quietly working away, and trying to stay unnoticed. He even made sure that his test scores and assignments did not draw any attention to him.

This didn't work. Mr. Baines noticed that Mason would rarely complete his work. One day, he asked Mason if he was not finishing his work on purpose or if he was just bored. Mason said that he didn't know, but secretly he did. At his response, Mr. Baines shrugged his shoulders and replied, "No problem."

Mason took to liking Mr. Baines, as he felt no pressure to perform in his class. More and more, he found his math classes both interesting and mysterious. It was something he wanted to dig into deeper, which was odd given that most of the other kids in his class hated math. He liked that they hated it, as it allowed him to feel like he was different from them.

Then, one day, Mr. Baines approached him in the hallway between classes and asked, "Would you be interested in participating in the school drama club?" Mr. Baines went on to say that participating in drama was a way to explore what the world was all about without having to reveal anything about yourself. This comment hooked Mason and he became more curious.

Reluctant at first, Mason showed up to the drama studio, just watching from the back. It was different than he had expected. There was lots of laughter, and it seemed like everyone was just playing around. After doing this twice, Mr. Baines approached him and asked if he would help out with the props. Once Mason was familiar with the stage, Mr. Baines asked him to read some lines from a skit they were rehearsing. Mason discovered that it actually was not as scary as he had imagined.

Soon, Mason was participating in several humorous skits, and he quickly discovered the world of living outside of your day-to-day script. It was like he was free to become the role, rather than being trapped in a character pattern forged by his upbringing and circumstance.

Drama was definitely not "macho," yet it was invigorating. He sensed that he could experiment with letting go without attempting to be in control of his energies all the time. Most importantly, he did not feel any sense of being judged. He also became acutely aware that not only could he act out different personalities, but some of these personalities resonated with him as if they were operating in the background of his primary personality—the serious-minded loner, the shy-yet-driven young man. He also discovered that, while he was roleplaying, it felt real. At times, it felt like he was wearing a mask. He reflected back on what Arnold the psychologist said—that we all wear masks, and that we can learn from them if we know what they are.

The most memorable experience he could recall was when he participated in a skit that had no script. A group of five students were encouraged to take the statement, "Today is the best day in my life" and add to it whatever came to mind. The only guideline was that whatever they added could not be negative. After a couple of rounds, what was being added each time became increasingly more laughable. Bursts of laughter started to flow from the group to the point that they had to stop for a few minutes to catch their breath. This was the second time in Mason's life that laughter had showed up when he least expected it to. Humour made him feel lighter and gave him a break from taking life too seriously. This was definitely something he wanted to experience more often.

It dawned on him that acting or making things up is what people do most of the time. Mason was not altogether clear how this applied to him. His opinion on others was that people seem to live their acts, not their lives. Maybe that was what he was doing too. When the drama group started to plan for a public showing, this was a line he could not cross. He started to fade away into the background and stopped attending altogether. He found that it didn't make much of a difference whether he kept it up or not anyway, as he would be graduating soon.

Finishing high school had no real impact on him. He was just going through the paces and dutifully following his mother's request to stay in school. Graduation also was a non-event for him, as he chose not to go to the ceremony. It didn't seem to matter, as he had no significant others in his life to share this experience with.

What to do next? A twelfth-grade education was not going to amount to much in the world of employment, and he felt no desire driving him toward a career in anything, with the possible exception of psychology. Math was too abstract to lead him in any direction, except perhaps in furthering his education at a university level. He ruled out this possibility, as he felt that university was too big a step to take. He had no idea how he could afford it, nor was he even confident that he was university material.

Nothing was really on the horizon for him, and being in a group home was stale and rigid. He tolerated living there at best, and he spent as much time as he could out of the home. He really did not have any friends there, and more to the point, he didn't feel the need for any. His group home caregivers, while supportive, really left him to his own resources, not making much effort to try to get to know him. Maybe it was Mason who kept them at a distance, like he did the youth in the home. It felt like he was still living in a bubble of his own making.

He thought deeply about these issues: *Where do I start looking for the answers to what my future will be? The world seems too mixed up and uncaring to me. When I look back, it gives me no clues, and when I look forward, there is nothing that attracts my attention. Never mind, I need to start with what little I do know about myself.*

Firstly, how can I know what to do next or what lies ahead for me, when I am mostly hiding out in my shadow? Then how do I reconcile this pattern with my urge to take flight—to be on the move, away from something that might expose me for what I really am; somebody who hides in his own shadow. If this is not confusing enough, what about my buried urge to challenge my life circumstances, to step forward, to be courageous enough to go beyond my fears of being inferior? What about my desire to discover what I really might be capable of? Are these three patterns like masks, like Arnold suggested? One might be the hibernator, the other might be the runner, and the third might be the adventurer.

It was a turning point for him in many ways. High school done and his days at the group home numbered, the path forward was unclear yet, in some uneasy way, exciting.

He was reminded about what Arnold had said, "There will come a time for you to let your courage surface. When this time arrives, you will feel the pressure to step out of your shadow to seek out your true nature. Your true nature, in many ways, is the opposite of what you have been doing. Instead of retreating, you will find yourself getting angry at yourself for not doing what you are capable of doing. You will challenge yourself to do what you have not done before.

You will find a way to accept others and interact with them rather than judge them. Self-doubt will be replaced with self-approval. The behaviours that are not you—like hiding out—will have run their course."

Chapter Five

⚜ Stumbling Forward ⚜

L EAVING HIS GROUP HOME was an easy decision to make, as social services wanted him to go anyway when he turned eighteen, which was just six months away. Taking only what he thought he needed, he set out on a Greyhound Bus to Victoria, drawn by the larger population and the expansive ocean surrounding three quarters of the bottom end of the island. The ocean was like a magnet drawing him in, stimulated by his early readings on dolphins and his fantasy interest in swimming with them.

A week after arriving in Victoria with a temporary welfare cheque in hand, he found a small one-room basement apartment near the university. A few days after his arrival, pondering what to do next, he took a walk along the seawall down by the fishing docks.

On a whim, and exercising some courage, he approached a fisherman standing by a trawler and asked if he was looking for any help. The fisherman looked him up and down and asked him for his name.

"Mason Walkway, sir."

Without hesitating, the fisherman continued, "Are you prone to sea sickness?"

Mason said that he didn't know, but he blurted out that he could swim. Pausing for a few moments, which seemed like forever to Mason, the fisherman said that he could use a deck hand for the summer, if Mason was interested.

So, out to sea Mason went. The work at sea was a struggle beyond his expectations, as the crew worked up to sixteen hours a day. Mason became very well acquainted with seasickness. When the sea was rough, he spent many hours steadying himself by trying to stay focused on the horizon when he could. There were many times, too many to count, when he had to hang his head over the guard rails. Somehow, he overcame seasickness—perhaps because when he was working non-stop for so many hours a day, he really did not have time to stay sick. By the summer's end, he had learned to adjust to the rolling seas, he had developed a healthy respect for the ocean, and he had learned to find solace in the rhythmic movement of the waves, day in and day out.

Despite the benefit of this experience he was conflicted about was how he could not find a way to reconcile his deep-felt connection to the ocean with that of being a harvester of fish. Not visually nor cognitively could he imagine or accept taking the life of a dolphin to satisfy human consumption needs. Mason sensed that his days of being a fisherman would be numbered.

Moving on, he was now ready to explore new horizons armed with a modest nest egg from his work as a fisherman. Living near the university, he often thought, *What if I could study to become a counsellor—or even more ambitious, to become a psychologist?* After indulging in this fantasy for a bit, he parked this unlikely dream in the back of his mind.

Then, a chance encounter with a second-year university student at a local coffee shop occurred. Mason was sitting alone when a tall lanky student named Ross asked Mason if he could join him, as all the other seats were taken. Ross was carrying a Physics textbook and wore a university t-shirt imprinted with the words "Science 72".

Mason nodded without saying anything and continued to read his book on dolphins. Then, it occurred to him that this might be an opportunity to find out more about the requirements for being accepted as a student at the university. Once Ross had settled into his seat, Mason let a few minutes go by before apologizing for not introducing himself. The student said, "No problem, I do it all the time. Hazard of being a self-absorbed student."

Encouraged by his openness, Mason asked, "How did you decide to go to university? What were the entrance requirements?" The student perked up and shared openly what grades he had from high school, which left Mason feeling slightly more optimistic about his own situation. After the student told him the minimum grade requirements, Mason felt that perhaps, just *maybe*, his grades were good enough to make him eligible. Ross also mentioned that both his parents strongly encouraged him to become an engineer as did his high school counsellor.

Mason thanked Ross for this information. Leaving the coffee shop, on his way back to his apartment he felt a refreshing surge of optimism that just perhaps going to university might be worth considering. Clearly, he had no real foundation of support or frame of reference to explore this possibility. Yet what did he have to lose by checking it out? There was no pressure from anyone to achieve or pursue anything.

The following day, armed with a renewed sense of courage, Mason decided to approach the university registrar's office and make an appointment to check out admissions requirements. He had no idea how he could afford to go to university even if that were possible, but he thought at the very least he would find out more about his potential.

He was given an appointment for the next day and was asked to bring his high school transcript with him. The admissions counsellor assigned to him reviewed his transcript and stated that his grades fulfilled admission requirements. She then inquired about his financial capabilities and family background. After he shared a brief overview of his parents' mixed cultural history and his modest savings from his summer work on a fish boat, the counsellor sat back, pausing for a moment, then said, "Given your background, you may be eligible for educational support from your father's band."

Mason was confused. *How is it that, being only part Indigenous, he would be eligible for special education funding that included living expenses and tuition costs?* Deep inside, he loathed the idea of being seen as needy. *Why did Indigenous peoples get offered educational perks that were not available, to the best of his knowledge, for non-Indigenous students from poor families, or children who had been in care and did not have supportive parents?* Even more confusing was that he was left with the impression that Indigenous students got preferred admission status, and that their educational achievement levels were set lower than for non-Indigenous students. The counsellor appeared eager to access information about his father's date of birth and his Indian status number. Mason indicated that had no clue about when his father was born, how to get his status number, or if he even had one.

The counsellor suggested that he go the Native Friendship Centre, and they would assist him in finding out about his father's band status. The interview concluded with the counsellor suggesting that he return next week for a second appointment after visiting the Friendship centre. She asked Mason to give his word that he would do so. Now, Mason felt obligated. He was reminded of his mother's words: "When you give your word to do something, then you honour it." Still quite unsure whether this was a path he wanted, or even a path he could take, Mason battled within himself whether to follow through with going to the Native Friendship Centre or not. He had developed a built-in aversion to taking handouts, given his experience of how inadequate he felt when getting handouts from the Salvation Army many years ago. While he was grateful at the time, it never felt like he deserved anything he got. He certainly didn't feel entitled. Mason sensed, now more than ever before, that he had to make his own way. He needed to legitimately earn the right to gain entry into the university.

Even more challenging for him was getting his head around being committed to four more years of study, given that he found high school quite boring. Never mind the distinct possibility that he may not be university material! Why try to do something you could possibly fail at? Then, catching himself, he wondered what had happened to his courage.

Cluttering up his internal conflict on this challenge was the overriding lack of resolve or clarity around just what he would choose to study if he enrolled at the university. He was interested in the sciences, but outside of the challenge of mathematics there was no burning desire to become an engineer, a biologist, a physicist, a forester, a chemist, or a medical doctor, even though those careers could provide a source of income and a life's work.

Mason definitely did not want to study to become a teacher after so many classroom experiences that left tell-tale markings of their boredom and lethargy. What would be the purpose of going to university, then? After debating with himself for three days and still not being clear on the matter, he finally decided at the very least, he was weirdly honour-bound to follow through with the admissions counsellor's suggestion.

Off he went to the Friendship Centre, and upon inquiry, was asked to come back the next day, as the person who could do the research was not in that day. The next day rolled around, and Mason was becoming less and less enthusiastic about pursuing this avenue. But for some unknowable reason, he pushed himself anyway and went to the Friendship Centre for the second time.

This time, he got to meet with a young Indigenous female by the name of Millie, who told him, after taking his history, that it would take a week to collect the relevant information and determine if he was eligible for university funding.

Mason next returned to the registrar's office out of a commitment to let the counsellor know that it would be at least a week before he could find out if funding was available. The counsellor said that this was a problem, as the university was to commence in one week. The counsellor asked Mason to return the following day, as she needed to consult with the Dean of Admissions.

Returning the following day, the counsellor informed him that he might be eligible for an interim bursary and that she had arranged an appointment for an interview with the Dean later that afternoon.

This was getting beyond him, as Mason had no idea what a bursary was or why he was still pursuing this pathway. Honour-bound again, he waited patiently until the appointment time, and then he showed up at Dean Harris's office.

As he waited for the appointment, he was interested to learn that the Dean of Admissions was also the Dean of Science. He held a professorship in the field of mathematics, which also perked his interest.

Mason was greeted by an elderly, grey-haired, soft-spoken man wearing a bowtie. With a curious yet encouraging manner, he asked Mason about his reasons for wanting to go to university.

Mason declared that he had a strong interest in mathematics and astronomy, but he also wanted to explore the field of psychology, possibly to learn about how human beings function, and especially to learn why they suffer so much.

Dean Harris then asked Mason about his family and living situation. In an emotionless manner, Mason shared that he lived alone and that both his parents had passed. As far as he knew, he was half Indigenous, due to his father's origin as a Blackfoot Native. Dean Harris then asked him if he had any relatives in BC, to which Mason responded that there were none, although he did know about an aunt who lived in Alberta. He mentioned that he had spent the last six years in foster homes and a group home.

When he heard Mason's story, the Dean apologetically said that he was not eligible for a bursary if he was possibly going to receive Band funding. But what happened next was totally unexpected. The Dean pulled out his cheque book and started writing a personal cheque. He gave it to Mason. Mason looked at it; he saw his name and the amount, written on the cheque was four hundred dollars. The Dean then told Mason that he could enrol in first-year studies as a probationary student using the money as a deposit on his tuition. Continuation as a student beyond the mid-term period would depend on his eligibility for Band or any other funding. Mason also was not to worry about paying it back, as the Dean was certain that he would pay this gift forward to someone else in need down the road.

Stunned and speechless at the thought that he was supported in this way, Mason left the appointment in a daze. *Where did this man come from? What was his motive? Why would a complete stranger give him a gift with no strings attached?* Nothing in his mind suggested that he deserved it. His life experience to date told him that you don't get something for nothing. Was this a random act of kindness? He wondered to himself, *How do we give without getting anything in return?* He recalled this also happened in his early childhood experiences with the Salvation Army. *Was giving without getting an underlying human value?* This was definitely a question he needed to explore further.

More and more questions tumbled through his mind yet no answers were forthcoming. Was this going to be one of the challenging aspects of the road ahead for him? Either way, it was clear that these questions would be important for his journey ahead. Exactly how, he did not yet know.

Then, the reality of becoming a university student and having to perform began to sink in over the next few hours. Presenting himself in a situation where he would be judged on his performance would be a departure from his past pattern of avoiding the scrutiny of others.

High school was not challenging for him, and he never felt that he was competing for grades. What little he knew about university was that it definitely was a competitive environment, and it was much tougher than high school. The drop-out rate for first-year students was over fifty percent.

Perhaps it was time to put himself to the test. In the back of his mind, he would hear his mother's words: "Do your best in school and never give up." Mason decided it was time to break out of his shadow, much like he did when he boldly took the job on the fishing boat.

There was no turning back now for Mason. He was university bound. He would enrol in the first year as a science student, taking courses in mathematics, physics, and psychology. Perhaps his relatively successful experience in high school with both physics and mathematics might give him a fighting chance of being successful in these courses. Psychology, on the other hand, was an unknown field to him, apart from the brief introduction he received from having had a firsthand experience with a child psychologist.

The last week before classes were to start, Mason ruminated excessively about the journey that he was about to undertake. Over and over again he found himself bouncing back and forth from feeling hopeful to being filled with fear of failure.

On the first day of classes, at his first class in mathematics he showed up at the lecture hall along with over eighty other students. It was daunting, to say the least. The math professor spoke for an hour and a half with no student interaction. When the lecture ended, he couldn't remember anything the professor had said, apart from what chapters in the textbook he had to read for the next class.

Very quickly, Mason learned that hard work would not be enough. University proved to be as difficult as he was told, and it was definitely anxiety-provoking. He was constantly worried about not being smart enough, never mind that he felt he really didn't belong. He had no reference point from his background to give him assurances that this was the right path to take.

Over the first month, his performance was borderline, despite his unrelenting effort to make studying more important than anything else. Day after day, seven days a week, he would study into the early morning hours, sometimes neglecting sleep altogether. On many occasions, he would read sitting up and eventually wrap his arms around himself and rock himself to sleep.

More and more, he was proving to himself that he was incapable and did not belong in university. It seemed that he was in over his head and fooling himself that he could succeed. Being at university was like being stranded on a life raft in an unpredictable ocean with nowhere to go. He developed no friendships and participated in no extracurricular activities. Essentially, he was a recluse. Back into his shadow, he thought. Yet, he was bound and determined to forge ahead.

Even more disconcerting was the news that he was eligible for university funding that would cover his tuition and living expenses for one year. So, once again, as he had with Dean Harris, he felt obligated to pursue university further.

His confidence was on shaky ground, as he was still uncertain whether he could be successful at university level.

First term exams were a disaster despite his study efforts, which were far beyond the normal. He did manage to pass his psychology courses with average grades and a math course with a first-class grade. He failed the two other courses he was taking. Mason was allowed to continue to the second term, but something had to change. He could not tolerate the idea of quitting. Hard work alone was simply not going to work.

He noticed how he had ignored his hygiene and basic nutritional needs. Looking into the mirror—which was something he rarely did, even when brushing his teeth—it struck him how untidy he looked. He seldom combed his hair and his clothes were wrinkled—not to mention unclean. He wore the same clothes for days on end. He thought that he looked like a street person.

His shadow had returned. Only this time, it was a different shadow. This shadow was not something he could retreat into; it was something more ominous. Now, it was a shadow that disowned his new unfolding self rather than protecting it. In a moment of clarity, it occurred to him that this shadow contained all the things he did not like about himself. This shadow rejected his newly developing boldness and courage to become a significant person. It was sabotaging his desire to come out of his old closet.

This triggered a memory of what Arnold had said to him when he was living in a foster home. "When you fully come out of your shadow and take off the mask that you are wearing, it will be very challenging. You will come face to face with the inner demons that you have protected yourself from experiencing. When this happens, you must not fight these demons. You must recognize them as unreal creations that arise from decisions you made about yourself when you were young. Those decisions may have made sense at the time. Decisions like 'nobody cares about me. I am inadequate. I don't count.' These decisions were made in order to protect you from your own fears. They will no longer apply when your courage to challenge the world you live in shows up."

This is a wake-up call, he thought. *It is time to regroup and stop fighting myself. It is time to shift and move forward with an attitude that I can do it. I just need to trust my developing self to do its best. I need to open myself to finding out more about who I really am and capable of being.*

This shift started by changing his study habits. Instead of studying as if nothing else mattered, he backed off. He still put in long hours of studying, but now he started to engage in some peripheral socializing with other students. He started showing more interest in what fellow students were talking about. This interest eventually helped Mason engage in the conversations and participate in after-class coffee sessions at the student union building as well as taking up chess again as a hobby. Every afternoon after classes he would show up at the student union building and join in with a group playing chess. This was in stark contrast to first term, when he would immediately decline any invitation to join any group or even go for coffee with anyone except himself.

Chapter Six

⊰⊱ Relationship Crucible ⊰⊱

A NOTHER IMPETUS FOR CHANGE occurred when the Social Psychology course he was taking required students to pair up to work on a semester-long assignment focusing on psychological issues related to cultural integration. As it turned out, Mason was paired with an extraordinarily attractive and athletic-looking student named Sylvia. Without any hesitancy she approached him, and confidently suggested that they meet weekly for two hours at the library over the course of the semester.

The professor had instructed that at their first meeting, each partner was required to tell the other their background, why they were taking this course, what their major was, and what they enjoyed doing recreationally.

Sylvia opened by sharing, "I am currently majoring in marine biology, although medicine also interests me. My father is a medical doctor. The Social Psychology course was just one of a number of elective humanities courses open for me to take as part of my degree requirements."

Intrigued by her confidence, Mason was keen to hear her talk some more. He asked, "Why did you choose this one, specifically?"

Sylvia smiled. "The course outline appealed to me mostly because I'm curious about how different cultures develop. I am an only child born and raised in Ontario in a strict very devout catholic family so I don't know much about other cultures."

Mason responded, "From what I know, Ontario has some of the best universities in Canada. What made you decide to come here to study?"

Sylvia replied, "My parents didn't want me to study this far away from home, but since marine biology has been my childhood passion, I was able to convince them to allow me to study out here on the west coast, close to the ocean. Besides, I wanted to get away from my home environment and spread my wings a little."

Mason didn't want her to stop sharing. Summoning up all the courage he could muster, he asked, "What do you do when you're not studying?"

Sylvia responded, "Well, I'm a member of the University Swimming Club, and I like taking long hikes in the wilderness." She then leaned forward over the table they were sitting at, looked him straight in the eyes, and said, "Okay, Mason, now it's your turn."

Taken off guard by her boldness, he was lost for words. He could not take his eyes off her. Her gaze was penetrating, and it felt as if her energy was enveloping him, taking over his body. She broke the trance by placing her hand on his wrist with a twinkle in her eyes, suggesting that it was perfectly okay if he wanted to wait until he felt ready to share.

At that juncture, he finally took a deep breath and awkwardly blurted out, "I am working on completing a degree in both mathematics and psychology. Psychology is my primary interest, although I am uncertain about where it will take me career-wise. Mathematics appeals to me, as I am interested in knowing how the world works scientifically. Regarding Social Psychology, my mixed cultural heritage has me searching for answers to the many questions I have about my cultural identity, as well as that of others across all cultures. I grew up in foster homes in BC, due to both my parents passing away when I was quite young. I live alone off campus, and I like to spend my spare time like you do, hiking and swimming…or doing anything to do with the outdoors."

"Great," she said. "Come join the team. The swim club meets every second day."

Mason was hesitant to reply at first given his aversion to joining groups and his lack of confidence in his swimming ability. Finally he blurted out that he was not comfortable with competition. Sylvia pressed further and assured him that, while the team was competitive, members really only competed with themselves and their desire to do their best.

This "doing your best" caught his interest, as he reminded himself that this was what his mother had always encouraged him to do. He finally consented to give it a try.

When Mason showed up to his first swim meeting later that evening, Sylvia grabbed him by the arm and introduced him to James, her swim coach. He was a tall, athletically chiselled man who looked like he was in his mid-forties. Almost immediately, Mason felt a sense of relief, as the coach had a peacefulness about him that seem to radiate a respect for others. He thanked Mason for attending and encouraged him to simply swim lengths in the open lane for as long as he liked. James said that if Mason had any questions, he would be happy to talk further with him.

Mason attended three swim sessions over the next week, as Sylvia bugged him to do so. He found himself agreeing to go because she was so engaging and enthusiastic—not to mention sensual. She seemed genuinely interested in becoming more than a friend. He could sense that she was attracted to him, and he could not deny that he found her to be very attractive. It felt like she was a magnet drawing him in at every breath.

At the fourth session Mason attended, James approached him and asked him if he had any questions, or if he would be open to any feedback from him. Mason did not know what to say except that he enjoyed swimming, but after watching the other swim team members; he felt that they were much more capable than he was.

Towering over Mason, James put his hand on Mason's shoulder and told him that some of team had been swimming for over ten years as members of some swim team, so they were very experienced. He then told Mason that he had been watching him over the past week. He said that he didn't often come across a person who demonstrated a natural talent for swimming. Mason was one of them. James went on to say that if Mason was interested and willing, he would like to coach him.

Mason was hooked. Swimming seemed to be like meditation, where his thoughts got suspended; everything seemed to flow naturally, and he felt in charge of himself. His negative thoughts about academics were left at the edge of the pool, which was tremendously relieving for him. Mason committed to swimming every other day. It also offered him the opportunity to spend more time with Sylvia. It soon became more than a friendship, as Sylvia agreed to become a study partner and go out on dates together.

Returning to his apartment late one evening after watching a movie with Sylvia, Mason could tell that something had shifted. His attitude had somehow changed, as had his view of university. Something clicked; he felt a growing sense of confidence. Learning suddenly became enjoyable instead of never-ending hard work. He started to look forward to his classes, his curiosity became more acute, and he felt a hunger to learn as much as he could from every minute spent in class. His interest in studying also shifted, as he found himself going to the library to study rather than studying at his apartment. At times, he could not wait to go to the library and crack open a book.

His relationship with Sylvia started to be more intimate as the term went on, to the point that they were now out on dates every weekend and studying together on an almost-daily basis. This was the closest he had ever been to anyone. The way she smiled at him when he was not looking radiated a feeling of warmth and acceptance that he had never felt before—not even with his mother. His body had come alive with passion, and his mind was open to making a commitment.

Then, suddenly, just after mid-term exams, Sylvia became quite ill. She needed to be hospitalized. She was diagnosed with mononucleosis with liver complications. After three weeks, she was released from the hospital to the care of her parents. They had arrived a few days after her hospitalization. Their plan was to take her back to their home in Ontario so she could recover. Mason remained in the background, as he felt that they did not approve of him. He wasn't sure why, except perhaps that he was not catholic and had a mixed native background. Sylvia was quite weak and frail-looking, and she seemed to downplay her relationship with him. As he had learned to do in the past when he felt excluded or rejected by others, Mason retreated to his shadow, numbed by a sense of powerlessness to do anything about the situation.

Before leaving for home with her parents, Sylvia intimated she would want to rekindle their relationship when she got better and returned to her studies. After she left, Mason struggled with a sense of guilt for not being more caring toward her. He wondered how she coped with her illness, yet he could not find it within himself or the opportunity to ask her how she felt about it. As well as not being able to express his concern for her ill health, he was also unable to get in touch with any feelings he had towards her regarding her moving away and returning home with her parents.

After about six weeks, he surfaced again as his numbness had gradually faded away. He returned to socializing again, but this time he noticed that he was much more cautious about allowing himself to become too connected to others.

As his first year was coming to an end, Mason's long-distance correspondence with Sylvia became less frequent, and by the end of the year, she had stopped responding to his letters. It seemed to Mason that she had lost interest, even though he felt that he had not, but once again could not say this to her. There was still a strong desire to contact her, which he resisted for fear of experiencing further rejection. He was not sure that he could endure this. He felt that the only way he could accept this loss was to bury his feelings for her and let the relationship slip away.

As summer approached, Mason experienced a strong urge to make contact with Sylvia again. He thought of getting on a Greyhound Bus and travelling to Ontario with the intent of recapturing his relationship with Sylvia. These urges disappeared as he quickly buried them under a ton of reasons for why he should not act impulsively, as it was out of character for him. It was best not to feed these urges in any way. He needed to work on his deep wounds, fears, and illusions before making any commitments to others.

Chapter Seven

⚜ Critical Thinking ⚜

A S THE ACADEMIC YEAR came to an end, Mason success-fully completed all of his courses. He felt that he had found his academic legs and his confidence had increased significantly. Funding was then secured for his remaining three years of undergraduate study, conditional on his continued successful performance.

Looking ahead to the next year of study, Mason now felt committed to continuing his study of both mathematics and psychology. Mathematics challenged him to explore the baseline framework of science, plus he wanted to honour the impact Dean Harris had on him. But psychology intrigued him more. He became more curious about what function the psyche plays in performance, perception, learning, and personal, as well as moral, development, not to mention his own development.

What he uncovered over the next three years was the purity of mathematics and the immense underlying impact it has had on scientific advancement. While difficult to make use of in his day-to-day student life, it still had a strong appeal to him. Even though many times throughout the four years of study it was difficult to make sense of the complexity and abstract na ure of mathematics, he persevered. The perspective offered to him by one of his professors helped him to be patient. The professor mentioned, "Understanding the efficacy of mathematics requires that one simply weave together the abstract concepts and over time they eventually will coalesce into a pattern that has both cohesiveness and clarity."

In the beginning, Mason found that the psychology courses were interesting but not really exciting. The course on motivation was ironically uninspiring. Abnormal Psychology, considered the cornerstone course, was dry. The Behavioural Research course seemed wanting, as it was soft science at best.

What captured his interest most was a course entitled "Perception and Time." The part of the course that interested him most was the part that addressed how different beliefs, patterns, and cultures by humans could create different perceptions. The different windows of perception historically proposed by Aldous Huxley were very intriguing, challenging the primary scientific view of an objective observer. It proposed the concept that time was different for different cultures. Standard scientific time was fixed but psychological time was not, making time relative and not a fixed entity. This led him to take any courses available that focused on exploring human psychobiological and spiritual development. Fixing human mind-body problems attracted him to explore everything from psychoanalysis to spiritual healing.

Despite the intrinsic value he was getting out of his courses in psychology, he was disturbed by how immensely difficult it was to put these teachings into effective practise. It was abundantly evident to him that the study of psychology focused disproportionately on the barriers to human well-being and far less on human competency and self-sufficiency. He surmised this was so because schools were largely teaching to support students' work in jobs that endeavoured to fix human problems, helping people to cope with their lives, and change people's perception of life's problems.

Psychology seemed to treat intuition as a fantasy realm, and transformation as interesting but impractical. Human competency took a back seat to a heavy focus on human suffering. Cognitive functioning combined with behavioural management was also of primary importance. Human potential was addressed but mostly in the context of what was in the way of actualizing human potential.

This prompted Mason to read anything related to existential, transpersonal, or humanistic psychology in his spare time. These avenues were not considered substantive and were relegated to the fringe of mainstream psychology. And, of course, these avenues would not do anything to support him to find a job.

There was so much to consider. Theories in the social, psychological, and biological sciences seemed disconnected, often competing or even contradicting with one another. No unifying platform addressing human existence was evident to him. As such, he could not bring himself to get totally committed to any one theoretical paradigm of thought.

Even the medical sciences were symptom driven, authoritarian, and pathologically biased more often focusing on parts while ignoring the whole. Health and healing seemed focused on intervention and paid almost no attention to prevention. In summary, he thought that illness trumped wellness.

Indulging in weird tangential thinking, Mason wondered, *Are we second-hand people controlled by history, the bureaucracy of fixing, making better, my way is better? Religion was also compartmentalized, with each sect competing to righteously attract humans into its organizational fold based on dogma, fear-driven rituals, and blind faith. What a smorgasbord of human paradigms!*

Puzzled and confused once again, Mason began wondering what role psychology played in healing and why there was so much preoccupation with human suffering.

He encountered many students in the Student Union Centre having coffee and telling one another how difficult their lives were, how their families suffered, and how they suffered being a student. How there was always a shortage of time, courses were difficult, professors were confusing, money was a problem, the workload was too heavy, and competition for grades was very stressful.

Mason, on the other hand, had learned to not give much thought about how difficult life was for him; this only interfered with intent on being clear-minded on what he was doing. He concluded that his life and background were how his destiny had unfolded; that really could not be altered, nor it did it need to be. What was still unclear for him was what would turn out to be his career path.

After his relationship with Sylvia ended, student life did not produce any new opportunities for intimate relationships. Mason shied away from any opportunities that did show up from time to time, as he was not willing to experience rejection again. Most of his student social connections revolved around swimming at the local aquatic centre on the weekends, or playing chess at the Student Union Centre.

His summer months were spent reluctantly working on the fishing boats or, when he was in port, kayaking and doing weekend hiking trips up local mountains or out in the back woods of Vancouver Island. He was drawn to the outdoors and thoroughly enjoyed being in nature. Occasionally, he would get involved in hiking trips and group kayaking, but for the most part he preferred to be by himself.

Throughout his student years, he made a few friends who, like him, tended to be "loners" and never made demands of him. He liked it that way, although there were times when he wanted company but was not willing to go out of his way to seek it.

The four years seemed to go by quite quickly, and then he was done his bachelor's degree. Graduation was a nonevent for Mason, as he chose not to attend the graduation ceremony. There was no one to share it with, much like it was for his high school graduation.

Completing the degree was confidence-building, but outside of that, it felt like it didn't make a huge difference in the world he lived in. There was not much that he could do that interested him, having only a bachelor's degree in science. It was time to move on and explore his next horizon.

He knew that he did not want to become a school counsellor or a social worker, especially given his own past experience with social workers. He briefly explored medicine but quickly ruled it out, as it seemed far beyond his grasp.

With a baseline background in psychology, the idea of becoming a healer or a psychologist like Arnold started to percolate. Native healing was of particular interest to Mason, although he had no idea how to pursue it. He reflected on how many times he had heard of the suffering of First Nations peoples and their need to heal the wounds of their past.

Mason thought, *Can someone like me learn to become such a healer? How would I know if I was destined to become a healer and what would I need to know and master to be accepted as one?* These questions were definitely not addressed in traditional clinical psychology.

He did know from his studies that exploring the impact of trauma was a primary cornerstone of therapeutic healing, which a healer would have to address both with themselves and others. This presented a major stumbling block for him, as he had a strong aversion to going backward in time. This was, of course, related to his own past experiences and traumas. He recalled how many times others, such as caregivers and social workers from his past, had often spoken to him about his past traumas and reminded him that he would eventually have to address them. Arnold had said the same thing.

On another front, how could he really know the healing needs of others directly, and not just through books? Given that he avoided developing relationships with others, how could he know their healing needs, being at arms-length?

To gain some degree of balance with his troubling questions, Mason continued to swim and took to mountain biking. Like swimming and running, cycling offered him a space to let go of unwanted thoughts and permitted him to go with the flow of just living moment to moment. As often as he could, he rode his mountain bike on wooded pathways or along old logging roads, always looking for new roads to explore in the backwoods of Vancouver Island. He found it relaxing to be away from civilization and spent time among the trees and around the ocean.

Out on his mountain bike, Mason would ruminate on how generally unimpressed he was with psychology but not mathematics. Psychology seemed to include a mixture of different philosophies and was shrouded with competing theories, while mathematics was esoteric and had an abstract purity to it. He was often reminded during his studies that the first degree in psychology only provided a basic foundation. For more in depth and intriguing aspects, one would have to go to graduate school.

What's next? A bachelor's degree in science was only a starting point, not an end point. In the meantime, without any attachments, he took on part-time summer employment as a tree planter. At least this got him out in the wilderness, which resonated with his desire to be connected to nature.

Now that university life was behind him, he started to spend more time reading books on subjects related to human soulfulness and unity consciousness. This ignited an interest in participating in philosophical debates at a local coffee house. Mason found it fascinating to hear what others had to say about philosophical or psychological topics, which allowed him to fine tune his own perspective. At these debates, he met many open-minded, passionate thinkers. Mason himself was reluctant to be passionate or opinionated about anything, choosing to feed off the enthusiasm of others. These encounters served to keep him loosely connected to others. This balanced the solitude he experienced while he was out in the wilderness for extended periods of time. There were a few occasions where he was invited to extend the dialogue with others away from the coffee house, but he always found an excuse to decline the invitations.

A local jazz club also became an infrequent hang-out, as jazz resonated with Mason's contemplative nature. He often found himself sitting with regulars for hours at a time, just listening and engaging in the occasional idle conversation, which suited him just fine.

Chapter Eight

❈ The Four-Fold Way ❈

O N A LATE SUMMER afternoon with no commitments, Mason went off for a long bike ride. The ride took him out on a gravel logging road, winding through old-growth wilderness. He was not sure where it led to, but that didn't matter. He needed to be away from civilization to reflect and ponder what to do next.

Pondering what may lie ahead for him did not gain any traction, as he found himself getting lost in random thoughts that had no pattern. It occurred to him that he might just be getting caught up in trying to outride the thoughts coursing through his mind.

After about an hour out on his bike, he noticed a long, open shed ahead of him on one side. It was completely open at the front, and the closer he got, he started to notice colourfully painted masks similar to the ones Arnold had shown him at his clinic several years back. Sticking out from the shed was a large, round, clean cedar log about four feet in diameter. It was spread across wooden cradles. It appeared to be in the process of being carved, as he noticed that the part being carved at the bottom end bore a vague resemblance to a woman. His curiosity got the better of him, so he stopped to examine it. And then it dawned on him that perhaps it was a totem pole in the making, like the ones he had seen in a *National Geographic* magazine.

Getting closer, he confirmed his suspicions: sure enough, it was a soon-to-be totem pole. He had also read about totem poles in his Social Psychology course. Totems were a well-known part of the West Coast Native cultural tradition. Beyond that, he didn't know anything about them. Mason wondered why totem poles were significant and a West Coast Aboriginal phenomenon. They were known to exist in other places as well but, from what he knew, not to the same extent.

No one appeared to be there. He had the urge to explore further, so down went his bike. Looking to see if anybody was around and seeing no one, he walked toward the totem. On the way, two other smaller—but upright—totem poles in the background caught his eye. They were painted in very rich red and black colours, with some of the yellow cedar left exposed. The smell of the yellow cedar carving chips scattered around the totem poles wafted through the air, leaving Mason with an earthy, grounded feeling.

As he looked around, he noticed that the whole area was heavily treed, predominantly with large, very old cedars that towered hundreds of feet up into the sky. He guessed that some of them were at least five feet across at the base. How old they were, he did not really know.

The totems drew him towards them. They were mystical looking and reeked with culture. He was so engrossed in this experience that he almost jumped out of his skin when he heard a deep voice behind him say, "What do you want to see?"

Abruptly, he turned around and encountered an older, serious looking silver-haired man with what appeared to be a carving tool belt strapped around his waist. His hands were calloused and knurled up. Mason assumed that he was the carver of the totem poles.

Mason responded "I have not seen a real totem before, only in books. I am curious about the importance of totems to Indigenous people."

"What is your name?" The Carver asked.

"I am Mason Walkway."

The Carver inquisitively asked, "How did you get to be named Walkway?"

"My father was from the Blackfoot Nation in the prairies."

"What are you doing here on the West Coast?"

Nervously, Mason blurted out, "Both my parents have passed away and I have been attending the university here hoping to become a counsellor or maybe even a healer."

He went on to say that he had studied psychology at the university. But he was not finding it to be helpful in his search for the answers to the many questions he had about mental and emotional health, curing, and healing.

The Carver stared upward and did not speak for what seemed like several minutes, leaving Mason feeling more uneasy. Finally, he pulled out a carving tool from his belt and thrust it toward Mason, startling him again. What is he doing? Mason wondered.

Then, after a few seconds, the Carver told him to hold his carving tool. Mason grasped it from his hand without thinking of what he was doing. The Carver then waved for Mason to follow him over to the totem pole lying on the ground.

When they arrived at the pole, the carver picked out another carving tool from his belt that was scallop shaped. Speaking in a much softer tone, the Carver said, "Let's see if the totem pole might shed some light on your questions."

"Totems are carved for many purposes, in many different ways, by many cultures. Some think totems tell a story. In our culture, that is not the primary purpose. The West coast totems are monuments. Here they are carved to acknowledge historical events or honour people of distinction in our community. Sometimes, they can be carved to represent the healing of a community wound, or even a wound between cultures.

"The woman at the base is meant to be an invitation for us to heal our wounds with kindness. She is embraced by a healing blanket, which represents the interweaving of many Indigenous cultures across our land. The blanket also possesses a thread connecting all peoples to our Indigenous cultures.

"The wolf above is to remind us of our need for strong family ties and our desire to communicate effectively, to honour one another, and to exercise good intelligence. Importantly, it is a symbol of a free and powerful spirit within us. It symbolizes our natural capability to trust our hearts and minds as we seek to support one another toward being whole and complete, and to be in charge of our destiny.

"I am carving the bottom third of the totem pole. The top third will be carved by my son when I am finished the bottom. I will then continue carving the middle portion."

He went on to say, "It is also misunderstood that the totem pole has shamanistic intentions. It does not. It can, however, symbolize the desire for healing and harmony between peoples, which is the case with this totem I am carving. This pole will also share our community's message that we welcome all people to our lands so that they might get to know us and experience our culture."

Mason was engrossed by the words of the Carver. "In your culture, what is required to become a healer?" Mason asked.

The Carver did not answer this question. Instead, he asked: "Where do you live?"

Mason explained that he lived in a basement apartment not far from the university. The Carver then asked, "Do you want to know more about native healing?" Mason felt like the Carver was reading his mind because this was what he was going to ask next.

"I know a little about the medicine wheel and the focus on holistic and spiritual healing, but only from what I have read in my psychology studies on native healing. I know healing lodges exist in First Nations communities, and natural healing is culturally embraced. I really don't know much more than that, but I am really interested in finding out as much as I can about aboriginal healing practices."

Instead of addressing Mason's response to his question, the Carver said, "In our culture, we have healers." He pointed to the carved woman and blanket at the bottom of the totem pole. "Sometimes, we refer to them as medicine men or women, but that is becoming less and less common, as modern white man medicine has all but overtaken cultural healing. Now, we refer to them as healing elders. To be acknowledged as a healer, one has to be accepted as such by the community as a whole."

Mason then shared his dilemma. "I really don't know what direction to take right now. My studies have been helpful. But I still don't feel like what I have learned gives me a clear picture of what I want to be doing in the future."

"What questions do you have?" asked the Carver.

Mason felt tongue-tied. But then, unexpectedly, he blurted out one question, which ran into another. "I want to know how healing works when separated into compartments, such as body, mind, and spirit. What are the most effective ways to ensure that healing works? Can anyone objectively and independently be a healer? These are some of my questions, but not all. I know there are shamans, cult healers, medical healers, spiritual healers, body healers, emotional healers, mental healers, faith healers, and more, of course. Which one fits for me, I don't yet know."

After a long pause, the Carver asked if Mason knew anything about sweat lodges. Mason said, "I have heard of them, but I only know they have something to do with cleansing the mind and the body."

The Carver went on to say that sweat lodges were open to anyone who wanted to experience what healing was for them, regardless of race or creed. No invitation was required, as simply showing up meant you were welcome to participate.

"Perhaps you may first want to consider attending a sweat lodge ceremony as a way to explore some of your questions?"

"Where and when do they occur?" Mason asked.

"They occur in our community, as in many other Indigenous communities. Here in our community, we have a sweat lodge on the last Saturday of every month, which will happen this coming Saturday. If you are interested, Crystal, a university student who happens to be from our community, will bring you to the sweat Lodge next Saturday at 10:00 a.m. I will give you a number and you can call her if you like."

Taking Crystal's telephone number, Mason thanked the Carver for the invite. The Carver gently responded, "It really was not an invitation; it is something you could consider experiencing along your path."

With that, Mason parted ways. With much to think about, he cycled back to his basement apartment. He was intrigued, but not convinced that this was for him. His mind went back and forth on the merits of doing a sweat lodge. He did not know what to expect or what value it would have for him. When he got back to his apartment after two hours of cycling, exhausted physically and mentally, he was more confused than ever. Frustrated by his indecision, Mason finally decided to bite the bullet and call Crystal to make arrangements for the pickup.

When Crystal showed up Saturday morning, Mason was startled. She appeared to be a few years younger than him, with fair hair and a slight build. She was dressed in black baggy sweatpants and an oversized grey collarless sweatshirt. Her femininity was definitely meant to be downplayed. In contrast, Mason was attired in striped track pants and a bright red hoodie. Mason noticed that she definitely did not look Indigenous.

When she first introduced herself, Mason immediately felt at ease. There was a childlike excitement in her voice and her attitude as she mentioned how honoured she was to meet him and to be going to a sweat ceremony with him.

She motioned him to her car, which was an older Volkswagen Beetle. Once on the way, she mentioned that she was also a student at the university, in the First Nations social work program.

Crystal had a calm demeanour about her that Mason liked. She exuded a self-confidence that he felt he did not have. There was nothing pretentious about her, and that put him at ease. He felt like he could easily communicate with her, even though he did not really know her.

Crystal was a non-stop questioner for the better part of their trip. She wanted to know everything about his interests in psychology and how he met the Carver. At first, Mason was guarded in his replies to her questions, a well-practised habit that he had acquired.

Interspersed with her questions, she announced that she was in her second year of a two-year First Nations social work program. Her plan was to return to work in her community as a social services worker in the fall. It was a brand-new program, so she shared that there were no guarantees that she would be hired by her band office. She went on to ask Mason if he had ever been to a sweat before, and Mason said no.

"Have you attended many sweats?" Mason asked. Crystal mentioned that she had attended one roughly every three or four months over the past three years. She went on to say that she was a member of the band that they were driving to, but she lived off reserve. Mason didn't ask yet, but he wondered if she was half native like he was.

He found himself staring at her until she noticed and asked, "Why are you staring at me?"

He apologized for being rude and went on to comment, "I am part Blackfoot from my father's origin, and I could not help thinking that perhaps you too were part native?"

Crystal replied, "Yes, my father is Coast Salish, and my mother is of Dutch descent. Both my father and mother live on reserve. I get asked this question often."

Mason felt a growing attraction to Crystal, which unnerved him, as this was not what he had expected. He found himself sharing more than he was used to, telling her about his questions about healing and his interest in possibly becoming a healer. He was careful to note that these were developing ideas, and he was by no means clear about what pathway to take moving forward.

Crystal replied, "Your willingness to attend a healing sweat tells me you want to know everything you can about healing and human suffering. Doing a sweat may answer some of your questions from an Indigenous perspective, but I am sure that it won't answer all of them. Thank you for agreeing to come with me."

During quiet moments along their journey, Mason noticed a small leather bag hanging from the rear-view mirror. He had detected that it seemed to give off a smell that was unknown to him but was nevertheless pleasing. He had the urge to ask her about its purpose. "What is the smell coming from that pouch?" he asked, pointing his finger towards it.

Crystal responded, "It contains sage for cleansing the mind and the body. When we get to the sweat, we will engage in a brief cleansing ceremony before entering the sweat lodge."

Arriving at the sweat lodge, Mason observed twelve people, all engaged in random conversation around an open-pit fire. There were five women, who were all middle-aged except for Crystal, and seven men of all ages.

Crystal directed Mason to a middle-aged Indigenous man with a shovel in his hands. He appeared to be tending the fire. Inside the fire were large soccer-ball-sized rocks showing signs of getting red hot. Crystal introduced Mason to Daniel Littlelight and stated that he was the fire keeper. Daniel acknowledged him with a nod and turned away to tend the fire. Mason felt uncomfortable being next to Daniel as his presentation was seemingly gloomy and quite serious. It led him to think that maybe Daniel was not pleased that he was there attending the sweat.

Focused on the fire, Daniel pointed with his shovel. In a gruff voice he then stated, "When they are hot enough, seven rocks called grandfather rocks will be placed in the sweat lodge centre pit." Pointing to the dome-shaped construction completely covered in animal hides about twenty-five feet from the fire pit, he continued. There was also only one way in or out—a small opening permitting only one person at a time to crouch to enter or depart.

Daniel continued, "The sweat will be conducted in four parts, each will last for about an hour. In each round, the sweat Elder will focus on something important about healing and then the Elder will instruct everyone to take a break from the sweat and leave the lodge. After the break you will re-enter the lodge when the Elder instructs you to do so. Before starting the next round, another seven grandfather rocks will be placed in the sweat lodge centre pit."

Crystal, likely noticing the uneasiness in Mason interjected in a more upbeat enthusiastic way, "Sometimes, when there are too many people, regular attendees step back so that new people can participate in the healing sweat. The maximum this sweat can accommodate is fifteen people. I am happy that everyone here today will be able to participate."

The Fire Keeper then stated, "Since you are the only person here today who has not attended a sweat lodge before, take the towel you were asked to bring with you into the sweat. You enter the sweat only when the Elder sweat leader arrives and asks you to do so." Daniel went on to say, "It is our custom not to speak in the sweat unless asked to do so by the Elder."

After about half an hour, an elderly man with braided hair and wearing sweatpants and a t-shirt arrived. He introduced himself as William and said that he would be conducting the sweat today. After a brief conversation with the fire keeper, he invited everyone to form a circle. Placing himself inside the circle, he lit a small bowl of sage and fanned it with an eagle feather until it smouldered. Moving around the circle, he cleansed each participant with the sage smoke, front and back, using the eagle feather.

Mason had known about this practise through his Indigenous readings, but this was his first experience participating in a cleansing ceremony. It was simple and very humbling. William then asked all the men to follow him into the sweat and indicated that all the women were to follow in after the men.

When the fire keeper started to bring in the glowing hot rocks, the Elder mentioned that if, at any time, anyone felt the need to leave, they could do so without any questions asked. One just had to say aloud that they wanted to go out. After the seven rocks were placed in the pit, the flap to the lodge was drawn down, making it pitch dark, save the light from the glowing rocks. The Elder then spilled water on the rocks, creating a plume of steam that billowed upward and spread throughout the lodge. It got hot very quickly.

William the Elder went on to talk about how there would be four rounds today, with a break between each round when new rocks would be added. While speaking, he spread sage over the rocks and gave thanks to mother earth and what he called the grandfather rocks.

The sweat elder explained to the attendees that the rounds would follow the four compass directions, starting with North, then the East, then South, and finally the West. The first round would focus on self-healing. The second round would focus on one's relations. The third round would address one's community, and the fourth would cover gratitude.

As the lodge elder offered thanks to the wisdom of the elders, he spoke about the spirit world guiding participants along the pathway of respect for all living beings, honouring their connectedness to nature and valuing family. Most importantly, he invited everyone to allow the sweat experience to purify their mind, body, and soul.

As the sweat progressed, his level of discomfort increased depending on how much water was spilled onto the hot rocks. Getting out for a breather between each round was relieving and kept him wanting to move forward with the experience. He found that being in the dark throughout the rounds with the door closed was humbling.

In no particular order, participants were invited to share their thoughts and feelings if they wanted to as they related to the focus of each round. He felt passively alert and attentive while the sharing was going on, yet he was not focused on the verbalizations of the participants. It seemed that the stories were told anonymously. Mason felt that he could listen without needing to respond. His general tendency to be judgemental somehow was suspended. Mason chose not to share.

There was no desire to do so, yet he knew that he likely could if he was more open and less controlling of his thoughts. *How ironic*, he thought. Being in a womb-like structure totally in the dark, protected from being seen or revealed, was much like hiding out in his self-made imagined cocoon, which he was quite familiar with. Yet the difference was that other people were there with him too! They were unafraid to share, but he was. This was beyond his ability to comprehend.

Mason sensed that what participants were sharing was not pre-rehearsed; the words seemed to flow spontaneously; a stream of consciousness, perhaps, that really seemed to belong to the sharer only indirectly. It was as if an inner voice was speaking through them, and their words simply got absorbed in the sweat lodge. Others listen were just there as compassionate bystanders. Something about the lodge experience was soulful, or even spiritual. He sensed that the sharing had cathartic value and offered participants the opportunity to let go of resentment, as well as offer appreciations to others in their communities.

Getting further absorbed in his thoughts, he surmised that some tangential similarities existed with the catholic ritual of confession. He recalled that his mother often talked about confession, even though she was a non-practicing catholic. Maybe these confessions and acknowledgements from the sweat participants would assuage some guilt, address some of their sadness, and get them to let go of some resentments. There was remarkable enrichment to be found in making amends and acknowledging others. Mason clearly witnessed the inspiring way this traditional healing was appreciated by the community.

At the end of the sweat, he felt that his body was somewhat cleansed from the experience, but his mind was far from released from its own machinations. He felt that this was a challenge he had yet to face.

Mason approached the Elder sitting around the outside fire and asked him about the Indigenous healing realm. He noted that he was particularly curious about what Mother Earth and Father Sky had to do with healing.

The Elder spoke in a sombre, pensive way, as if he was sharing rhetorically. He said, "In aboriginal cultures, Mother Earth is revered as the ground of being. Mother Earth is always accepting, always nurturing, and unconditional in her willingness to accept and absorb our suffering. The sweat lodge serves as a womb, and Mother Earth embraces us unquestionably without any judgement, knowing that our true nature is always worthy of acceptance. Father Sky offers us the opportunity to let go of our ordinary, limiting mind and know that we are much more than our suffering. Father Sky reflects our true nature back to us in a timeless way, without beginning and without end." The Elder went on to say, "Father Sky is difficult to know directly. It can only be gazed at without thinking."

Thoroughly mystified Mason went on to ask about the purpose of heat in the lodge experience.

The Elder responded, "Heat is essential to melt away our resistance to letting go of our suffering. Heat dissolves rigidity, softens us, and leaves room for our spirit to show up." He used the example of a sugar lump. Putting it in hot water was necessary for the sugar to dissolve and become one with the water.

Mason kind of got the meaning, and then went on to ask about his own personal dilemma, albeit indirectly. "What training or experiences does one have to take to become an aboriginal healer?"

The Elder, once again in softer tones, and this time more directly, said, "The journey of being and becoming a healer is not a simple one. All four Directions need to be embraced, as you experienced in the sweat lodge. They are interwoven."

The Elder then got up and said it was time for him to leave. He offered Mason the salutation, "All my relations." Somewhat hesitant but emboldened, Mason asked the Elder if he could talk with him more at a later time. The Elder advised him that it would be best for him to return and continue his conversation with the Carver on his questions about healing.

Driving back with Crystal, Mason found himself watching her again, as he had done on the way out, intrigued by who she was. *Would he connect with her any further?* He felt a pulling inside that told him he wanted to stay connected and find out more about her heritage. Meanwhile, she turned to him and asked if he would like to go for coffee next week. Mason agreed, and they set a date for the following Saturday.

Their first coffee date was followed by several others, as Mason found Crystal to be easy to engage with. Her smile and overall enthusiasm were infectious. After a few weeks they made a habit of walking the trail that encircled the university campus before going for coffee. Their last trail walk around campus proved to be a turning point in their developing close friendship. Stopping for a coffee afterward, the conversation became more personal. Mason was caught off guard as Crystal asked if he wanted to become more serious and intimate with her, as she was not sure about his intentions.

After a long pause, Mason responded, "Getting close to others is not something I have practised much. It seems that I gravitate toward relationships that are informative, but I shy away from any commitments or attachments. My social workers used to tell me that I have serious issues with abandonment. This is the way I have been for a long time, and I don't know any other way to be or what to do about it."

As he spoke, Mason noticed Crystal's head drop down and from what he could detect she appeared to be saddened by what he was saying.

"I do know that when I see you, my heart starts to race. It makes me very uncomfortable, and I feel very vulnerable. When I get vulnerable like that, I retreat into my own bubble. I guess that way I can avoid the risk of being rejected by anyone."

Mason stopped speaking, noticing tears flowing down Crystal's cheeks. Confused and not knowing what to make of what was happening he blurted out, "Why are you crying?"

Crystal responded, "What you have said saddens me. Not because you are not willing to get more serious with me, but because I sense what you are missing."

Mason was speechless, so he just looked at Crystal with an empty sense of bewilderment. Crystal slowly stood up and said, "I am your friend now and always will be. Let's stay in touch as much as you want to." Then she left.

Mason felt an urge to go after her but remained frozen in his seat and just stared as she walked out of the café. Something was not quite right with how he could not find the courage or the words to share what was going on within him. He had no idea what he needed to do about it.

As was his tendency in all his relationships, Mason chose to discount his feelings for Crystal. In this way he did not have to address how his response towards her lacked compassion and most likely was disrespectful regarding her feelings for him. He felt twinges of guilt about being a coward but could not face condemning himself any more than he was doing. Despite Crystal's invitation to keep in contact with her if he wished he could not bring himself to do so.

***

Taking the sweat lodge Elder's advice, Mason rode out to the carving shed for the second time. On this visit, the Carver was busy doing some finishing work while his son was starting to do prep work on the top part of the totem pole. Noticing Mason's approach, the Carver stepped back from the pole and asked Mason to take a walk with him. As they walked, Mason mentioned the sweat Elder's suggestion that he further explore the questions he had on healing.

The Carver asked, "What are your questions?"

This time, Mason was better equipped to ask practical and clear questions. He responded, "The pathways of becoming a healer through science seem to be discounted by First Nations cultures. Is there a way that makes more sense to First Nations people?"

The Carver replied, "In our culture today, the pathways to learning to become a healer have almost disappeared, being replaced by modern day white man's medicine. They do exist however, but they are not easy to travel. Few choose to take it. For you, given your background, it is unlikely that you will find a way to take this pathway."

At this, Mason's heart dropped into his stomach. "What do you mean, unlikely? Isn't there anything I can do?"

The Carver smiled. "If the creator supports you to take this pathway, you will know it, but not for a long time. Our Elders have told us that Nature is the way to enter the healing path. The first task is to become whole again by connecting with Nature. They say that one must not seek to become a healer. Healing is not an event. Healing never stops and never ends. The healer's journey in our culture involves travelling the Four-Fold Way."

"What is 'the Four-Fold Way'?" Mason asked.

"The Four-Fold Way begins by establishing a footing as a Peaceful Warrior. This pathway is not about fighting. It is about courage and being challenged by nature to use your own humble power to work *with* nature, not against it. The Peaceful Warrior becomes mature through conversing with Nature. Like the traditional scout, it is his purpose to explore unknown territories and be alert to receive moment to moment information from the environment. Travelling this path, he needs to learn to become a listener without needing to hear, a gazer without having to see, a feeler without having to feel."

"This sound both intriguing and daunting. It suggests to me the Peaceful Warrior is not focused on himself, his abilities, or talents. The background becomes his main focus; not the foreground." Mason replied.

"This is true, and difficult to achieve given the self-centred world we live in. Developing a strong connection with Nature can prepare the ground for the second pathway to unfold. On this pathway, the Peaceful Warrior becomes saturated in learning all the ways healing occurs. It is important, on this pathway, for him to discover what works in healing and what does not. Learning just what he might find interesting and what agrees with his thinking is not enough. All healing realms can teach him about the journey with the healing we all experience. Most important in this learning is for him to uncover the underpinnings of natural healing."

Mason responded, "This sounds like trial-and-error learning and a need to keep an open mind and not get stuck in being the expert."

The Carver replied, "Yes, this can be so, although the Peaceful Warrior is careful not to be trapped by his opinions or assumptions, which form the basis for trial-and-error learning. Otherwise, learning is just learning and applying learning is exploring.

The third path the Peaceful Warrior travels is generally done over many years. On this pathway, his purpose is to selflessly contribute to the healing of others. While it may seem to be straightforward and easy to do, it is not. The Warrior must remain clear that it is a privilege to participate in the healing of others. He must not fall in the trap of being a master healer and viewing himself as powerful. This trap is experienced by most travelling this pathway, which ends in them no longer being able to continue the Four-Fold Way."

Mason responded, "I can clearly resonate with the idea of assisting others who are suffering is a privilege. What I am puzzled by is how much emphasis is placed on being a seasoned or experienced healer in our society at large."

Replying, the Carver said, "This is something that I am aware exists and can interfere with those who seek to take the Four-Fold Way.

Moving on, the fourth pathway lies on sacred ground. Few have been known to travel this path. It is travelled when the Peaceful Warrior evolves into the Visionary Warrior. Here is where the magic of healing can be known and understood for what it is. It not known as a mystical, metaphysical, or religious pathway, as some may mistakenly think. Its essence cannot be captured with words. The best way it can be travelled is with the guidance of wise story-tellers who have travelled this path. Through the telling of stories, they open the Warrior to experience glimpses of the power of this pathway. Any attempt to try and become a Visionary Warrior actually moves you further away from being one.

Choosing the Four-Fold Way, like the four directions, takes one on a journey which has no beginning and no end. All pathways can and do operate in an interwoven way throughout one's journey."

Overwhelmed by the depth of this roadmap, Mason remained speechless. He could not find the words to respond, choosing to nod appreciatively. He had no idea how he could or would incorporate this information, not to mention what to make of the Four-Fold Way.

Changing the focus, the Carver said, "I noticed your attention was drawn to the masks hanging on the shed several times. You may want to visit the natural museum, as they have quite a display of masks, which might interest you." Mason turned to the Carver, gave him an offering of tobacco—as Crystal had mentioned was a tradition when one engages in conversation with an Elder—and thanked him for his wisdom. With that said, they parted ways and Mason returned to his bike for the ride home.

On the way back, he thought about the Carver's comments about his interest in masks. It reminded him of his experience of wearing the native masks during one of his sessions with Arnold many years ago. Perhaps, by visiting the gallery, he might find out even more about his own character development.

Chapter Nine

❊ Natural Healing ❊

As THE FALL APPROACHED, Mason's deliberations about what to do next were front and centre for him. For the Peaceful Warrior journey to unfold, employment was now necessary. He needed to take care of basic living requirements.

Through his search, he came across an intriguing advertisement posted at the University Student Services Centre. The ad indicated that the provincial department of Social Services and Justice was looking for an outward-bound Counsellor to do wilderness expeditions with young offenders. Mason thought this might just work for him, especially as it would allow him to commune with nature.

Despite not having any experience in this field, he applied. He was banking on there not being much interest in this type of job; given how challenging and scary it would be working with young offenders in an uncontrolled wilderness environment. The job entailed taking up to eight young offenders at a time out into the wilderness for repetitive three-day survival training in the back hills of the West Coast. Additionally, the job involved providing life skills, training, and alternative education when the group was not out in the wilderness. Young people would be mandated by the courts to attend this three-month program.

Much to his surprise, he was offered the job. Working alongside two other counsellors, Mason's first year on the job turned out to be a steep learning curve regarding human behaviour. Most disquieting was how destructive young offenders could be, and how defiant and irrational they were in general. He had countless encounters with anger, rage, sadness, defiance, and self- destructive patterns from the young people. The participants rebelled at the drop of a hat over just about anything. It didn't help that being forced to attend this program meant that someone was going to wear their resentment.

Engaging in outward-bound experiences with these youth was continuously challenging. Even though nature can be embracing and calming, it also can be harsh and unforgiving. This latter fact did not seem to register right away with these young people, as they tended to exercise oppositional behaviour without any clear sense of what they were doing and what the consequences might be. Setting safety rules and rules of conduct backfired more often than not.

Mason recognized himself in many of these young participants. He remembered, on occasion, feeling angry at the world, trusting no one, and lashing out at the closest target. But even though he remembered feeling this way, Mason did not know how to reach these younger, more volatile versions of himself. Sometimes, the survival challenge became too much for them, resulting in behaviour that was reckless and harmful.

Etched in his memory was the experience on one of the survival outings, of one young person who decided to simply quit hiking out in the middle of nowhere because the weather was bad, his pack was too heavy, and hiking was too tiresome. This young person took off his hiking boots and backpack, and he threw them off a cliff before running away into the wilderness. After several hours of searching, Mason and his female co-counsellor found him crying in a rock cave with cut up feet. Fortunately, he allowed Mason to tie his oversized running shoes to his feet. He then reluctantly followed them back to their group campsite a few kilometres away.

At the campsite, Mason's co-counsellor bandaged up his cuts and massaged his feet until he fell asleep. The following day, thankfully he was more contrite and more compliant. He continued to create challenges on the three-day expedition but pulled himself together enough to finish the trip without further incident.

As he accumulated more Outward-Bound experiences, Mason discovered that he could not change the young offenders' behaviours by attempting to convince them of the error of their ways. Common sense made no sense to them, as they distrusted anyone who had an agenda to make them wrong or label them as "bad."

Encountering one setback after another, he finally realized he could not be a supervisor of their behaviour and a pseudo-counsellor at the same time. He had to find a way for them to discover the value of learning to be totally self-sufficient.

As it turned out, he came across a provocative article in a journal on delinquent behaviour that suggested resistance could be used as a resource. The paper recommended that, when confronted with aggressive or defiant behaviour, the counsellor should find ways to redirect the young person's aggressiveness or resistance onto something that can make a difference for them. The challenge, of course, is to find out what in the moment can make a difference for them.

Deciding to give it a try, Mason discovered that it worked if he did not get caught in taking aggressive behaviour personally. Mason learned that this unusual concept required patience and, when in the wilderness, a willingness to let nature become an ally. The Outward-Bound Program then became a way for the young people to find their own way with Nature's assistance. It was obvious; Nature's power was immense, far exceeding any human-conceived psychological healing strategy.

After the first year in the job, Mason became aware that what worked best was to not give up on, discount, or reject the young people for their bad behaviour. He felt a deep sadness for their troubled lives and a desire to challenge them to discover their own goodness.

As they became more comfortable with the wilderness, most of the young people almost inevitably reached a turning point and mellowed out. Their confidence in surviving in the wilderness increased. They slowly became more accustomed to taking responsibility for their behaviour and actions, as opposed to their past patterns of blaming the world for all their troubles. Nature had a calming effect on them, and it became evident to them that they could not fight Nature and get their way.

Another unexpected bonus was that being away and gaining distance from their community and home problems gave them a break from their wayward and disruptive life patterns. They seemed to benefit from nature's natural wisdom encouraging them to take charge of distancing themselves from getting embroiled in the chaotic, problem infested world they came from. Nature became their ally in healing themselves. Counselling was ancillary and, more often than not, counterproductive.

Mason learned how to stay out of the way enough to allow them to find solid ground and self-confidence. Telling them as a counsellor how to do life differently just didn't work.

Part of the Outward-Bound Program was participation in weekly encounter groups and mandatory school attendance. Mason thought these elements were what the adult world thought the young people needed; not what they *really* needed.

The encounter group experience was supposed to promote self-awareness and accountability through constructive peer confrontation. It was an ordeal at the best of times. Interestingly, the young people actually seemed to look forward to confronting their peers, even at the expense of being confronted themselves.

Schooling was another matter. At best, it was tolerable to the young people, and very trying for the teachers. Mason found that the biggest challenge was not the students; it was getting the systems-oriented teachers to abandon their traditional ways.

Working as an outward-bound counsellor had taught him that his most valuable asset was his ability to just go with the flow rather than trying to make things happen. Reflecting on his own adolescent years, it was a pattern he had developed which kept him safe from getting embroiled in conflict with others.

On another front, he recognized more and more through his interactions with the young people how their behaviour was largely compensatory given their life circumstances. He could see himself, if he were in their shoes, responding in similar ways.

Taking the backdrop of Nature coupled with working with troubled young people, Mason became aware that this experience was very therapeutic for him. He could see more clearly how he had developed various isolating and resistant patterns of behaviour given his own developmental experiences. Nature was an amazing teacher, revealing to him some of his character flaws, which the young people quickly reminded him of. He could not imagine a better way to start on the path of a Peaceful Warrior.

Chapter Ten

 Good Medicine

B EING AROUND THE OCEAN a fair amount, Mason felt an urge to know more about what lay beneath the waters. Having a strong attraction to water, Mason wondered what it would be like to explore the underwater world. Using his holiday time, he enrolled in a four-week scuba course offered by the YMCA.

At first, he was struck by how silent it was underneath the ocean, apart from the sound of his own bubbles. He liked the idea that communicating with other divers was restricted to sign language or dive signals transmitted through a four-foot buddy line that tethered two divers together. The quietness resonated with him, as it allowed him to notice more of what was happening around him.

Diving also seemed to have an impact on reducing his tendency to ruminate and over think whatever he was focused on. His thinking slowed down and, occasionally for brief moments, it would stop altogether. Time also felt like it was slower under water. An hour's dive seemed like two hours. The only break in that awareness was when he looked at his oxygen tank reading to check the time he had left.

Once Mason was in the water, everything seemed interconnected. While many different undersea life forms existed, they all seemed to belong. Yes, the predator-prey cycle was evident, yet there was no sense of panic. It was like it was supposed to happen. There was a balance and rhythm in the coexistence of all life forms, each depending on one another for all to exist.

When he was simply diving, curiosity was the driving force; it was like he was a visitor in a world that reacted to him but did not judge him. On occasion, he caught himself smiling and wondered why.

During his dive training, Mason was teamed up with a man a few years older. This man, John, had just learned how to swim! Mason could not resist asking John, "Why do you want to become a diver if you're barely able to swim? Aren't you afraid you might drown?"

John responded with a mischievous grin on his face. "I am more afraid of not living fully than I am of dying." John went on to say, "Diving is not swimming as one might do on top of the water. When you wear a wet suit, the buoyancy it provides acts like a life vest. Being able to swim is important for sure but drowning is far less likely when you are wearing buoyancy equipment."

Seeing Mason's perplexed glance, John continued. "Besides, doing what seems most difficult and seemingly impossible has always attracted my interest."

After the dive, they decided to find out more about each other over coffee. Starting the conversation knowing that Mason had been a university student, he asked, "What did you study at university?"

Mason replied, "I just completed a degree in mathematics and psychology. I am not sure where that is going to take me. Becoming a counsellor of some sort is what interests me at the moment. The road ahead is unclear for me."

John mentioned that he was a family physician just starting his practice but was not sure yet what area of medicine he wanted to specialize in.

"What made you decide to become a physician?" Mason asked.

John told him that medicine was his lifelong passion, as his father was also a doctor and he felt driven to follow in his footsteps. However, what he discovered in his studies and practise was that he was not to primarily become a healer. What he learned was that his job as a physician was to focus on curing or remediating diseases of the body. Healing, on the other hand, was what the patient did, given the right environment. John went on to say that the downside of medicine was the tendency to be myopic and focus almost exclusively on cures, using science as an umbrella to diagnose complex human physical, social, and psychological problems.

"It's deduction-based," he said. "For the most part, you get in the habit of treating the patient as an object to investigate; you repair them like a body mechanic or offer advice that most doctors find a challenge to follow themselves. Most disheartening is the preoccupation with addressing deficiencies rather than competency capability. And lots of doctors use drugs as the go-to panacea for fixing intractable problems. It is a seductive process that encourages blind faith in the physician."

Mason interjected, "What aspects of medicine appeal to you?"

He replied, "Surgery is the heart of medicine to my mind, and following that, it is trauma treatment. Giving patients an opportunity to recover from acute and chronic, physically disabling tissue and bone breakdown is rewarding and meaningful.

What fascinates me most are the causes of illness and death. Healing is only of peripheral interest in my practise of medicine. It is mostly a by-product of what happens as a result of everything else I do."

Mason commented, "So it seems what you are saying is the science of medicine is of most interest to you and healing comes secondary."

John went on to say, "Relief from pain is considered by many to be the primary goal of medicine, which can be achieved by promoting or facilitating healing. Healing is ongoing throughout life, and medicine plays only a small part in healing."

This was not what Mason expected to hear. He had come to believe that medicine was mysteriously complicated, like the language it used, and that physicians were beyond reproach. He erroneously thought that they were healers of the first order.

Mason decided to share his sense of uncertainty about his direction in life. He mentioned his strong interest in being involved in a healing profession but acknowledged that his options seemed limited. To progress along this path would require going to graduate school, or maybe even medicine. This was not likely to happen, as taking his education any further would require finances he did not have.

John responded, "Sometimes, the journey we take has walls that we must go over or go around. Never give in to these walls. They are only barriers to overcome."

He then shared that he encountered a wall when he failed his second year of medical school. He had many excuses at first, but he finally realized that the excuses were "poor me" excuses, and if he continued to allow them to determine his future, it would indeed be a very bleak one.

"Giving up could have been an easy option. But I did not want to be run by failure or victimized by this failed event. If I couldn't fix this problem for me, how could I fix or help to fix other people's problems? This was a turning point for me. I pulled up my bootstraps, let go of my self-pity, and allowed humility to guide me. I mustered up the courage to approach the Dean of Medicine, offering no excuses, and asked to be reinstated. I expressed my commitment to do whatever it took to complete my degree successfully. On this basis, I was reinstated as a probationary student, and then I went on to complete my medical education."

Mason was struck by this story and was stimulated to look beyond the barriers he had perceived to be insurmountable in moving forward with his own education. Inspired somewhat by John's story, perhaps medicine could be a pathway ahead for him. But after thinking about it, he wasn't sure that he wanted to end up practicing medicine as John described it. On the other hand, psychology seemed to have many more avenues and was more eclectic, which resonated with his intuitive desire to become a healer, not a hands-on fixer. What hurdles did he need to jump to further his education in the field of psychology? He decided that he needed to explore this further.

Changing the subject, John asked Mason if he would be interested in participating in a weekend human potential workshop with him this upcoming weekend. The workshop would be happening at a retreat centre up island a few hours away. John went on to indicate it was designed to be an in-depth workshop experience uniquely tailored to those in the helping professions. The focus would be on psychological well-being from a holistic perspective. John further mentioned he had attended a previous human potential workshop at the same centre two summers ago and it had made a huge difference in his continued medical studies as a struggling student. Mason quickly accepted. This felt like a good opportunity to explore the realm of healing with like-minded people. His growing sense of trust in John made it an easy decision.

The weekend approached. After an early morning drive up the island and off a dirt side road, they arrived at the Centre. The Centre's main building was built from logs and appeared very rustic. Surrounding the Centre were several small cabins. The facility was set in a valley overlooking the mountains on one side and the ocean on the other. Arriving at the front door, they were greeted by a very tall, bearded man. He was casually dressed and looked like he was in his mid-sixties. He hugged John, as both already had known each other from John's previous workshop experience. Turning to Mason, he vigorously shook his hand and introduced himself as Charles. He went on to say that he was delighted that John invited him to attend the workshop. With that he motioned for them to enter the Centre and then introduced them to the eight other participants.

After some casual dialogue over coffee and a short tour of the facility, all were ushered into a large room facing the ocean. The room had twelve chairs set in a circle with large cushions placed in the middle. Off to one side was a round table with blankets and tissue boxes. They were all invited to take a seat.

The workshop began mid-morning with Charles asking them, in no particular order, to share a little about themselves and what brought them to the workshop. One by one the participants spoke about themselves which, for the most part went right over his head as he was preoccupied with rehearsing what he was going to say about himself.

Mason waited to be the last to share and at that point his anxiety was so high he stumbled with his words, struggling to make sense out of his purpose for being at the workshop. A feeling of embarrassment overtook him as he felt his life script was quite shallow compared to what he could glean from what the others were saying about themselves when he was able to listen. He heard himself say that he was an Outward-Bound Counsellor and that he was intending to explore the possibility of further studies in psychology after having just completing a science degree. In respect to what he wanted out of the workshop, he stated that he was not altogether clear except that perhaps he could learn from others about how to become a healer.

Listening to the other participants he was surprised to find out two of them were practicing psychologists and one was a child psychiatrist. In addition, there were three social workers, an ICU nurse, and a chiropractic student. All had attended a workshop at the Centre in the past.

The workshop unfolded over three days, each day lasting approximately fourteen hours. In many ways, it was a classical marathon group that gradually broke down the participants' resistance.

One of the most profound moments occurred on day two, when he shared his history in greater depth and disclosed that it was difficult for him to trust others and let them know anything about him. Unexpectedly, he found himself blurting out that he preferred to remain an enigma to others.

"Why would I trust others? They just leave me to my own resources and more often ignore me anyway." He couldn't believe what he just said. He loathed the idea of being a victim of anything.

The group responded in a way that he did not expect. They had comments such as, "It's not about others ignoring you so much as it is you denying that others can possibly be interested in you."

Others said, "It seems to me like you are just rejecting yourself before you imagine others will reject you."

After the feedback from the group, he realized that emotionally trusting others would unlikely happen if he could not discover a way to trust himself.

Charles's comment particularly stood out: "What other people think of you is not your business; it's theirs."

This stuck with Mason, as it made intuitive sense, but he was not quite sure how to practically make it work in his day-to-day life.

Another takeaway from the group experience was how the participants revealed that everyone suffers at one time or another. If you were not suffering, or if you were too joyful, something was wrong with you. Life was a struggle, first and foremost, not a gift, even though we would like it to be otherwise. It appeared that almost everyone there was on a personal journey to discover how to suffer less or not at all, and how to find out how to manage their lives in a world full of human conflict.

Mason silently felt an upwelling determination not to allow needless mental suffering to run his life. Notwithstanding this intent, creeping into his thoughts he heard an inner voice say, *Okay, just how are you going to accomplish that?*

At the end of the weekend, Mason was able to tell the group that this workshop had some similarities to the sweat lodge experience he recently had, but it was personally more intense and made him feel much more vulnerable. He said that it felt like he was being revealed for who he was, which at first scared him but as the workshop went on, he discovered what he was really scared of was his shadow; of being inadequate. Over the course of the workshop he felt a gradual letting go of his shadow, discovering that being inadequate was all made-up. Overall, he felt the experience was very cleansing.

When the workshop came to an end and he departed with John to return home he realized he wasn't what others said or thought he was or even what he had previously thought he was. Who he was was still not clear to him. The challenge remained. What pathway was he to travel on to uncover his real potential?

***

Three weeks later, Mason met up with John at a coffee shop with the intent to review the weekend group experience. After a warm greeting and some casual catching up, John offered his take on the workshop experience.

"Overall, the experience of the workshop was very sobering. It made me realize that the way I have practised medicine has been too self-serving."

Mason was surprised to hear this. He had only known John to be very considerate of others and generous to a fault. "What do you mean?" he asked.

"I have known this for some time, but I have let it slide, choosing to continue on as always, and rushing people through appointments because of the pressures of the practise. In so doing, my level of caring and empathy for my patients has been very low and, embarrassingly, sometimes non-existent. Given self-imposed time constraints and working with a 'doctor knows best' attitude, I have been symptom-focused and driven to tell my patients what they needed to do. I spent precious few moments listening to what they may really want."

Mason asked, "How do you handle being an expert, knowing most people sideline what they really want, trusting that you know better what is good for them? That your judgement is superior to theirs?"

"It's interesting you should ask that Mason. I am not sure I know how to respond except it does not work for me to be in this position. For a long time now I have felt stuck, as the medical model is so rigid and structured. I have been conditioned to think that objectivity is considered essential to diagnosing medical issues accurately. Compassion is considered acceptable but dangerous. I now am much more aware of how I have subjugated my desire to be part of the healing process to remain focused on what I know cures and trying to fix human ailments."

Mason inquired, "Speaking of compassion, how do you address death and dying?"

"Mason, it is extraordinarily important for me to be respectful and considerate towards others around death issues. When I encounter such concerns, I go out of my way to spend as much time as possible with these situations; something, as I have said, I have not done with the so-called 'run of the mill' medical issues.

The workshop has awakened in me a resolve to alter how I am practicing medicine. So, I have changed my scheduling, allowing ten more minutes per patient than I previously scheduled. This has allowed me more breathing room to be curious and inquisitive, and of course more present. It has resulted in remarkably different qualitative experiences, both for me and my patients. It seems that my patients are generally more animated and enthusiastic than before, especially when it comes to following my suggestions for their healing. They are also way more appreciative of the extra time than I thought they would be. Some have even said this has been the first time a doctor ever really listened to them. This experience has encouraged me to become even more curious. Sometimes, I even ask patients what they think would work best for them."

John's revelations and responses to them startled Mason. "What you have said reassures me the world of healing is still alive and well. Your candidness is refreshing."

When it was Mason's turn to share, he told John that he felt lighter, yet more grounded after the workshop. He also felt like he got a cursory glimpse of the power of human connectedness and how genuine empathy was a catalyst for healing personal wounds.

Mason continued, "However, as the weeks have gone by, my old patterns of searching for something other than what was going on in the moment have returned. The halo effect the workshop leader had warned us about has dropped away. Now, some of my former heaviness has returned. I find myself looking for peacefulness rather than allowing it to be here in the present moment. The experience was still very meaningful, and it showed me that I need to be less self-absorbed and more curious about how to contribute to the well-being of others. I also feel that I have become more aware that I would not be so good at fixing other people's problems, as I am too impatient with my own physical and mental health issues to be truly very effective in dealing with others at this time. The big bonus was that the experience increased my enthusiasm for continuing my exploration of ways to become a healer."

John responded, "I know what you mean about the halo effect. This was my second workshop at the Centre, and both times I have been jolted out of my habitual way of thinking and being, only to for the most part return to my old ways. Each time, though, something has changed within me that I cannot put my finger on. So, I feel that some benefit of the experience has incrementally been ingrained. These experiences have not been quick fixes for me but incrementally have served to clarify my intentions and my purpose being a physician. What thoughts occur to me about your journey is perhaps you might give yourself room and let the journey of becoming a healer not be so daunting."

Not knowing what to say, Mason and John remained silent for a few minutes. Mason felt the need to change the topic and said he was baffled how medicine seems to primarily focus on the body, psychology on the mind, and religion on the spirit or soul almost to the exclusion of one another. Like they were separate tracks that seldom flowed together.

"Where and how do the mind, body, spirit, and soul get woven together in the process of being healed and being a healer?" he asked.

John paused, "Healers with that perspective existed, but I am personally unaware of its existence in mainstream medicine or psychology for that matter. I am fascinated by the possibility, but I do not see a clear pathway to take that kind of journey. Perhaps in the Far East that paradigm may well exist and be valued, but not so much in our western way of living."

After some lighter sharing, Mason and John parted. They agreed to do a dive on the following weekend.

When the dive day came, they both decided to go to a nearby "breakwater" protecting a harbour. The day was crisp. There was a clear blue sky, and the rays of the mid-day sun danced and shimmered across the blue and turquoise waves. It was a cool spring day, but it was not cold. The mountains along the peninsula were snow covered and stood out, capturing their attention as they were preparing for the dive.

Down they went, exploring the rock shelves and sandy bottom, noticing many different indigenous species of small fish and a small octopus on the move. Then they stumbled across an unusual object shaped like a mummy with a rope attached to a large metal ring. Mason saw it first, and he signalled to John using the buddy line.

They both moved toward it. When they got close, Mason could not immediately believe what he was seeing. It appeared to be a pale blanched head poking out from a white sheet wrapped around the body of a man. Transfixed by the man's bloodless, bloated, and ashen white head, Mason kept at a distance. John, who was experienced at dealing with dead bodies in his medical training, moved closer to inspect the body. He then signalled that they should go to the surface. At the surface, John commented that the man had a big crush mark on the back of his skull. He surmised that it was likely he had been murdered and that they needed to call the police.

When they got to a phone at a nearby restaurant, John made the call to the police. The police arrived, took statements and told them to remain at the restaurant until a military dive team arrived.

When the military dive team arrived an hour later, they instructed John to dive with them to point out the location of the body. The body was brought up in a body bag and transported to the morgue.

During this extraordinary event Mason felt that time had stopped. There were no feelings surfacing that he could detect. It was almost as if he was not there in body yet witnessing something profound and unspeakable. For the most part he remained electively mute, speaking only when spoken to by the police allowing John to do all the talking. John seemed so calm and confident, interacting with the police and military dive team with ease.

What an unusual, unexpected experience, Mason thought. It actually aroused in him a weird sense of intrigue and interest in the mystery of death once again.

His mind wandered back to the time he found his mother dead in their living room. Similar to this encounter with death, he remembered being numb and feeling empty as well as being speechless at that time. Up to now, he could not bring himself to dwell on the passing of his mother for reasons he could not fathom. Perhaps he thought by not thinking about her he could avoid the deep-seated feeling of abandonment.

These thoughts were interrupted by John, who quietly and unpretentiously said, "I am used to seeing dead bodies, but it still impacts me deeply. In this situation, I cannot help but wonder what it takes to purposefully take someone else's life. I am intrigued about the human condition and the extent to which we may be unconsciously wired to be aggressive to one another."

This resonated with Mason, as it stirred in him questions about the criminal mind. He thought, *What would it take to cross over the line of life and death and purposely and violently end another's life? And what would it take for a person to take their own life? How would they cross over the instinctual survival line?*

***

After a week passed by, they met up again to review their unique confrontation with death. Mason started off by sharing how impactful the experience was for him. It raised many questions for him. "What happens after we die? Are we all just recycled material or is there a soul?"

John responded, "I really haven't a clue how to answer these kinds of questions. It is beyond my understanding. From my knowledge, our ordinary minds do not have a universally accepted solution to these questions. The mind is part of our evolutionary development. It is a framework that allows us to navigate in our world not so much out of it. The ordinary mind is actually quite limited, narrow, and finite. Therefore, so is our ability to fully address questions about what lies beyond death. Answers regarding the infinite seem to be beyond the capacity of our ordinary minds. Humankind has resorted to many faith-based or metaphysical solutions to the problem. And in most cases, these solutions have stirred up more questions than answers, leading to the conclusion that getting answers needs to take a back seat to faith in a belief system of your choosing."

This reply was deeper and more complex than Mason had expected. He was also not able to get any sense from John or, for that matter, in any of the readings he had encountered, about the relationship of the soul to the body. *Something for me to ponder on another day,* he thought.

In retrospect, this experience awakened in Mason questions related to his own mortality, something he had never consciously thought of before. Yes, he had fearful experiences. However, this was fleeting, and little thought was given to addressing the possibility of his life ending. It just did not seem to matter, as he realized that he had become driven by a need to seek experiences and accumulate information, and not to dwell on anything, as it would interfere with getting on with his next adventure.

Another week passed. Mason was back to mountain biking, this time out along an ocean trail. He got the urge to stop and sit for a while and watch the ocean and the mountains in the background. He listened to the waves crashing. His mind wandered. *Do the waves care if I am here? Do the seagulls think they are inadequate? Are the trees unhappy? Does nature in all its majesty fret about death like humans do? How is it that humans judge so much?*

What happened next was totally unexpected. His whole body began to shake uncontrollably, and tears started to fall from his eyes. *What was happening to him?* All he felt he could do was to allow the tears to flow and the shaking to continue almost as if it was not happening to him.

As the tears subsided and the shaking discontinued, ghost like images surfaced; first of the discovery of the dead man with John and then of finding his mother dead. These images seemed to interweave with each other, connected in some way. He wanted them to go away but they persisted. A sense of deep sadness for both his mother and this man then showed up, which he had not previously experienced. Being connected to others was a challenge for him he knew full well, yet he felt in a mysterious way connected to these images. His feelings of his own emptiness seemed to now join with theirs. Their loss of aliveness was both profound and unspeakable, as was his, even though he was still alive and they were not. Creeping into his awareness was a realization that he had responded to the loss of both his parents by in some ways dying himself, or the very least not allowing himself to fully live.

Returning to a more settled state a random thought then occurred to him. Could it be that he kept loneliness at bay and covered it up by rationalizing that aloneness was preferable?

What then surfaced on his mental landscape was a message.

You are not what you think you are. You need to let go of your own entrenched way of viewing yourself.

Was this message surfacing from his unconscious because he had let himself lose control? Then he remembered Arnold, the child psychologist, telling him one day he would come out from behind his mask of loneliness and when that happened he would feel vulnerable but very alive.

Just as quickly as this message surfaced, it faded away. So did the focus on his inner world. As he got up and walked back to his bike, Mason wondered if this experience would be repeated in any way. He felt certain that somehow this experience would have a major impact on his future development as a potential healer. Just exactly how he did not know.

Chapter Eleven

⚜ The Pursuit of Knowledge ⚜

F OR MASON, THE MOST recent events and conversations
with John started to spark a curiosity about pursuing his
university education further. Given his obvious fascination
about their unusual encounter with death, coupled with his
outward-bound experience with young offenders, John suggested that Forensic Psychology might be worth him checking out. Mason agreed with John; however, he knew that
such a program was not available in this province. If he was
to pursue this avenue, he would have to relocate to another
province or country. Given his financial circumstances this
would not be possible. Exploring further, Mason came to
the realization that if he were to discover ways to become

more capable as a potential healer more in depth learning was essential.

As a beginning step, Mason applied and got accepted into a master's level program in Counselling Psychology. To finance this education he continued on as an outward-bound counsellor, working on the weekends and in the evenings. Doing both a full academic program while being employed full time would potentially be pushing himself to the very limits of his capabilities he committed to doing both anyway. Taking on student debt was not something he was willing to consider. Challenging himself in this way would definitely require that he stay very focused and manage his time very carefully. Taking on this challenge was simultaneously exciting and scary. Failing at either endeavour would not be an option.

Planting one foot into his studies and the other into his work with youth, all other interests were discontinued. No cycling, no swimming or diving, and no chess. Interestingly, it turned out the psychology courses, in particular the course on the psychopathology, proved useful as he was able to apply some of the concepts to his work as an outward-bound counsellor. The backdrop of his work occurring in the wilderness contributed to balancing out his academic efforts. He felt that acquiring theoretical knowledge could be absorbed rather than just accumulated. The practicum courses offered provided a base to expand his understanding of human functioning beyond just the outward-bound domain.

As the two year program unfolded, he found that his curiosity was heightened to a degree he had never experienced before. Learning was refreshing and addictive. When the program finished, Mason woke up to realize that he had been in a trance like state throughout the program. While the workload as expected was very heavy, working in the wilderness on the weekends rejuvenated him to the point that he looked forward to his studies during the week. An added bonus was discovered as he was able to see patterns in the concepts and theories that could be practically applied to real life issues that showed up in his work with young offenders.

Now with a more skill-based platform, Mason felt his confidence rise yet he was still unclear about how his academic achievement could move him along the path of being a seasoned healer. In his mind he was still an apprentice; still far from being significantly capable of making a difference in the lives of others. He still was incomplete.

Even though he was now considered to be a trained counsellor, he felt his career options were limited and not very appealing. Reflecting back on his course work it became evident to him that the courses he had taken and practicums he had completed were baseline and at best preparatory to becoming a healer. The different counselling or therapy domains he studied, such as client-centred therapy, transactional analysis, behaviourism, cognitive behavioural treatment, crisis intervention, the skilful helper, and suicidology were all very impactful. But none of them stood out for him. He didn't feel ready to accept one approach or theory as being more significant than another.

As the summer approached, he learned of an elective summer course on psychology and hypnosis being offered at the university. The visiting professor teaching the course was from a university in southern California. He was well known as an acclaimed authority in the field of clinical hypnosis. What triggered his interest was the mystery surrounding the practice of therapeutic hypnosis. Quite possibly he surmised, learning more about hypnosis could increase his understanding of the realm of the unconscious mind. It was an opportunity that he felt he could not let pass by so he enrolled in the course.

As the course unfolded Mason discovered that hypnosis what not anything like he thought it was. It turned out that hypnosis was such a common feature of day to day living that it largely was ignored as a powerful tool to effect psychological change. He sensed the whole world of the unconscious was not overtly available to most of us unless we can discover how to connect to it via some oblique perhaps esoteric way. Practicing various induction techniques Mason felt he was just beginning to uncover some of the hidden powers lying dormant in the human psyche.

Near the end of the course Dr. Cohen unexpectedly approached Mason and asked him if he was interested in enrolling in a doctoral program. He went on to say at his home university in the US the doctoral program was well known for its very eclectic and humanistic focus. International students were encouraged to apply provided they had a tenured professor in the faculty of Psychology willing to mentor them. Dr. Cohen then added that if Mason was interested he would be willing to mentor him. Not knowing what to say Mason awkwardly responded by saying he was honoured and extremely privileged to be considered. He followed by saying that doctoral studies had never occurred to him as he felt it he had gone as far as he could go with his education. Mason mustered the courage and decided to ask about the entrance requirements. Dr. Cohen followed up suggesting that he should contact the graduate studies admissions office to find out if he would qualify and what would be required to get admitted. With that being said they agreed to follow up on his possible interest before the course ended the following week.

This unexpected offer of mentorship caught him totally off guard. It was all he could do to contain his excitement about the possible impact this might have on his journey ahead seeking to become a seasoned healer.

Very quickly though the excitement faded away being replaced with the sobering second thought that he may not be competent enough to engage in doctoral studies. His first inclination was to dismiss the possibility given the many barriers that he felt would be in his way such as getting accepted not to mention how to finance advanced education that was known to be quite expensive. Then, out of left field flashing through his mind were the words of John his diving friend from the past "All it takes is courage and commitment to explore beyond your comfort zone to overcome what might be insurmountable boundaries."

Deep down he knew this was a potential opportunity he could not pass up. He needed to press forward and search for ways to make it happen. As his mind continued to mull over the possibilities it occurred to him this higher learning pathway was an uncommon one to take for someone wanting to remain on a pathway to become an Indigenous healer. However, justifying its validity he rationalized that it was still aligned with the purpose of the second pathway of the Four-Fold Way—that of expanding one's knowledge base of healing.

***

Mason next learned that one of the primary entrance requirements to the doctoral program was the need to achieve a benchmark score on the Graduate Record Exam as set by the university graduate school department. This also he learned had been set at a level that roughly only twenty five percent of the applicants obtained marks that were acceptable to the university. Not to be deterred Mason began studying for the GRE in earnest as the next sitting for the exam was two months away. Studying for the GRE was challenging for him, as it essentially did not excite his interest in anything new.

The more he studied the more it took over his life. He found himself staying glued to his study desk taking breaks only when he absolutely needed to much as he had done years ago when he first enrolled as a freshman university student. As the exam date approached, Mason sensed he had prepared well enough and now he just needed to let the chips fall where they may and not get stressed out by the need to get an acceptable score.

Doing the exam went surprisingly well despite the pressure of it being time-limited. At the end he sensed he performed to the best of his abilities despite reoccurring inner doubts about his capabilities. These nagging doubts lingered in the background during the exam but remained largely buried below his level of consciousness as he was able to keep them at bay using some of the hypnotic techniques he had learned in Dr. Cohen's course.

***

Three weeks went by before the results arrived by envelope in the mail. During this period of anxious waiting, he ruminated excessively about his performance causing his sense of confidence to erode. At first he resisted opening the envelope, choosing to leave it to one side for a day. Not able to delay any longer than that, he mustered up the courage the following day and tore open the envelope. To his immense relief, the results of the exam indicated he had met the entrance requirements for the PhD program.

Now the next hurdle was to find a way to finance this very expensive education before submitting an application. Mason set out to apply for any scholarships that he thought he could be eligible to receive and applied for a graduate teaching assistant position but no immediate success in these domains was forthcoming.

On a long shot attempt he decided to approach his employer for possible contributory funding. He knew that it was not uncommon for the government to consider sponsoring employees with a paid leave of absence who wanted to upgrade their education to the master's level if it was relevant to the work they were doing although no precedence was known for them supporting doctoral studies.

What happened next was a total surprise. His employer consented to give him a two year leave of absence with pay. Now, the final requirement was to be accepted by the university graduate studies department. Mason submitted his application, and a month later he received a letter back approving his admission. He was on his way to higher learning and possibly someday becoming a certified psychologist.

***

After settling in a rented apartment at his new university in the US, Mason was struck by how students and professors there were so enthusiastic about their areas of interest and specialties yet at the same time noticeably laid back. This attitude certainly did not prevail during his university experience in Canada, where almost everyone seemed to be stressed and overly serious about everything.

The doctoral program he was enrolled in was designed to be completed over a three year period. Mason figured that he would need to push himself to complete all the program requirements within the three year period and if need be complete his dissertation upon returning to Canada. His plan was to extend his two year leave of absence for an additional year without pay. He felt he could manage the third year by stretching the funding offered over three years rather than two.

As he began his studies he experienced an upwelling of confidence quite unlike his university experiences in the past. Something was different this time. A shift had occurred; now, his doubt about his academic competency was fading into the background, being replaced with an intuitive sense of confidence that he had never fully felt before. He sensed his background experiences in the wilderness had something to do with his confidence preparing him well to go with the flow. He also sensed he was in the right place at the right time both naturally and purposefully.

Mason was able to cultivate a few friendships during his time at the university, but generally he spent very little time socializing, choosing to stay focused on his academics. Interestingly the friends he did make tended to be runners who encouraged him to spend his free time running with them on the extensive cross country trails located around the university. This gave him a much-needed break from his tendency to get too absorbed in his studies. Further reinforcing this interest was the reputation the university had for training some of the best cross country runners in the country. He could not resist the temptation to learn more about the "endorphin effect" experienced by long distance runners, as well as hearing about the many references made to it being a trance-like experience.

His first long distance formal run was a half-marathon fundraiser for children's cancer research. After that he was hooked, and whenever he could, he would go for long runs on the weekends through the countryside and along a twenty mile trail nearby a meandering river.

It dawned on Mason that while other students were socializing and attending to commitments outside of school, such as family, part-time work, or recreational endeavours, he was not nor did he have to. With no outside responsibilities, his biggest worry was in becoming too preoccupied with questioning what he was learning.

***

Reflecting back to when he first crossed paths with Dr. Cohen he naively thought that hypnosis would be just a sideline interest. Not so as the coursework in hypnosis and hypnotherapy offered by Dr. Cohen during his doctoral studies had a profound impact on him. Most striking was Mason learned that the unconscious mind was extraordinarily more powerful than the conscious mind. The fact that it could be meaningfully accessed to assist in healing was no longer just fanciful thinking. Dr. Cohen's perspective was that the day-to-day happenings of human beings were but a small fragment of their true nature. He would often tell Mason, "What we know to be our selves is scripted based on what we think." Hypnosis, he would say is actually a process that allows us to come out of our limited or ordinary mindscape and become reconnected to the larger field of awareness. The natural or unconditioned mind is expansive and unlimited, as it exists in the field where everything and all experiences are interconnected. It is this field that embraces, thereby opening one up to insights and a freedom to explore beyond the restriction of one's conscious beliefs.

Most notably, Mason would also hear Dr. Cohen say, that hypnosis was just one way to enter an altered state of awareness, where the enormous depth of the unconscious could be accessed. Psychoactive drugs were another, as was self-awareness training. Many other experiences were also valuable in accessing other states of awareness, such as the Buddhist approach to using meditation to address mankind's struggles with loss and, in particular, death and dying.

Dr. Cohen's perspective on hypnosis also resonated with Mason as he was completing a one-year course offered within the doctoral program entitled "Confrontations with Death." The course was based on the five stages of grief as they related to death and dying: denial, anger, bargaining, depression, and acceptance. Lectures were interlaced with trance inducing experiential retreats focusing on personal and interpersonal exercises on the meaning of death and dying.

On many occasions, it was pointed out to him in the course that to become meaningfully acquainted with death, one had to meaningfully become acquainted with living and dying from one moment to another. Conceptually, it made some sense to him, but practically, it was hard to experience.

The course made him more acutely aware that he needed to address his own unawareness about living and dying moment to moment. Being a counsellor of any measurable value to anyone facing death or experiencing death of others would no doubt depend on his active willingness to conscientiously address his own mortality.

Another main thread of experience of his doctoral experience occurred when he discovered a Gestalt Institute located on campus that was affiliated with the university. He learned through further inquiry that several doctoral students in his program had attended the Institute and highly recommended that he consider attending as well.

Deciding to go ahead and check it out further, he made an appointment with the director of the institute and was granted an interview after providing a reference from Dr. Cohen. After preliminary greetings, Mason asked if he could be accepted for instruction.

The director responded by asking, "Do you have any problems with who you are?"

Mason replied that he did not think so, and that he was mostly interested in other people's problems.

The director paused, before saying that he would be accepted to participate, but he needed to be aware that the primary focus would be on participant self-discovery with only a secondary focus on using Gestalt practices with clients or patients. He went on to say, "Gestalt training is not just about knowledge or theory, although knowledge could be a by-product. It is about direct exploration that would reveal in every experience that the whole was greater than the sum of its parts, and that in each part there exists the whole. Therapeutically, it is about reclaiming disowned attributes, emotions, and thoughts, and integrating them back into one's natural state of being."

Mason had recalled Dr. Cohen mentioning this phrase, "in the part exists the whole," which further fuelled his interest. He was intrigued enough to begin taking workshops at the Institute during his last year of doctoral studies.

The workshops helped him understand what the expression meant in a way that seemed more than plausible. Clearly, it highlighted how this was a far cry from what transpired in medically driven psychotherapy, and in many forms of cognitive behavioural counselling. Therapy, as he had come to know it, highlighted the importance of breaking down problems to their smallest parts and working on the small parts to the exclusion of the whole.

The Gestalt workshops were three hours long and were held once a week. The trainers were both seasoned therapists in private practice and part-time professors at the university. They tended to be quite supportive but very blunt, as they were quick to point out dead-end thinking, ego-driven preoccupations, and reductive thinking. Their focus was on personal responsibility and the facilitation of awareness rather than analysis.

"Analysis can lead to paralysis," they would say. They also presented as being very laid back and not overly serious about anything. Humour punctuated what they did, as they found humour in just about everything human. Mason looked forward to being challenged by these sessions.

During one very memorable and personally relevant session, the participants were asked to examine their shadows. It was not the same as the imaginary shadow that he had lived in when he was growing up, yet in a way this conceptual shadow encompassed it. This was a shadow where one disowns aspects of oneself and projects them onto others and the world at large.

As journal writing was a requirement for Institute participants, Mason and his peers were instructed to record at least two bothersome attitudes they observed in others from their practicum counselling sessions.

Mason remembered writing that he found it frustrating when people complained of being either inadequate or unlikeable. For the most part, he felt that they were making it up as an excuse or to justify their problems in life.

When it was his turn to share his journal writing, Mason was asked to own these traits he saw in others as if they were his. This experience awakened him to realize these *were* the traits that he most disliked about himself! The trainer then asked him to reclaim these projections and to recognize how inhibiting they were to his overall mental well-being. He was asked to recall how they might have originated, and whether they still applied now. Mason realized that they were made up a long time ago to protect him from being rejected. *What need did he have for them now?*

The workshop leader followed-up by asking Mason if he could find humour in this situation. At first, he was guarded and reluctant to let go, until others in the group started to laugh, which released him to do the same. It took him a while to stop laughing with the others. Overall, the experience left him feeling lighter, more integrated, and relieved of an unnecessary burden that he had been carrying for a very long time.

As his experience at the Institute unfolded, the more he came to realize that Gestalt therapy was awareness-based rather than rule-based, which resonated with him. It also focused on personally being accountable and not attempting to justify poor performance by your perceived limitations. It promoted being in the moment and acceptance of what is rather than what was or could be. Making mistakes is inevitable but not an indictment of one's capacity to be competent. There was a strong emphasis on re-owning aspects that people don't like about themselves and then laughing about how silly humans are to partition ourselves up into good and bad parts.

Also important—and somewhat contrary to his understanding from the many books on the subject—the therapist or counsellor does not cause change to happen for clients. The therapist or counsellor can at best be a catalyst or a mirror reflecting back to the client so they can see for themselves more clearly their own barriers for change. In so doing, the client can be afforded the possibility of uncovering their own potential to enact change in their unique circumstances. Mason had also come to accept that change is an ongoing process that the therapist or counsellor, in a privileged way, gets to participate in. It is a relational paradigm where the interactive energy can become synergistic.

Arriving at the final session of the one-year training, Mason felt apprehensive, as he knew that it was time to receive a summary review of his participation. The trainers made it clear that their comments to all participants were for reflection and personal development only. They prefaced their review by saying that the evaluations were not designed to grade anyone; they were to assist participants to become aware of their multi-faceted character development.

Hearing the summary reviews of the six other participants first, Mason became even more apprehensive. The candidness of the comments from the Institute leaders given to others was foreboding to the extent he sensed he may not want to hear what they had to say about him.

When it came time for Mason to receive feedback, the lead facilitator said, "It would be worthwhile for you to stop hiding behind your questions of others. If you intend to discover your true nature and self-worth, it would be of immeasurable value if you allowed others to question you instead of redirecting their questions. Others see that you are fearful of being vulnerable and exposing yourself."

Mason was speechless. *Was that what he was doing? Hiding behind questions? Was he that afraid of being seen by others? Could they detect his fear and self-doubt about himself?* What the facilitator shared was hard for him to hear, as no one had ever been that candid with him about how he presented himself. He felt embarrassed. He had been undressed in front of his colleagues with no way of defending himself.

Now, he asked himself what he was going to do about this feedback. He slipped away from the final class without responding to the facilitator's feedback. He had a strong urge to just bury the experience. But deep down, he sensed that it would be a mistake, as it would likely continue to show up as an issue down the road when he didn't want it to.

Then it struck him like a thunderbolt that he was still hiding behind a mask of pretending to be insignificant. In so doing he could remain reclusive and unreachable. In this way he could observe others without taking the risk of being put on the spot and revealing his true nature. As long as the attention on who he was could be deflected, then he did not have to address his own character idiosyncrasies.

Back at his apartment, he decided to shift his focus and take summary of his doctoral training so far. It was evident it did not directly address his principal driving interest of becoming a healer. It was primarily designed to groom him to become a certified psychologist or therapist, which would support him becoming gainfully employed and knowledge-able about human behaviour and the human condition.

The nine-month internship he completed at a psychiatric in-patient ward was also very eye-opening. The ward steeped in the medical model, offering a rather rigid, antiseptic environ-ment. The major treatment was psychopharmacology. Patients were objectified and labeled, and staff often referred to them by their diagnosis (i.e., "the manic-depressive patient," "the borderline patient," "the mood disorder patient," and so on).

After completing his doctoral studies, Mason felt that what he had learned was far beyond what he had imagined possible. Not only did he experientially and cognitively advance his understanding of the human condition, but he also got a powerful glimpse of his own conditioning and how it had impacted his ability to be in charge of his own well-being. Living in the shadow of his own potential had been significantly lifted. Now it was time to embrace the outside world with the courage to find ways to make a difference both in his life and the lives of others.

Chapter Twelve

❧ Unleashing the Apprentice ❧

Now a newly minted PhD, which suggested a certain level of mastery in the field of Psychology a master he was not. He still was a practicing apprentice in the realm of healing. Professionally however, it meant that he was perhaps a "somebody of significance," having successfully met the requirements for certification as a psychologist.

Having completed this chapter of his education with more time to reflect, as he was so easily predisposed to doing, he wondered if he had focussed so much on its completion that he lost sight of the pleasure of the journey itself. As his Gestalt trainers told him many times, he was still operating as a "human achieving" and not so much as a "human being."

Even though he was confident that he now had a solid foundation of treatment skills to work from, he was still unsure about how this allowed him to progress along the pathway to becoming a healer. Counselling and clinical psychology training was very meaningful, but had not yet instilled in him a sense of clarity regarding healing. He was still missing a sense of being whole or at one with his training to date. All the different parts of his educational training like a jig saw puzzle were yet to be integrated into some coherent operational foundation. It was clear to him he was now theoretically practised and knowledgeable about grief and loss, with a special focus on death and suicide and he now possessed what he thought was a thorough understanding of mental illness. In addition he had acquired a very workable body of knowledge regarding the criminal mind as well as a strong sense of the power of alternate realities through hypnosis. The underlying question still remained; could he make a difference with all this training?

Returning home he was initially excited to be re-employed by the government to work as an adolescent psychologist at an innovative new clinic called Integrated Services. As part of the clinic professional group, Mason was asked to take responsibility for providing psychological services to young people and their families where self-harm, including suicide, was a primary concern.

Quickly it became evident to Mason that Integrated Services, as a concept, was really a coordinative effort not an integrative one. Ironically there was really nothing integrated about it. Professionals across the spectrum of mental health care were brought under the same roof and encouraged to consider operating on the same page in the best interest of serving troubled youth and their families. The different professional perspectives, from trauma medicine, social work, special education, juvenile delinquency, psychological mental health, and welfare, struggled to find a common platform to operate from given their different operational and philosophical positions. The team he was on did its' best to work together despite the restrictive rules imposed upon them from their professional governing bodies.

Over the next two years, Mason seasoned his treatment skills working with what were referred to as hard-to-serve youth attending the Integrated Services clinic, much as he had done as an outward-bound counsellor. Only now he had more clout to make recommendations to mental health and social services authorities regarding treatment plans. It occurred to him that now he was being predisposed to wearing the mask of the "learned one".

In most cases, it was clear that the young person and their family wanted the Integrated Services team to shed light on their difficulties. They really didn't want this team of professionals to fix their problems for them. They wanted to be able to find a way to fix their problems themselves if they were indeed fixable. Even though clinic professionals could not be faulted for their good intentions, the involvement of too many professionals oftentimes overwhelmed those they were meant to serve.

Further adding to his evolving professional expertize at the clinic, Mason was contracted to provide trauma assistance and debriefing to police officers and ambulance paramedics in the community. The purpose was to address the profound impact of death and dying trauma work on first responders. The underlying goal besides optimizing performance was to potentially reduce the need for stress leave. Given that trauma debriefing was mandated, a hurdle in itself, Mason discovered very quickly that debriefing was like pulling teeth especially given the backdrop of an authoritarian organization where the general practise was to "suck it up" and hide any vulnerability.

Part of the service required Mason to attend crime scenes or loss of life situations in order to experience firsthand what the officers and paramedics were going through. This included suicides, fatal auto crashes, small plane crashes and drowning's as well as tragic domestic violence events. These experiences were noticeably stressful for him and at times they were difficult to handle, yet the impact on him overall was not debilitating as it appeared to be over time for some of the first responders.

After each exposure, he found himself at first reflecting on his own experience of the trauma as he had learned to do from his Gestalt Institute training, before engaging in trauma debriefing with the first responders. Clearing away his own perception and responses to a traumatic event allowed him the space to focus with greater clarity on the trauma event's impact on the first responders.

During moments of recollection Mason was often reminded of some of the most indelibly etched experiences with death he had encountered with his work with the first responders. One such encounter was a suicide of a young person hanging from a tree in a park on an early spring morning. Mason remembered watching the police officers cut down the person and noticed how their distancing behaviour patterns were similar to those he experienced in a hospital environment. The police officers seemed to depersonalize the experience as best they could refer to the young man as the "body" or the "DOA," and so on.

Humour also was present, although not directly related to the situation or in any way meant to be disrespectful. Rather, they would make comments about things happening in the news or the police department and make fun of the situation or themselves.

This behaviour was obviously meant to relieve their tension. However, Mason did not share the same emotional response. His past pattern, as he had experienced when his mother committed suicide and when he had stumbled upon the murdered victim during his underwater adventure, was to disconnect himself from his emotions and remain aloof, slow to react choosing to carefully contribute in a very measured and reserved way. This way of dealing with emotion had also shown up during the intense workshop training he participated in when he was enrolled in the university "Confrontations with Death" program.

Triggered by the memory of this suicide encounter Mason could not help but also remember another tragic event which took him far out of his comfort zone. In this event the Police Trauma Unit was called out on a suspected drowning of two young children who were playing on a partially frozen lake on a sunny day in the middle of winter.

Requested to be there to support the parents and the police he remembered arriving at the scene and immediately being drawn towards seeing two children, aged five and seven, laying face up on a tarp with a coroner in a white suit examining them. Stopping in front of the children he remembered an immense sense of heaviness had overcome him. He then recalled his mind going blank for what seemed like several minutes. It felt like he had withdrawn into a cocoon like he had done when he was a child growing up. Mason then recalled a numbness taking over him as he returned his eyes to focus on these two children. He had felt an urge to leave but could not move. He seemed to be frozen in place.

Remembering slowly coming to his senses, he found the courage to approach the parents and offer his condolences. He had asked them if there was someone he could call or anything he could do for them. They sat on the dock and just stared at him with an empty look in their eyes not responding. He remembered feeling tears start to well up from his eyes and then turning his head away for a few moments to compose himself before sitting down beside them on the dock. He recalled saying nothing for the longest time as intuitively sensed that no words he could come up with would make a difference.

As Mason remembered driving away from the lake that day the memories of the loss of both his parents, of finding a murdered man in the ocean, and the suicide of the young student found hanging from a tree all became intertwined leaving him wondering how he could make sense of senseless loss. Unlike previous experiences with death the deaths of these two children had impacted him the most. This time, unlike others, he had felt an immense upwelling of sadness and empathy for the parents. It shook him to the core. His discomfort was at the time palpable and unnerving, leaving him feeling emotionally vulnerable.

The death of these two innocent children heightened his sense of how difficult it was to care for others in such tragic circumstances. The parents' overwhelming grief had left him speechless. He felt that there was no consoling response he could have come up with that would have made their anguish diminish even slightly.

***

A year went by. Mason had become more aware of how his respect and empathy for the first responders had matured when doing his debriefings. His sensitivity to what they might be protecting themselves from experiencing when responding to tragic deaths became more acute and perceptive. The more he just reflected back to them what they were going through the more the first responders accepted him as someone who actually understood what they were going through.

It was becoming obvious to Mason that there is no right or clearly defined way to address the experience of death or loss. Each person needs to be respected in finding their own way. Although he seemed to be making progress as a professional assisting others in managing their distress with significant loss, Mason still was cognizant of the fact that he was still a practicing apprentice. The more he learned through experience, the more he felt he did not know.

During his time with the Police Trauma Unit, he began to question what happens when the energy that is so vibrant in life leaves the body at death. *How could he explore this further?*

This question triggered once again his memory of the encounter with death while diving with John, the medical doctor he had met several years back before going off to graduate school in the US. Mason decided to try to reconnect with him as they had not spoken with one another since. After tracking him down through the BC College of Physicians and Surgeons, he made the call and they agreed to meet and rekindle their friendship. During their conversation, John told Mason that he had gone on with his medical education and was a now a pathologist working in the Victoria coroner's office.

Meeting John at his office, they recounted their separate journeys' and reminisced about their past diving adventures. They then got around to Mason's question about energy and death, prompting John to suggest that he might find value in attending one of his autopsies. Mason was very apprehensive at first, but his curiosity got the better of him, so he agreed to accept the invitation.

John set it up for the following day. Arriving at the Forensic Centre, Mason was excited but nervous. He was not sure he was ready to participate in what he had imagined to be a gruesome exploration.

Prior to entering the examining room, Mason gowned up and prepped, and then John motioned him to approach the examining table. On the table was the naked body of an emaciated looking man, causing Mason to initially cringe.

John started the exam by speaking slowly, saying that today they would be simply doing a preliminary forensic examination of the body before them on the table. There would be no dissecting done today. Mason was relieved. John encouraged him to ask questions at any time.

John began, "Today, we have the privilege to examine some of the physiological historical factors as well as current trauma issues underlying the causes of death of this person who died two days ago. This privilege is sacred and deserves our total respect. What we discover can be revealing and meaningful both to our understanding of trauma death and to our forensic understanding of human functioning. This is a forty-six-year-old man who died from a drug over-dose. The file indicates that he was a chronic street drug user. There is some suspicion by the police regarding foul play in his death as the toxicology report indicated he had three times the lethal dose of fentanyl in his body apparently injected in his lower abdomen. No next of kin have been located. Today, we will only make an external forensic examination, looking for signs of injury and diseases that can be observed externally on the body."

As the examination progressed, Mason became more and more curious. In a surreal way, he was learning about life by examining death.

At the end of this very enlightening autopsy, Mason thanked John and they agreed to remain in touch. John commented that he very much wanted to be kept informed about his ongoing journey as an apprentice healer.

While Mason did not get any conclusive clarity from this experience as to what happened to the energy after death, what he did oddly experience was a felt sense of the deceased person's energy still being there. It was not in the body, but rather in the room at large.

This unusual experience triggered a strong desire to continue his work with trauma and probe further into the impact of death on the living. He also wanted to know more about the thoughts of those who take their own life or others'. For them, death was not the problem—living was.

Chapter Thirteen

The Journey East

CONSISTENT WITH HIS NOMADIC career pattern and his desire to continue his apprenticeship healer journey, it was time for Mason to move on. Wanting to exhaustively explore different counselling and therapy paradigms, especially as they might impact death and dying, Mason started to search for employment opportunities beyond the West Coast.

His encounters with suicide and death over the years had provoked and even skewed his interest in wanting to find out as much as he could about self-harm—including suicide—and what worked to prevent it. Underscoring this interest were of course the deeply ingrained personal experience of the loss of his mother to suicide and to a much lesser extent his own ruminations around drowning himself that surfaced when he was an adolescent in a group home. Factoring in his work with self-destructive adolescents during his work as an Outward-Bound Counsellor, his adolescent psychologist work with Integrated Services as well as his first responder trauma work convinced him that he needed to pursue employment where he could advance his knowledge and experience in this important area of mental distress.

Up to this point in his career, his professional involvement in providing mental health treatment to adolescents who were self-harming was not satisfying. For the most part, the intervention strategies he practised did not really work. What knowledge he had about suicide was not enough. To become more knowledgeable and effective, he needed to specialize in self-harm behaviour and practise in a workplace or hospital where they exclusively dealt with this serious mental health problem.

In his search for such a place, he came across an advertisement in the *Journal on Suicidology* looking for an adolescent psychologist to become part of an interdisciplinary team to work at a new intensive secure treatment centre that was being developed in Eastern Canada. It would be connected to a major hospital. . This team in question was in the process of being assembled.

This could be what he was looking for. He decided to pursue it further. Choosing not to engage in debating with himself about the pros and cons of showing up at the centre without securing an interview, Mason booked a flight and flew out to Eastern Canada where the treatment centre was located and showed up at the centre unannounced. His intuition was telling him that if he was meant for the job, they would all know it. It would be quite clear that his commitment and resolve would be undeniable. He also surmised that it would be highly unlikely that they would be interested in him sight unseen and it may be a stretch for them to consider someone unfamiliar with the unique cultural and environmental needs of a densely populated inner-city environment. It was a long shot, but it was a way to get his foot in the door. He was willing to take the risk.

Arriving at the centre, which was a four-storey brick building with no signage, he approached the receptionist and introduced himself. After he briefly shared his reason for being there, the receptionist apologized, stating that the director, Dr. Brighton, was in meetings all day. Mason thanked her and returned the following day, receiving the same message from the receptionist. Returning the third day, the receptionist invited him into the waiting room, which opened into an atrium that towered to the sky above through the centre of the building. She indicated that Dr. Brighton might have a few minutes between meetings, but she did not know if or when that would occur.

The inside of the building looked nothing like a secure treatment centre, leaving Mason puzzled about what their underlying operational philosophy of treatment might be.

After a few hours of patiently waiting, he was approached by a casually dressed man who introduced himself as Dr. Brighton.

He invited Mason to his office and stated that he only had about fifteen minutes to spare. After about forty-five minutes of lively discussion, Mason sensed that Dr. Brighton was taken by his boldness and perseverance, as well as his experience and credentials. Dr. Brighton apologized for having to end the meeting and promised to get back to him after discussing Mason's application with his treatment team.

Mason returned to BC thinking that he gave it his best effort. A week went by before he received a call from Dr. Brighton inviting him out for a second, more in-depth interview with the whole treatment team.

After this second interview, which lasted three hours, Mason was advised that they were required to review his application with their advisory board and that he would hear from them soon. Dr. Brighton added that they were seriously considering adding him to their treatment team. They asked him to stay one more day, and they would get back to him after the board had deliberated.

The next day, he was called in and offered the job. Mason felt affirmed, especially having been perceived as having the competencies they were looking for. The third path of his apprentice healer journey could now potentially unfold even more meaningfully than he had ever anticipated. As he left to return to BC and wrap up his commitments, he sensed that new horizons in the healing domain lay ahead of him. He felt privileged to be given the opportunity.

***

After returning to the west coast he took care of all his commitments and packed up his belongings and returned to Eastern Canada ready to plunge in with both feet. Very quickly he was thrust into the team's developing approaches to intervening in the lives of young people who were very volatile and very unpredictable. Some treatments seemed to work, while others did not. The challenge was to continuously reconfigure the treatments in search of more workable interventions.

In short order it became clearer to Mason that almost all adolescent suicides were impulse driven, making risk assessment a primarily post hoc effort. Seldom were suicide notes written and, more interestingly, when the attempt was unsuccessful, the risk of further attempts dropped significantly. Depression was a noted undercurrent, but it was not a predictor by any means. Time and time again, he saw that marginalized young people who experienced bullying, peer rejection, loss of family, and loss of important relationships would impulsively engage in self-harming behaviour as a severe reaction to their loss or rejection. Confusion and loss of self-worth, he felt, drove them toward a desperate need to end their unacceptable internal anguish. Dying was seldom their primary focus or objective.

At the other end of the spectrum, there existed a very small percentage of attempters who wanted very much to end their lives. These young people would engage in incrementally more risky self-harm behaviour to prime themselves for achieving their goal of ending it all. Whenever Mason encountered a young person who clearly had an unswerving resolve to commit suicide, their commitment would hit him like a sledgehammer. Outside of casting a safety net around them, mental health treatment seemed to be impotent. Drugs didn't work; they only interrupted their commitment to dying for short periods of time, if at all. Secure treatment seldom had an impact, and community interventions were largely ineffective.

During these times, Mason engaged in many debriefings with families confronted with suicide. He also participated in treatment planning initiatives with government agencies and other treatment centres, all of which made exploring the mystery of suicide all the more compelling. He increasingly felt that they were making progress in discovering ways to intervene in suicide attempts before they became successful.

As he continued to focus on suicide, Mason learned about a psychiatrist who was well known in the health sector for being incredibly knowledgeable about suicide and the continuum of self-harm. He was drawn to attend a workshop this man was conducting at a conference on suicide, entitled "Final Exit." At first Mason struggled to understand this man. He seemed to be both intellectually brilliant and at the same time iconoclastic. This one meeting led into several more, as they were both coincidently were asked to participate in a working task force on adolescent suicide.

Mason felt like he was a sponge, absorbing everything he could from this person about death and dying. As the task force came to an end, he realized that the exchange was almost entirely intellectual, albeit highly informative. What was missing was a sense of caring for those at risk. Suicide was objectified, not personified. Cases were examined forensically, with little or no effort to probe or address the meaning of death as a part of living. The "why" of suicide was still shrouded in assumptions and remained a mystery to him. The "how" of suicide was almost always the primary focus.

***

As time went by at the centre, Mason realized that he had drifted away from his intention to self-explore, getting caught up in his role as a psychologist focusing on self-harm. The perennial questions, "Who am I?" and "Who am I meant to be?" drifted in the backdrop of the demands of his work. As these thoughts passed and his questions melted away, he immersed himself even more deeply into his work.

After three years at the centre, his enthusiasm for the work started to seriously wane. Apart from being exhausted, no really significant breakthroughs in learning had occurred. It was time to take a step back and re-examine his work there.

Over his first three years he had worked six days a week and as many as twelve hours a day. Unquestionably, he was feeling burnt out. Contributing to his exhaustion was the disillusionment experienced that despite the intention that the centre operate from an interdisciplinary framework, it really did not. The medical model hierarchy at the centre was overarching and overruling, often mitigating collaborative effort in favour of top-down decision making. In this atmosphere, other health care providers at the centre often found themselves at odds with one another. When professional opinions and belief systems underlying their professional identity were challenged, collaboration suffered.

Remarkably however, the centre was seen by the professional community and government funders as being measurably successful. Mason could accept that the centre's acknowledged success was warranted. But it needed to be taken in perspective and understood against the backdrop of a history of very poor intervention outcomes. In other words, the bar of success was low from his viewpoint.

Mason was of the opinion that psychology had a meaningful seat at the health care table. Certainly, medicine was extraordinarily efficient at treating diseases of the body, but there was less success treating diseases of the mind and how they affected the body. Medicine was rigidly science-driven, and psychology was tolerated by the predominantly medical model-endorsing scientific community. It was standard psychiatric practice at the centre to first and foremost treat uncontrollable anger and rage with drugs. The interdisciplinary approach of day-to-day humanistic patient-centred treatment was secondary. Psychology, in particular, was seen as being only purposeful as a cognitive behavioural intervention. Mason remained frustrated by the political and bureaucratic forces that glorified medicine above all other fields of exploration.

Adding to his increasing discomfort at the centre was the sense that he was precipitously becoming more and more of a strategist and manager, and less a direct service provider. He came to the realization that he had allowed himself to lose a grip on his original intention of pursuing his visions of becoming a healer. His journey to become a healer seemed to have been side-tracked. *Had he sold out to authoritarian medically-driven fixing practises where one got acknowledged for assessing and diagnosing problems and not for healing?*

The impulse to professionally establish himself and build a reputation had eclipsed or overshadowed these intentions. He needed to regroup. It was time to confront his attraction to being an authority on aberrant human behaviour, as well as his overarching need to be a respected professional. Getting stuck in self-centred practicing was too limiting and too self-serving.

Critically thinking, which he felt he did too much of, Mason was of the opinion that symptom management of human suffering does not directly translate into action that ends suffering. You cannot end what never ends. One suffering transforms into another, perhaps less pronounced, yet nevertheless offering only a temporary reprieve. If suffering is in fact endless, one cannot fight this war armed with only techniques, strategies, and logic. He knew all too well that efforts to diminish suffering merely promoted temporary relief. The most common view he encountered from other professionals was that a little temporary relief was better than none at all. This underlying acquiescence had underscored what he felt was a pervasive shift toward coping and hoping. *How depressing! Can we get off the wheel of samsara as the Buddhists suggest we are on? Can we alter our perception of suffering and therefore our response to it? Can healing not be so stressful?*

Feeling exhausted by his consuming thoughts, he decided to take a break and go for a meditative jog. Refreshed somewhat from his run along the boardwalk, upon returning to his apartment he pulled out his favourite cushion and began to meditate.

During his meditation session his attention landed on the question he often posed to himself. *Could suffering end or be significantly reduced by disengaging our feelings from the endless thoughts that get attached to our feelings? Could we simply observe our feelings respectfully without thought?* Remembering his past research on psychological shadows, the concept known as character impeccability showed up on his mental screen. What he understood it to mean was: by not being attached to one's identity, one could minimize the experience of suffering. Then a question popped into his mind, *How does one achieve character impeccability such that you do not identify with any of your characters, you just simply notice them for what they are?* Mason's memory then triggered of the thought that perhaps the fourth pathway of the Four-Fold Way might well reveal some answers to these questions. He felt the desire well up inside to find a way to refocus his attention on the Four-Fold Way again.

The moving landscapes of thoughts nevertheless persisted. Now his conscious mind began to reflect on how so many professionals, including himself, had become wedded to theories or strategies on suffering such as systemic psychology, psychopharmacology, cognitive behavioural therapy, psychoanalysis, and hypnosis, among countless others. The professional strategy world was at times overwhelmingly confusing, given its propensity for one theory competing with another. The real impact of suffering seemed to be booted from one camp to another; no camp had universal acceptance. In a sense we end up shopping for relief.

Round and round again, Mason dwelled on the problem. *Am I missing something here? Can the truth about the origins of suffering and what can be done about it be revealed this way? Or am I just moving along the pathway of samsara like everyone else, turning on a wheel of suffering that spins off one karmic experience after another?*

Was it time to wake up and realize that his addiction to knowledge—to systems, to his never-ending search to become a more skilful healer—only produced more confusion, more disillusionment, and more self-absorption?

Am I nothing more than an idea-run traditional psychologist, thinking I know what to do based on my preferred theories, my systems conditioning, and my accumulated experiences? It was time to explore how to become more transparent to himself and fully address his desire to be a healer. This was highly unlikely to happen if he continued along his current path as a psychologist at the Crisis Treatment Centre.

What he thought he needed to do was find a way to get free from all propaganda and theories about human suffering. He wanted to stop searching outside for answers and commit to examining the relationship between himself and the world. Without an intimate, solid base of awareness of his personal relationship with suffering, was there really any meaningful basis of knowing what suffering means to others?

Stepping back from the probing intensity of his conceptual thinking, he realized his mental gyrations had got the better of him once again. His meditation session came to an end, leaving him with the feeling he had not really meditated at all.

***

A few more months went by at the centre before Mason learned about an International Hypnosis Symposium to be conducted in New York. What caught his attention was that sports psychologist, Erik Mette, would be delivering the keynote address. Mason had come across Erik's work on using hypnosis with Olympic athletes a few years back. Erik had a reputation of assisting world-class skiers, cross-country runners, and tennis players achieve peak performance as well as address performance anxiety and pain management.

The conference he thought might just be timely for him to attend given that he was now running marathons. Long distance running had become an addiction ever since one of his co-workers at the centre, Anne—an art therapist and avid runner—got him to join up with her and her running group out of the nearby YMCA. The group would run almost every lunchtime, work permitting, and they would do a long twenty mile run on the weekends. Having enjoyed running in his youth, he became re-addicted to running—to the point running marathons had now become a passion.

Then it occurred to him this symposium might offer him some insight into his questions related to human suffering and healing, if only from an athlete's perspective. He felt a strong impulse to register for the symposium. The next day, following his intuition, he signed up. This would be an opportunity for him to take a break and get away from the centre's demanding workload, not to mention his tendency to be obsessive about it.

Chapter Fourteen

❧ The Turning Point ❧

THE SYMPOSIUM EXPERIENCE WAS incredibly inspirational as one speaker after another did demonstrations on hypnosis, as well as talked about how to use it to promote healing and well-being. Attending Erik's workshop, entitled "Peak Performance in Sports and Health," Mason was immediately struck by how humble and unassuming Erik was. There was a clarity and simplicity about his presentation that was extraordinarily appealing. The humility he exuded was also disarming, as he invited questions from the participants without coming off as an expert. He did not adopt an authoritative stance, and calmness prevailed as he spoke.

Mason felt strangely attracted to every word Erik voiced, as he felt he either instinctively knew what he was saying or that he had read about what he was saying many times before. Not able to contain his curiosity Mason asked Erik at his workshop "How does the athlete transcend the conditioned mind?"

Erik responded, "Peak performances best occur beyond the conditioned mind, as the conditioned mind is time-bound and, as such, enamoured with the past. Memories of past experiences have a way of interrupting the flow of energy, as does the desire to do better rather than doing just the best they can in the moment.

When the athlete focuses their awareness on the limitations of their ordinary conditioned mind without condemning it, they have the opportunity to move beyond it. They then can begin to trust their training. When the present moment prevails, time seems to slow down or even become irrelevant. Athletes who experience peak performances beyond what their conditioned mind thought they were capable of generally cannot explain how it happened."

Mason nodded, and it was clear that Erik had the room in the palm of his hand.

Erik went on to share, "It can sometimes best be explained by what it is *not*. It is not like the trance impact of habit-driven behaviour, such as driving a car and not remembering the route you took. It is a moment-to-moment awareness without a conscious need for an agenda. When this in-the-moment state of awareness occurs, a state of flow can take over. To actualize this state of being is an *uncovering* process rather than a *discovery* process. This trance-like state can be achieved by anyone willing to let go of habitual thinking as the only baseline way to achieve extraordinary performance results.

The pathway is simple, but the approach less so. Paradoxically, one cannot master the whole natural unbounded mind with strategies derived from the condition-bounded mind. Hypnosis, meditation, and yoga have been known to promote access to the natural or whole mind, and in so doing can promote the possibility of peak performances as well as good health."

How compelling, Mason thought. "Could this information and perspective be also beneficial in assisting those caught up in a world of suffering?" Specifically, he wondered whether hypnosis, meditation, and mental mastery could be employed within the treatment centre. He didn't think it was likely. He could not imagine the treatment team being enthusiastic about hypnosis.

Over his own on-and-off-again exploration of hypnosis, he had become aware that hypnosis had often been compared to meditation, biofeedback, and guided imagery. In this context, he agreed with some experts in hypnosis, who suggested that all hypnosis was a form of self-hypnosis and akin to meditation.

Mason recalled going through episodic periods where he regularly practised mindfulness meditation and how hypnotic that was. His practise would ebb and flow, based on work distractions and his lack of commitment in general. The virtues of meditation were well known, yet he somehow felt that he had to overcome his preoccupation with life in general being an ordeal before he could enthusiastically sit down and meditate. There was something not quite right about this need to compel himself to do something that he knew was good for him. Was he unconsciously resisting and if so, for what reasons?

In the past, Mason had resisted taking direct instruction on how to best practise meditation. Instead, he chose to craft his own unique way of engaging in meditation, formed from a wide variety of book-learned techniques. He never considered having a guru, mentor, or master to instruct him. Extraordinarily stubborn and rigidly committed to finding his own way in life, he did not believe that having a master would work for him.

He was accepting that non-religious Buddhism was agreeable to him, especially its focus on compassion—a human trait that he felt was underdeveloped in him. But he definitely did not accept being tethered to any dogma, ritualistic belief system, or discipline. Traditional Buddhist rituals involving the taking of a master, following a strict disciplinary way of living, and practise were not something he could allow himself to do.

***

The return trip from the symposium provided him with several hours to reflect on the impact the workshop with Erik had on him, as well as what he learned from other presenters. What repeatedly crossed his mind was how it seemed evident—in fact, obvious—that meditation in some form was essential to healing and to performance. Coupling this with the thought that he may well be at a turning point with his position at the centre, Mason had the overwhelming urge to step back from his work and find a way to gain clarity about his practices as well as his purpose in being a psychologist.

During his attendance at the symposium, he had learned about an upcoming six-week intensive meditation residency program entitled, "Death and Dying and The Roots of Suffering." It was being held at a Buddhist retreat nestled into a valley in the Southern Appalachian Mountains.

The title of the program seriously captured his interest. Fortuitously, he heard more details about this event from a psychologist who sat next to him at a workshop that promoted the virtues of meditation as an adjunct that enhanced hypnotherapy. What he remembered that really turned his interest way up was the psychologist's testimonial about the retreat. He mentioned with engaging enthusiasm that he personally found the experience ground-breaking and life-altering. He went on to say that it had generated a level of clarity about his practice that he had never experienced before.

That was enough to get Mason committed to attending the retreat if he could arrange for the time off. Since he had not taken holiday time off from his work at the centre for the last several years, perhaps now was the time to take a two month leave of absence and seriously address his direction in life.

After securing a reluctant approval from the centre's board of governors, Mason enrolled in the program. During the weeks prior to the commencement of the retreat, he discovered more details about the program that reinforced his belief that he was making the right decision to attend. Consistent with what the psychologist at the symposium told him, he learned that the residency program was very flexible and accommodating.

Traditional meditation, or "sazan," was an option, but everyone who attended was free to choose to meditate in whatever way worked for them. That included meditating while taking nature walks, running, eating, observing others, and one's own mind. While there was a daily agenda, it was flexible and voluntary. If one wanted to, they could simply spend the day by themselves. The intent was that time would not be a controlling feature of the retreat. One could meditate as much or as little as they liked. The focus was on using a mindfulness approach to meditation with informal guidance as opposed to being trapped into arcane and disciplined Buddhist rituals. The only rules imposed would be for participants to refrain from drugs, social intimacy, and using cell phones. Given the surroundings, participants would also be encouraged to take nature walks or hikes in the mountains on a daily basis.

Arriving at the centre tucked away in a valley between two mountains the setting was idyllic. The valley was sparsely treed, and several streams flowed down the mountains and wound their way down the valley off behind another mountain some miles away. Wildlife was plentiful.

Most stunning was to see big horned mountain goats traversing the mountainsides.

The main centre building was a large log cabin with a huge central area for formal talks and fireplace chats and a communal eating area. Surrounding the log building, terraced down the slope of the mountain, were ten cabins for the residents. There was no electricity, and each cabin was heated by wood fireplaces.

As the retreat got underway, every student was assigned a preceptor who would engage in a dialogue with the student after each meditation session. The preceptors were Buddhist monks, always dressed in red robes. They were under the guidance of the "sensei," or the retreat centre principal. Every morning started with a short meditation session, followed by a talk by the sensei on something to do with death or dying, or on the causes of human suffering. These sessions would be didactic, offering the opportunity for participants to ask as many questions as they liked.

At the beginning, Mason discovered that, at best, his past participation in meditating was comparatively quite superficial. The freedom to meditate daily without time constrictions and with no set methods during the first two weeks revealed a depth of meditation he never knew existed.

In the third week, the primary focus of meditation was on addressing personal experiences with suffering and loss. The conversation would be focused on the students' personal experiences and what they had learned about themselves when focusing their meditation on their past suffering or losses.

Mason spent this week almost entirely focused on the loss of his mother and father. It was like riding an emotional rollercoaster. Anger, sadness, and guilt all cycled through him as he meditated or tried to meditate. The preceptor showed a depth of empathy that was beyond what Mason had ever experienced before. It was like he was his twin, who immediately knew what he was going through.

Every emotion was respected, and every confused thought was honoured. His preceptor was completely focused on him; no judgements were made, and no consoling was attempted. There was just total attention, as if nothing else mattered. After three days of repetitive sharing of his losses, the emotions began to subside, and the walking meditations he chose to do in nature became increasingly more peaceful. His long-buried feelings were no longer buried. He felt opened and vulnerable from the persistent focus on releasing his inner anguish. This openness had, in a refreshing way, precipitated a shift as he could now allow these events to just be significant events in his past that had unfortunately happened. The trauma impact had melted away.

Then another shift occurred when he became aware that the preceptor was like a mirror reflecting back to him his feelings, thoughts, and visual memories. It was like he could now sense how everything and everybody was all connected. An all-encompassing wave of self-acceptance and calmness flowed over him. The preceptor became more curious about the inner peace that he was now experiencing. This led to several sessions spent exploring ways to tailor his daily meditation in ways that would maintain, reinforce, and enhance his ability to achieve a calm state of being.

During the remaining three weeks, the meditation sessions became more natural and easier to engage in. Each day now ended with a question-and-answer didactic session by the centre's sensei on the events of the day. The sensei invited discussions on the origins of suffering, focusing on how it is driven by fear, grasping, and self-absorption. What actually transpires at the moment of death was also discussed and pointed out to be humankind's ultimate mystery.

The sensei was clear in saying that Buddhism does not provide theories of an afterlife. When questioned about the meaning of life, he would tell stories of how this question was addressed by his venerated ancestors over the centuries. He would occasionally inject a "koan," or saying, in his dialogue that reflected on dying and how profound this moment was for everyone, whether they are aware of it or not. Mason remembered him saying, "Dying and living are one. Living each moment, dying then takes care of itself."

Arriving at the last day of the retreat, Mason found that he could not organize his thoughts to capture the essence of the experience. Knowing this would be a likely experience for all the participants, the last day was set aside for all to retreat to a quiet space and write down their experiences in a journal.

Journal writing was something Mason did from time to time, but it was not a regular practise. Writing anything was, at best, an ordeal, as he often found words were inadequate in communicating his underlying perceptions. Intuitively, he knew that words could express the truth but could not fully capture it. Words as symbols only recorded a fraction of what he was experiencing, even when the experiences were very meaningful.

Despite his awkwardness and hesitancy with writing, he put pen to paper and surprisingly discovered that the experience just flowed without much effort. The words just tumbled out on to the pages one after another, highlighting what he had discovered and could declare about himself. Most poignant were the following passages.

The way I have avoided the fear generated by believing that I am inadequate was to project this fear onto others, perceiving them as inadequate in their own suffering.

I recognized that my assessment of others' suffering was just a collection of opinions or assumptions based on my accumulated knowledge.

I realized that my belief that doing my best was not good enough was based on an unrealistic belief that I could get better at being me.

My fascination with death was driven by seeing it as a mystery to be solved. I recognized that I had avoided embracing death and facing it for what it is; our human condition and where life and death are one phenomenon.

I also was aware that self-knowledge cannot be attained by attending one retreat or another. It was clear to me that there is no method or system or psychological training that I know of through which self-knowledge can transparently be

*obtained. These methods or systems only provide informa-
tion about my character patterns, which by and large resist
change. Acquiring self-knowledge happens only when I am
open to explore without fear of condemnation.*

*For me, demonstrating empathy—a genuine caring for
others—has been an off and on experience, depending on
the setting. When in the community involved in trauma
response, it seems to come naturally. When in a more clinical setting, it takes a backseat to being primarily objective
and diagnostic. I now understand more clearly that this
contradiction and lack of congruency has long ago been
deeply rooted in my own distancing pattern with being
empathetic toward myself.*

*The practise of being a compassionate witness was a concept
that I had come across many years ago, but I really only
knew it to be a concept. At this retreat, I experienced the
compassionate witness in action through my preceptor in
a way that truly drove home the power and impact of just
what being a compassionate witness was all about. Yet,
it still was a concept, and I could not find the words to
describe what a compassionate witness was. When I asked
the sensei, he stated that it is best known by what it is not.*

Returning home, he knew the path forward was going to
alter. In which way he did not know yet. He could return to
the centre and continue his work as a clinical psychologist;
or, as he had done several times in the past, he could find
another path to travel that might lead to him discovering

what to do to make his life more congruently meaningful. He was at yet another crossroad.

With two weeks remaining before he had to return to the centre, Mason was unexpectedly presented with an unusual request. He was asked if he would consider volunteering to provide fill-in coverage for the psychologist—who was going away for two weeks on holiday—on staff at the Aides Hospice. The hospice was dedicated to assisting those in the final stages of their illness with AIDS. The average length of stay was six weeks.

Feeling grounded from his meditation retreat, percolating through him was a desire to find something meaningful and contributory to do with his final two weeks of leave of absence. This request presented to him seemed to be a perfect fit. He felt ready and willing to take up this challenge and agreed to offer his services.

On the way to the hospice, his thinking landed on the thought that this was also an opportunity to drop his mask of professional identity and just be *Mason. Could he get to know the residents as they were not how they were or what they were in the past? Could he just let simple awareness and compassion guide him to be there for them as they faced impending death?*

Arriving at the hospice, he was greeted by the director, who thanked him for agreeing to fill in. He was taken on a tour of the residence and noticed flower-filled vases in every room. All the bedrooms were painted in the colours of the rainbow and were tastefully decorated. They all had a warm, attractive feel to them. He was told that, prior to their arrival, residents were invited to bring a wall hanging or picture of their choosing which they then could place on their bedroom assigned to them at the hospice

In many ways, the hospice triggered his memories of his own group home experience as an adolescent. The staffing set-up and amenities were remarkably similar as far as he could remember. The only major difference he noted was the addition of an in-house pharmacy.

Following the tour, he was introduced to the staff and residents one by one. Without exception, every staff member spoke of how privileged they were to be there with the residents. There was no sense of the sadness or stress that he expected to find at the hospice. The residents were remarkably cheerful despite their end-of-life circumstances. Communication was upbeat and supportive, almost as if they were all members of the same family.

Also unique about the hospice was that nobody seemed to be in a hurry. The focus was on minute-to-minute, person-to-person interactions, with no apparent agenda. Reminiscing seldom occurred. Laughter was pervasive, as residents and staff cracked jokes and made fun of one another in light-hearted ways. There was almost no talk about end of life or life after death.

Like his retreat experience, the hospice was infused with unconditional respect. When a new resident arrived, all the other residents would embrace the new resident with a sense of unconditional caring that was beyond words. Staff always remained in the background and, as best they could, would allow the residents to be in charge.

At first, communication was challenging for Mason, as his ingrained programming as a psychologist was to inquire and search for solutions to problems. Here at the hospice, he was respectfully asked to shift his inquisitiveness toward finding meaning in who they were and what they were experiencing each day.

Reflecting back over his two-week experience at the hospice, it became evident to Mason that the residents were teaching him the art of living through dying. Each resident interaction was a learning moment about how to be with someone completely without judgement and without an agenda. He recalled how one resident would ask him to walk with him without speaking, while another less able to be mobile would simply ask him to sit with him while he gazed out the window and talked about how beautiful the trees were. Another resident looked at him with wide-open eyes and smiled while asking him to hold her hand. She thanked him for his kindness, letting him know just being there took her attention away from her pain. It also became obvious to Mason that they wanted him to recognize them as worthy and capable. It was their soulfulness that they wanted recognized, not their deteriorating physical health.

Faith played a part for some. Yet the overriding sentiment was that they were there to complete their lives with meaning, dignity, and respect. Their spirit was alive and well even though their bodies were coming to an end for them.

In an extraordinary way, the experience had released from within him a deep sense of compassion beyond empathy for the residents at the hospice and for others who he knew were suffering. Prior to this experience, his journey within the mental health landscape rarely revealed within him a deep and abiding sense of compassion for others. Empathy he was familiar with, but compassion seemed missing in action.

On a more sombre note, despite the upbeat vibrations that prevailed at the hospice, there was still a blanket of fear that existed—while untouchable and sidelined, it was nevertheless palpable. The fear of loss was multi-faceted—not just about impending death, but also loss of face, loss of family, loss of physical capability, and loss of purpose. In so many situations, families had ostracized or disowned these residents, leaving them feeling worthless and abandoned. At times, being there with them as they shared their feelings brought him close to tears. Abandonment was something he knew all too well.

The converging impact of this unusual volunteer experience with the six-week meditation retreat had clarified for Mason that he had gone off track from his intended desire to become a seasoned healer. Without any clear intention, he had redirected his focus towards becoming a specialist in trauma treatment and crisis intervention. It was now obvious to him he had become addicted to the idea that he could make a difference in the lives of others by taking on the mask of being an expert or specialist. There was no question that this path he had been on had merit. It was just not the path that resonated with his deep underlying intention to make a difference as a genuine unfettered healer. With this awakening, Mason realized that he could not continue doing what he was doing at the treatment centre. He needed to refocus on his lifelong mission and move on.

Chapter Fifteen

❊ Letting Go ❊

MOVING ON THIS TIME would be difficult. Despite the meaningfulness of his involvement at the Crisis Treatment Centre and the gains achieved in minimizing the suffering of others, it was time to let go of making the centre the focal point of his life. No one seemed to understand this when he stumbled around with his verbalize his reasons for leaving. Some felt that he was abandoning them. Some were angry because he was dismissing the importance of their work. Others were mystified that he would simply end his promising career with nothing planned.

This time, unlike his past adventures, Mason did not have something to go to; he had no job, and no family or friends drawing him back to where his journey in life started. There were no new tangible career adventures that captured his interest.

Departing for the West Coast without planning for the future felt freeing, yet it left him with a sense of uncertainty. Was this the right move to make at this juncture of his life? He did not know. But he was clear that experiencing new, unknown horizons was the driving force spurring him onward.

As he planned his move, he wondered, *Will this move help to further clarify my understanding of myself? Will it afford me the opportunity to address my preoccupation with being right, being an expert, my addiction to knowledge, to possessions, my envy, and my pseudo pride in being a somebody of significance? Will I transcend these embedded and conditioned low energy patterns, or will I continue to recycle through them? Is it possible for me to transform; to move my energy to a higher plane?* These were just some of the questions ruminating around in his head on his long cross-country train ride back home.

Back on the West Coast, Mason had plenty of time to further contemplate what might be worth experiencing next. For the first time that he could remember, there was no pressing need to do or experience anything right away. He sensed his ego had become minimized in some way or at the very least parked in the background of his awareness.

He settled into a cabin he found for rent off the coast of Vancouver Island. The cabin was nestled among tall Douglas fir trees on a windswept cliff overlooking the ocean. The serenity it provided allowed him to meditate on the questions he had posed during his journey home. The idea of self-actualization or residing in the power of the moment was to be the central thought of his meditation sessions, around which he would allow other thoughts to float in and out of his awareness.

Initially showing up in his mindfulness meditations were thoughts about the countless workshops and seminars on human potential he had attended over the years. It was clear that they had had an accumulative impact on him, but in many ways it was not enough. Moreover, all the self-help books he had read and the theories on transcendence, self-actualization, self-awareness and being fully human he had learned about had gradually faded away into the background, giving way to his old character patterns. At best, these explorations resulted in temporary well-being—a temporary awakening. He was still wearing the same old masks.

The more he meditated, focusing on his journey in life, the more obsessive he became about it. What he was looking for was spontaneous, randomly flowing thought in his meditation. This was not happening now. It was time to take a break from his meditative experiences being driven by obsessive thinking about his journey in life.

Over the next two weeks, the summertime weather was warm and enticed him to be outdoors in the wilderness. Mason replaced sitting meditation with longer mountain bike rides on the West Coast ocean side trails. The early morning rides were refreshing, as he chose to stop often and take in the scenery. He became particularly entranced on several occasions when he stopped to watch the seagulls ride the thermals, seemingly just playing with the wind.

He found that these early morning rides allowed him to regain his mental balance; his thoughts were more and more focussed on the environment around him and less internalized. He was thankful for the shift in focus it offered.

His late-in-the-day rides were a different matter. Try as he might to stay externally focused by making the rides more challenging, his internal ruminations regained a foothold in his awareness. Repeatedly, one thought would prevail over all other thoughts, telling him he could not continue to practise psychology the way he had done over the past two decades. This pattern needed to come to an end.

Leaking through and surfacing to his consciousness was the thought of another pattern he had developed in his career. It was evident to him that he had the tendency to move from one field of psychology to another. And along the way he would learn the tools of the trade but not be fully and completely dedicated to any one domain. He had dabbled in so many areas spanning forensic psychology, suicide, trauma intervention, humanistic psychology, child development psychology, and human performance psychology. All had captured his attention, but none had been sufficient to keep his attention alive and thriving over time. He knew that, in many ways, he indulged in the entrapments of being a psychologist as an entitlement to speak about many areas of human functioning without truly being an expert.

Once again, he came face to face with his mask-wearing being a person of knowledge rather than being just a human being. Who he really was, he did not know. Could he discover his true nature in greater depth by taking a visionary journey of some sort, or was this just imaginary, delusional thinking?

Surfacing from his intense preoccupation with self-exploration, he wondered, *What is it that I really want? If it is not to become a healer, what's next? What is the visionary way? If I were to commit to exploring the Visionary Warrior pathway, how would I start? What kind of resources would I need?* He simply did not know the path forward.

It became clearer to him that when he ruminated excessively, it was his ego operating and that would not lead him to his calling or to the truth. The truth could not be told, but his ego tried to tell him that it knew the truth. What a paradox!

His conditioned mind wanted him to be different than he was—more intelligent, more clairvoyant, better than he was, and, most of all, more respected. It wanted to separate him from others and protect him from the fear of being exposed, hurt, and ignored.

He knew that his tendency toward self-absorption and being driven by fear of inadequacy were the gatekeepers of his identity. He knew that he was nothing special, nor was he clairvoyant by any means. These thoughts so plagued him on his long, late afternoon mountain bike rides along the coast.

Discontinuing his late afternoon bike rides, Mason returned to just meditating. In the beginning, his thoughts were quite balanced and flowed from one thought to another in random fashion without any particular focus. He felt encouraged that he could watch his thoughts without getting stuck in them again. This did not last for long.

His attention soon landed on the issue he had about being a follower. Reflecting back over the years, he was aware that he had built up a seemingly impenetrable wall that prevented him from deferring to or depending on others. He was acutely aware that he wanted to find his own way in life. In this regard, he could not bring himself to search out a teacher—or guru, for that matter. Learning from others, he could do. What he could not bring himself to do was subjugate himself to a master. He felt that his ingrained stubbornness was necessary to protect him from being manipulated by others.

Besides, he thought, even if he were open enough to look for spiritual or visionary mentor, where would he begin his search? Even more importantly, to what extent were there any genuine visionary mentors out there to find? He was not aware of there being any breeding grounds for mentors of the visionary kind.

Shopping around for one was not the answer, as this in itself could become an obsession where one runs the risk of becoming a spiritual tourist. He was absolutely certain that he did not want to become a "spiritual junkie."

The more he meditated, the more he was just ruminating about his past and increasingly becoming puzzled about his future. This was troubling as he felt stuck going around and around in a circle. Instead of trying to eliminate this dead-end focus, he decided to become even more focused on it in his meditations. His central thought would now be to go with the flow without judging or condemning his thoughts, and to simply observe them as best he could as they unfolded.

As the summer was coming to an end and mountain biking had been temporarily suspended in favour of dedicating his time to meditating, another shift occurred. He discovered that trail walking along the coast paths near his cabin allowed him to slow down his thoughts. It started to become a daily practice.

On his first walk, thoughts of past memorable encounters with people who had a significant impact on getting him grounded in life started to surface. Then, unexpectedly, he found himself imagining all these people were gathered together and sitting around a large round table. The table was the same treatment room table he had sat at with Arnold, his child psychologist, so many years ago. Giving his imagination free reign, a movie of his making started to unfold. Crossing his visual landscape, he first saw Mr. Baines, his maths and drama high school teacher. In his mind, Mason heard him say, as he had done in the past, "You are not just the characters you play or have played. You are free to choose and enact whichever character that shows up in your awareness. Nonetheless, they are simply characters representing aspects of what you have experienced. They are by no means who you are. Your characters are the way you play out your drama in life, based on your memories, past experiences, and habits, which generally become unconscious over time."

An inner voice within him replied back, "The primary character operating my way of life up to the present is that of being a professional psychologist. My concern is that this character has run its course. I don't know which character, if any, to promote next."

Mason then heard a reply from Mr. Baines. "You always will be unclear, as characters are illusive and unreal. For you to engage in the play of life does not mean that you have to be attached to any character. Characters are like monkeys; don't feed them, and they will be interesting, but they won't bother you incessantly."

Following this dialogue, an image of Dean Harris showed up. Running across his mindscape was the memory of Dean Harris's generosity and compassion towards him when he was starting out as a university student. His unconditional gift had left an indelible imprint on him.

Upon recollection, he was reminded how he had, from time to time, found himself doing the same thing for others without any preconceived intentions. It brought to mind his anonymous financial gifts he had made to the AIDS hospice, as well as the crisis accommodation fund he participated in that helped street youth exit the streets when they were ready to do so. He also recalled the free counselling services he had offered over the past decade to First Nations peoples who had experienced the trauma of residential schools.

In the imagined words of Dr. Harris, Mason heard, "Giving from the heart not the head will then have no strings attached to it. The heart is today. The head is filled with yesterday and the promises of tomorrow. The moment you think about giving, there ceases to be a creative reality operating, and it becomes judgement. There is immeasurable freedom when one just gives as it occurs to do so."

Next, John's infectious smiling face showed up. He heard John, his old diving partner, say, "Good medicine comes from within. Do not succumb to doubt. You will get trapped in what you know, and you will cease to be courageous in discovering who you want to be."

Mason replied that he felt that ending his attachment to being a psychologist was like a character death. John followed up, "Your biggest challenge regarding professional identity is surrendering to it coming to an end now rather than having it become a far off event on some horizon."

Shifting his focus, an image of the Carver appeared. The Carver sat in a soft, accepting posture, holding an unpainted mask of a human face. He sensed the Carver was gazing at him and it felt like he was looking right through him. The Carver remained silent. The Carver reminded him of the masks people wore, and how it was important to respect them. He also reminded Mason that the pathway of a healer was not an easy one to travel. Taking the Four-Fold Pathway was just one of many paths he could travel. Pathways did not make a healer. They could be a roadmap, but they could never be the territory. Most importantly, Mason recalled that the Carver encouraged him to carve his own pathway. No teachers or advisors were necessary.

This last point hit home as he recalled the many times he had engaged in teaching others, either through workshops, consultations, or in treatment group experiences. He always felt that he was window dressing and falling short of achieving anything significant. *Why so?* He thought. He would hear the Carver saying, "People hunger for information but not awareness. You cannot teach awareness. Being open to your own awareness can be your best teacher."

The next to show up at his imaginary gathering around Arnold's table was Erik, the sport psychologist who had showed Mason his signature way of being both humble and joyful at once. His pioneering work using hypnosis seemed to exist in a separate paradigm outside of mainstream psychology.

Remarkably, he heard Erik say, "Competency cannot be a goal, nor can it be an achievement. Doing your best ought not to be guided by outside results, but rather by mastering one's internal reality. Achievement is not a competition. It is what happens when your mind and body are inseparable. This occurs when one can watch the disturbed, competitive mind without getting disturbed."

When the walk came to end, Mason realized his unconscious mind—in a trance-like manner—had revealed to him some of the inner workings of his state of being. Each of his mentors had revealed to him something about himself, and now it was up to him to put everything together.

Over the following two weeks Mason's daily walks were uneventful but remarkably peaceful. He felt more grounded as the thoughts he was having just showed up and disappeared, not being hooked by any of them. It left him feeling primed and ready to explore new ideas and new territories.

To start, he decided that it was time to seek out new perspectives on healing by broadening the scope of his readings.

A few weeks after the trance walk, Mason came across a remarkable little book as he was researching Indigenous healing methods, entitled *The Four Agreements*. The author, Don Miguel Ruiz, a Mexican physician, was known in his culture as a master healer. The Four Agreements were offered as a basic framework to navigate the workings of the conditioned mind. It was boldly prescriptive; an aspect of which Mason initially was critical— yet its simplicity was what was appealing.

Mason understood the agreements as practical guidelines for managing one's confusing and unreliable conditioned mind. They were not hard and fast rules for living, as all four agreements could be understood in as many ways as there were people choosing to apply them.

Reviewing these agreements was an opportunity for him to check out what they meant to him personally. Could they assist him to redirect his tendency to go off-track and become self-absorbed, rather than remain focused on self-awareness?

The first agreement, which Miguel considered to be the most important, was "Be Impeccable with Your Word." This agreement resonated like a tuning fork with Mason. Essentially, its underlying message was that words are not the truth. They are a reflection of the truth. He took that to "be impeccable" meant to be clear and clean with words, using them rather than letting them use you. Miguel suggested that to be impeccable, one needed to speak with integrity. This, to

Mason, meant saying only what you meant. One needed to avoid using the word to speak against oneself or to gossip about others. Miguel suggested using the power of your word in the direction of truth, but not *as* the truth. Mason took integrity to mean being whole, and that in all parts exists the whole—a concept he knew well from his training in Gestalt Therapy.

The second agreement, "Don't Take Anything Personally," meant that what other people say about you is never *about you*. It's about who they are, and it's a projection of their own reality. This agreement intimates that when you are immune to the opinions and actions of others, you won't be the victim of needless suffering.

Mason interpreted this agreement to also mean, "Do not take your own character, or the characters posturing as your identity, personally either." They are not *you* in essence; they are only an approximate or incomplete description of you—an attempt to describe the indescribable you. In summary, you are not the sum of the characters you have played throughout your life; you are much more. Reading about this agreement felt like the culmination of the treatment lessons he had first learned from Arnold.

The third agreement, "Don't Make Any Assumptions," disturbed Mason as he struggled with how he engaged in assumptions in his own life. Remnants of the egregious and ingrained assumptions he made about himself still existed. Most prominent were the assumptions, "I am damaged goods, and I am not good enough," despite much evidence to the contrary. They still lingered in his background. Making these kinds of assumptions, he realized, was a way of diverting himself from exercising the courage necessary to take full responsibility for who he was.

To a lesser extent, he was carefully guarded against making assumptions about the actions of others despite his clinical training, which allowed assumptions to be made if they were couched as hypotheses and subjected to the rigors of peer scrutiny. Given his propensity for being an iconoclast, Mason chose to take a neutral stand whenever possible and not render his thoughts with contrived or scientifically-backed opinions.

In the professional world he played in, he found himself quietly resisting the traditional practise of rendering diagnoses, which was really just being an expert making assumptions. He felt they were all too often justified based on professional privilege or experience. This was considered to be a baseline unquestionable practise from which advice would be given and judgements made.

And finally, the fourth agreement, "Always Do Your Best," simply suggested that doing your best would always be good enough. This was something that Mason had struggled with, erroneously thinking that he always needed to do better. He reminded himself that he had, up to this point, adopted an attitude of pursuing excellence in his life. In so doing, he was trying to make a mark in his world rather than leaving markers. Excellence was always around the corner; it was not quite reachable. The message he got from this agreement was that excellence was not something you get to. Excellence was who you are when you were always doing your best.

Despite his habituated pattern of wanting to do better, he knew deep down that he really wanted to be grounded in doing his best without reservation, without condemnation. Being addicted to doing better was just that—an addiction.

For Mason, this book highlighted that more than just knowing these agreements was required; much more. To begin with, he needed to completely, without reservation, give up, to surrender his attachment to being a victim of his life's circumstances. Then he needed to release himself from his ingrained patterns of avoiding his vulnerabilities and his tendency to self-depreciate. The thoughts that controlled these patterns were disabling, not enabling.

Surfacing for air from his deep dive into exploring the underpinnings of his own character, he needed to lighten up and get out of his head. The urge to get out on his bike, along with a desire to run again, surfaced. Upon his return to BC, he noted that his passion for running—which was a core aspect of his daily life at the Crisis Centre—had been suspended, taking a backseat to mountain biking, meditation, walking hikes, and, of course, his primary focus on mental self-exploration. Sensing his body's uneasiness, he started to add running back into his daily activities.

Chapter Sixteen

❦ Self-Reflections ❦

O N ONE OF HIS daily rides on his mountain bike, Mason passed by a Buddhist temple out in a rural area. Curious to explore further, he decided that on his next bike trip, he would stop by and check it out.

Before he made his way there, he reread several chapters from Alan Watts's book, *Become What You Are,* and Chögyam Trungpa's *Transcending Madness,* as well as the chapter on compassion from the *Tibetan Book of Living and Dying.* Back to being driven by knowledge-seeking, he thought, *Oh well, let's see what this experience brings.*

Entering the temple grounds, it was startling to see how colourful it was. There were long rows of multi-coloured flags, flapping in a gentle breeze leading up to the temple.

Two gold embossed, twelve-foot wooden doors led into the temple. Inside the temple was a two-storey gold Buddha statue. The temple was immaculately maintained inside as well as out. Mason pondered for a moment the role ritual and ceremony played for those seeking awareness in a Buddhist temple.

A few people were milling around outside, as well as about half a dozen or so inside. They were of all ages and dressed casually. No one was talking, which was strange, as no formal ceremonies were being conducted, and there were no signs suggesting that those visiting needed to exercise nonverbal communication.

Mason noticed a pond surrounded by benches with a curved bridge. On the other side, he noticed a shaved headed Buddhist monk dressed in a red sarong sitting cross-legged on one of the benches close to the pond. Mason didn't know why, but he felt the urge to go over to him. As he approached the bench, he decided to sit down on another bench next to the monk. No words were spoken for what seemed like ten minutes.

Finally, the monk, a middle-aged man of about fifty, threw a coin into the pond. After pausing for a few moments, Mason broke the silence in an uncertain, yet curious voice. He asked if he had thrown a coin into the pond as a ritual.

Surprisingly, the monk responded inquisitively, "Did you hear anything?"

Mason naively responded, "I heard a splash."

The monk responded, "What did you see?"

Without thinking, Mason said, "I saw ripples in the pond."

Then, the monk surprised Mason again when he asked, "What do you see or hear now?"

Mason did not know what to say at first as he felt he was being challenged and caught off guard. Then inexplicably he blurted out "interconnectedness."

Silence followed for several minutes. The monk then stood up, bowed, and departed without a word. *Strange encounter,* Mason thought. He did not know what to make of it.

Deep in contemplative thought on his way home, it occurred to Mason that Buddhist doctrine suggested primordial awareness could not be accessed by a conditioned mind. One needed to be free from the ordinary conditioned mind before primordial awareness could be experienced. Being in this natural state of awareness, one could reflect on and review the workings of the conditioned mind without being conditioned by it. Mason was able to get the gist of this esoteric concept but had yet to find a way to experience it directly.

He recalled a quote from his recent readings: "Total awareness cannot be grasped consciously; we cannot give it a stable form; it has no clear-cut boundaries; we cannot describe it in words."

As this experience with the monk was a riddle of sorts, perhaps it also was a message to his ordinary conditioned mind that other realities existed. That awareness was not amenable to analysis; it did not need to be justified, evaluated, or made sense of. Awareness could not be introspected, as it would then not be awareness—it would be just an attempt to make sense out of experiences from the internal workings of a *thoughtful* mind.

The state of awareness, according to his readings, cannot be cultivated or acted upon as a goal to achieve. Attending a temple, meditating, doing virtuous acts of kindness, or being pious or an ascetic was not a recipe for awareness. These were rituals or behaviours designed to manage or quiet the ordinary mind—to get our behaviour and thoughts out of the way so that we might discover ways to uncover our true nature.

As he also had come to know, it was not a state of becoming aware; it was a state of *being* aware. It was of the moment, moment to moment. There was no "I" that was aware. Awareness was passive alertness; it was choice less, effortless. He had heard say that it was the most powerful antidote to address suffering.

Mason decided not to try to figure out what this unusual Buddhist monk interaction meant. Perhaps it would be best to let the experience sink in and not dwell on it.

Mason felt that that no system, school of thought, or practise such as Buddhism or Indigenous healing could teach him how to be self-aware. These platforms offered the means to gain an understanding of one's patterns. In that way, they could prepare one to do one's own self exploration work. He was convinced that he needed to be his own witness, his own explorer.

What appealed to him about Buddhism was how they made compassion the cornerstone of their practise. Compassion was still somewhat elusive for him, as he struggled to be compassionate toward others. In the past, he realized that he had talked to others about the value of allowing compassion to be baseline for self-awareness. Yet compassion did not fluidly course through his veins. It was still largely a cognitively-driven intention.

Mason was mindful of what the Buddhist "sensei" at the retreat he attended said: "One does not have to find compassion. It is deep within all of us. It is not lost, just covered up."

In his search for a more in-depth understanding of compassion, Mason had come across the intimations of Mother Theresa, who was known to be preeminent in her demonstration of compassion towards those who were dying. What he gleaned from this exploration was that compassion was not unique to any one person. Compassion is who we are as humans when we are not self-focused. If we let go of the fear of needing to be somebody, to be known, and to be respected, compassion naturally shows up.

In his education and professional experiences related to death and dying of others, empathy showed up many times for him. With this backdrop, Mason felt he had a deeply ingrained sense of value for human life, but he did not feel he had a corresponding deep sense of compassion. When it did show up, it ebbed and flowed. No telling when it would do either.

He reminded himself of how he justified not being compassionate toward himself. There was no need, as long as he was constantly on the move. Self-caring only indirectly showed up when he was running, cycling, or being active, and even then, it was only of passing interest. His primary interest by staying active was to challenge himself physically in order to reinforce his identity of being physically capable.

Arriving back at his cabin by the ocean, after his visit to the Buddhist Temple there was nothing for him to do except contemplate who he was in relation to the world he lived in. He had no obligations and no plans yet for what he would do next. This state of neutrality freed up his mental landscape, allowing him to meditate without an agenda. His twice daily meditations, daily cycling trips, and running every other day filled up one day to the next. Occasionally, he would ruminate about the need to be productive and back on the apprentice healer pathway but, for the most part, this preoccupation did not last long.

A month went by and he became increasingly more tranquil just focusing on the environment he was in moment to moment. It was like he had entered a trance where his conscious mind had taken a holiday, allowing his unconscious mind to percolate through. What then started to surface through his day in and day out meditative experiences was a message that who he really was in relationship to others and the world around him was seeking clarity. At first these intimations were benign but, within a few days of them happening, they became more energized.

This prompted him to explore what he was doing with his relationships to people, things, and himself more deeply. Now was the opportune time for him to begin doing this. To begin this exploration, he would start by exploring his relationship with the outside, objective world, then people, and then move on to his relationship with himself. Remembering his Gestalt training, in particular the concept that "in the part exists the whole," it would be important for him, he thought, to get a picture of how each area of relationship was interwoven to reveal the whole of his relationship world.

This would be a shift in his meditative practice from allowing thoughts to come and go to having a conscious agenda which would be new for him.

As he began this different meditative approach, the first issue that showed up on his radar was his relationship with money. Money had a depressing effect on him. Coming from his beginnings, where money was scarce, he operated as if there would never be enough in his life, despite the fact there always was. Mason was fearful of becoming penniless and destitute, and he doubted his skills at managing his own resources.

Consequently, money as a problem always lurked in the background of his existence. The more he focused on money, the clearer it became that he was driven by the need to hold on to it. In an interesting way, holding on to money made no sense given the frugal way he lived. There always seemed to be a push-pull with money and possessions. They hampered his freedom to just be, yet they offered him the freedom to explore new horizons and experiences.

Giving money away was, at times, difficult to do, and he felt that it required a phoney altruism to make donations to others in need. Impulses to contribute were most often screened through his belief that it would leave him short of money. He was attached to money and, at the same time, he did not want to be. What a paradox! On a more upbeat note, when he did donate anonymously, the attachment to money disappeared.

The next relationship issue that showed up after several meditative sessions on money was his relationship with knowledge. To begin with, Mason was aware that he had an addiction to knowledge. Reflecting on his journey with knowledge, it was also a love-hate relationship. He was aware that knowledge fascinated him, and he felt driven by the desire to always seek more of it. Mistakenly, it occurred to him that knowledge was power rather than being a means to having power. This was a fact in the material world, but not so much, he thought, in the psychological world. While knowledge could generate wealth, it also could generate confusion. The accumulation of knowledge actually did not produce clarity or understanding, except on a superficial material level. If anything, his search for more knowledge was driven by his need to clear up his confusion with having too many conflicting ideas which actually were created by the pursuit of knowledge itself. This was a closed-loop entrapment with no seemingly available exit point. Acquiring more and more knowledge, he also knew, was a way to distance himself from his past and find a future that would allow him to feel complete and worthy, which it did not accomplish. Seeking knowledge was not an unworthy pursuit; it just was taken too seriously and given too much importance in his life.

At the next mediation session, he reflected further on knowledge and his relationship with others. He became aware of how he used knowledge to fortify his perspective on what he thought he knew. He also was aware that, from time to time, he would be tempted to embellish his knowledge as a way to promote his expertise. Even more concerning was how, on occasion, the gaps in his knowledge would be filled in with assumptions he could not back up. What this actually revealed was how predisposed he was towards donning the mask of being the expert whenever he felt the overpowering need to be acknowledged. When this happened, it was clear to him he was trapping himself by wanting to be perceived as more capable than he was. Taking a moment to reflect on how this might come across to others, it occurred to him it was a distinct possibility he could be perceived as being somewhat disingenuous. This troubled him deeply, as it was the opposite of what he wanted to be.

Not wanting to let self-condemnation take over his self-exploration and cloud his awareness, he shifted his focus, recognizing he could learn from this pattern by taking a step back from it. Knowing that knowledge creates the foundation for opposites, it also presents an opportunity to explore ways to merge the opposites without having to be an expert in the process.

At the next session, what captured his attention was the awareness that knowledge always seemed to bring mixed blessings. In a fast-moving world, its value was undeniable. Ideas stemming from knowledge were addictive. On the other hand, for Mason, knowledge accumulation was always a chore, as he actually preferred knowing by doing as opposed to knowing through books and traditional education. Having an education seemed to dampen his irrational fear of being stupid; he had been labelled as such many decades ago, and that fear was now buried underneath this accumulated veneer of knowledge. In an ironic way, he also knew that his endless pursuit of knowledge actually inhibited his pursuit of self-awareness and meaningfulness beyond his identity as a psychologist.

Now a week into this meditative focus on relationships, what showed up next was his relationship with his cultural heritage. What first surfaced was the awareness that he viewed his Indigenous background in a cursory way. It was interesting to him that he was part native and had only infrequently participated in Indigenous culture, yet Indigenous culture had had a profound impact on him. Still, he sensed that he could not motivate himself to fully assimilate Indigenous worldviews into his way of life, even though he unquestionably respected them. It felt like he was on the border between his two cultural backgrounds. In an inexplicable way, he wanted to feel a connection, a sense of belonging, yet he also didn't. Belonging to any culture or belief system was a problem for him, as he did not want to be limited by the identity restrictions they would impose. To belong meant to be obligated and abide by beliefs he could not support, which he was unwilling to do. It was not that the beliefs were not meaningful and valuable to others; it was that he did not find them so for himself.

At his next meditation session, his focus shifted on to his family of origin. What showed up was a shadow over his father and a blanket over his mother. They were like vague images—not fully fleshed out, to the point they stirred up no sense within him of being emotionally connected to them. With no grounded relationship with parents or siblings, Mason sensed no deep and abiding interest in family. Not having much of a family of origin story to tell, there was no real interest in creating a family of his own.

Following this session, his attention was drawn to his relationships with others. Socially, he enjoyed people, except when they were aggressive, emotionally needy, or too self-absorbed, which he experienced more often than not. Ironically though, these were the traits that most interested him in work as a psychologist and which he could not tolerate within himself. Mason felt he had no difficulty with and enjoyed engaging in professional or recreational friendships. But his desire to have intimate relationships had clearly been repressed. This avoidance was underpinned by a strong underlying belief that allowing himself to experience intimacy would expose him to the risks of being rejected or abandoned. This he could not tolerate, as he decided long ago not to let himself get too close to others for these very reasons. Etched in his memory was the sense of being abandoned by Sylvia so many years ago. This was his very first intimate relationship, which ended when she left college and returned to her hometown due to a serious illness.

As his mind continued to focus on relationships, it occurred to him that he could handle personal rejection but not when there were emotional strings attached. Reviewing his past attempts at developing relationships through dating experiences over the years, on every occasion the relationship would end before romantic intimacy started to show up. It was obvious that those he dated lost interest in him, largely because of his trepidation in allowing himself to be intimate or become emotionally vulnerable. This was a pattern he could not seem to break.

As his daily self-reflection unfolded, next on his mindscape was his relationship with his career as a psychologist and his life-long desire to serve others in a healing capacity. The identity of being a psychologist offered him a sense of security in an unsecure, uncertain, and unpredictable world. The work was always challenging, but not always rewarding. He wanted something more from it. He felt driven to seek another identity as a healer. This had not happened yet, making him more aware of the insufficiency of any path he might identify with.

Reflecting on his relationship with assisting others as a psychologist revealed to him that his at arms-length concern for others was genuine. His desire to be of value to others in need was unquestionable and, as far as he could tell, it was without reservations within the scope and role function of being a psychologist. Still, something was missing. Some deeper capacity to contribute, he felt, existed; he had experienced it on rare occasions but could not call upon it to show up.

***

After meditating on relationships for several weeks, Mason decided to give it a break for a few days. He knew without any doubt how susceptible he was to being consumed by his addiction to self-exploration. Up to this point, this daily experience was unforced, leaving him with a sense of being open-minded and enthusiastic about what he was doing with his meditation. It actually did not feel like meditation. It felt like he was simply observing himself at arm's length.

Looking out at the ocean, Mason experienced the urge to go swimming. It was a clear, sunny day and he had not gone swimming for some time. Grabbing his swim goggles, he hopped on his bike and rode down to the ocean. The ride lightened his mood. The warm wind that whipped by him was refreshing, as he meandered his way along the path that took him to the ocean. He arrived at a small beach tucked away between two rock outcroppings. The water was cold at first but very quickly he became comfortable, just swimming leisurely without a direction in mind. The water was crystal clear, inviting him to hold his breathe and submerge to explore the ocean beneath. Diving down about 15 feet, he headed towards a rock ridge where many varieties of rock fish were congregated. Crossing his mind was the many memorable dive experiences he had with John so many years ago.

Returning to the surface, he decided to find a comfortable spot on the closest rock ridge and take in the breathtaking views of the ocean and Olympic Mountains beyond. After several minutes, his focus shifted to reflecting on his relationship with his thinking mind. The mind, in so many ways, he felt, was not user friendly. Thoughts would repetitively occur that were not wanted. Some thoughts interrupted other thoughts and some thoughts just popped up unexpectedly, redirecting his attention away from what he wanted to focus on. *Who exactly did not want these thoughts? Who was the thinker of thoughts?* He mused. He knew that the conscious mind was the warehouse of the known. It was the known that trapped him into compartmentalizing knowledge that frustrated him. It was the unknown that intrigued him.

The thoughts coursing through him revealed that his mind somehow did not fully belong to him. It was neither inside nor outside of him. So where was this mind? Could he have a relationship with this mind at all? It was obvious that he could not make contact with this mind of his bodily senses; it had no form and no identifiable location.

Was it possible that the mind was a conduit for a universal, limitless intelligence? Were humans using the mind intelligently, or had they only consciously tapped into a very shallow pool of mindfulness? This was the perennial mystery that sages, mystics, religious icons, and philosophers had struggled with though history. Was it possible to know the unknowable dimensions of the mind? Or were these thinkers on a mental tangent, searching for what was not lost and therefore could not be found? Such an unfathomable mystery this was for him! If one is stuck at the shallow end of the pool, how does one get to the deep end?

Mason sensed that to ask these rather profound questions suggested they were worth exploring. Allowing the conditioned mind to run us, both for good and bad, meant that we were continuing to allow our existence to be separated into parts. Choosing to have his mind seek out a relationship with itself may be only one way into the deep end of the pool where there is no distinct mind—just intelligence in the form of awareness.

Acquiring insight had been a preoccupation for Mason for as long as he could remember. The more questions he asked, the more questions arose about the questions he asked. Could there be intelligent action without a questioning agenda? This question about questions was the most interesting of all.

Taking care not to get too caught up in the minefield, Mason's awareness drifted toward reflecting on his relationship with virtues. The virtues of being considerate, kind, generous, peaceful, honest, and trustworthy had been cognitively accepted by the mind. Mason noticed that these virtues were largely encompassed within his identity as a psychologist. In this manner, they were more contrived and, at times, disingenuous. Interestingly, when he was not being this psychologist identity, these virtues naturally showed up.

Shifting the focus again, Mason landed on thoughts about his body's relationship to his mind. His body was kind of dragged along in life by his mind and its machinations. As such, the body was sometimes like a donkey to be ridden and used, and not a temple by any means. Characteristically, it was a source of self-indulgence for the mind to get caught up in·suffering the exigencies of day-to-day life. The concept of "mind over matter" was enacted as "mind over body" when it came to disciplining the body through excess stress, such as running a marathon and forcing the body to stay awake to study. This state of affairs begged the question, *Can the mind and body be just one entity?* He did not know.

Mason decided to continue his self-exploration of his study of mind by reflecting on his relationship with concepts such as the soul, the spirit, and transformation. The soul was not understandable to his mind. He was attracted to the concept but did not indulge in any effort to explore its meaning outside of interesting stories about the soul through his readings.

His spirit nature he perceived as non-spiritual and considered to be simply his enthusiasm for always seeking new experiences and new challenges. He was spirited but did not possess any spirits.

The mind wanted to craft him into a master healer. It also wanted him to become other than he had been—someone more significant and more powerful. It was driving him to seek ways to transform how people experienced suffering and to prevent needless suffering. The mind would tell him that if he could transform himself into being a master healer, he could transform others. Transformation, he thought, was a future event—an ultimate end goal.

With a somewhat clearer understanding of his relationships with his external and internal worlds after doing these reflective meditative experiences, Mason felt like he had begun to reset himself in some ways. It was both uplifting and freeing. In a relieving way, there was a growing feeling of being at peace with his relationships. Now that he was more aware of the masks he had adopted throughout his life, there was nothing he needed to do about them except be mindful of them. He did not need to fix them or change them in any way. By accepting them as they were, without judgement or condemnation, his true nature could naturally come out of hiding. The field of unconstrained awareness seemed to have opened up somewhat.

He was now inclined to begin the search for new experiential opportunities. He was particularly open to seeing if he could be of meaningful service to the mental and emotional health needs of First Nations peoples. Not knowing where to start looking, he decided to revisit the experience he had many years ago with the Carver.

Chapter Seventeen

⋙ Carver Revisited ⋘

WITH NO AGENDA AND no pressing commitments, Mason decided to take a trip on his bike and retrace his journey to the Carver's shed, which he had taken over two decades ago. Off he went down the old road, which was now paved. The further along he went, the more houses and buildings appeared. Eventually, he arrived where he thought the carving shed used to be. A large building, with a sign above it reading "Native Healing Centre," had replaced the shed. In front of the building—that looked like a long house—was a thirty-foot totem pole, which he recognized as the same totem pole that he had seen being carved so many years ago.

Mason approached the entrance, not knowing what to expect or who he might meet inside. Entering a reception area he noticed in the centre of a large domed room with cedar rafters he a young Indigenous woman sitting at a desk surrounded by a semi-circular very thick table made of varnished cedar with live edges. He went over and introduced himself. In a cursory way, he shared his experience at this location many years ago.

He asked her if she might know the whereabouts of the person who had carved the totem pole situated in front of the Centre. He went on to say that he had met the carver of the totem pole at his carving shed, which was situated where this building now stood many years ago. He asked the receptionist if the Carver was still alive. The receptionist said that she could not tell him much, and asked if he would wait a minute. She went off down a hallway to check with the Director of the Centre.

When she returned, she asked if Mason would follow her to the director's office. Arriving at the office, he was greeted by a woman he immediately sensed he already knew but could not quite place the experience. She looked at him inquisitively and introduced herself as Crystal, the Director of the Centre. Hearing Mason's name, she took a step back and smiled warmly. "You have returned," she said. "I knew someday you would. I am so happy to see you again!" Awestruck, he was without words. He just stared, not believing what he was seeing. Crystal motioned him to come and sit with her in her office, saying to him they had much ground to catch up on.

Snapping out of his trance-like state, he now realized who Crystal was from his past. He had connected with her, at the Carver's suggestion, several decades ago and they both had participated in a sweat together. His memory came back to him how they parted after he was unable to move forward with their budding relationship. He remembered vividly how captivating she was back then.

Her office was adorned with native carvings and masks. It reeked of sage, which brought back memories of the sweat they had done together. She invited him to sit at a coffee table that had a sage bowl in the middle and beside it an eagle feather with the stalk trimmed with colourful beads. She invited him to share his memories of the Carver, as well to tell her about the journey he had taken since their memorable encounter so many years ago.

As Mason shared, Crystal bent over toward him with an intense yet gentle interest. Mason, comforted by her engaging receptiveness, found himself sharing his background and his somewhat unsuccessful quest to become a healer. He briefly shared the teachings he had received from the Carver and how it had led him on a twenty-five-year journey. This journey, as best he could surmise, was guided at least in part by the Carver's statement that it would be important for him to allow his journey to unfold without it being goal-driven.

"It was difficult at first," he said as he explained being a Peaceful Warrior, then a learner/teacher, and finally a practicing healer. All were interconnected but did not result in the outcome he had intended. "The final pathway, that of being a Visionary Warrior, I have not travelled yet, nor have I discovered a way to do so."

After providing a chronological overview of his journey and his experiences across the country, she sat back and sighed. "You have had an amazing journey, not anything like I had imagined." With that, she shared her own journey over the years as a social worker and now mother of three grown-up children. "I have been at the treatment centre now for ten years and every day it is a privilege just to be here and contribute in whatever way I can."

Pausing again after sharing her experiences in greater detail, in a soft and compassionate way—and with a deep sense of reverence—she said that the elder who carved the totem had passed to the other side. But his son, who also was involved in carving the pole at the entrance, had taken over as Master Carver. He has continued the family tradition of carving at a new shed about ten miles away. The new carving shed had been constructed to acknowledge and honour his father.

As their meeting was coming to an end, she asked if it would interest him to attend a sweat ceremony this coming Saturday. How amazing that would be to revisit that experience with her. Mason stated that he would indeed be honoured to attend. He then thanked her for opening the possibility for him to reconnect with her and his past experiences. Departing, he sensed that he would want to make a return visit to this place.

Mason showed up for the Saturday sweat lodge, not knowing anybody outside of Crystal. He quietly participated through the four-hour experience. And as before, he did not share in the sweat lodge. Upon completion, Mason approached the Elder who had conducted the sweat, a tall man in his early sixties, and asked him if they could talk. The Elder said that he would be happy to do so and invited him to attend a talking circle that he was conducting in a few days for Indigenous people attending the centre.

Mason showed up a few days later at the appointed time and discovered that the attendees were all from the local prison; they were on temporary release to the treatment centre. As residents of the centre they were there to address their historical trauma issues as well as substance abuse issues. Eleven in number, the participants all male, varied in age from their mid-twenties to their late forties.

The talking circle was conducted using a talking stick, which was a way to ensure that the sharing was not interrupted as long as the talking stick was in the possession of any one person. Only the Elder would be permitted to ask that the stick be passed.

When Mason's turn came to speak, he was nervous and hesitant, as it was his pattern to be a listener and resist exposing his own feelings and thoughts.

Once he started to speak, it was like the floodgates had been opened. In an anguished way, he shared, "My life-long journey of becoming a healer has only partially been achieved, largely because of the way I have gone about it. My overriding approach has been to accumulate as much knowledge and experience as possible, and in doing so I have lost touch with my original purpose. Gradually, over the years, I have allowed myself to become addicted to my professional identity. In so doing I have largely ignored my own healing needs. I have traded self-healing for being an expert on crisis intervention and the suffering of others. Most revealing to me has been my denial that I have suffered at all! Suffering is only what other people do. This warped pathway I have taken has resulted in my hiding away from my own sense of the truth. Instead, I became preoccupied with what the truth was for others."

As he went on with his sharing, he could not help noticing how several of the participants were nodding and offering encouraging glances, as if they were seemingly approving of what he was saying. This made him feel motivated to continue.

Mason went on to say, "At times, I have felt phoney. I have traded what society authorizes me to be, with the genuine me going missing in action. The genuine me is still largely unknown, continuing to be shrouded in illusions of wanting to be a somebody."

Mason concluded by saying that he was thankful for the Indigenous encounters and "learning's" he has had over the years, and that he felt honoured by them. He regretted that these immensely important experiences had been overshadowed by his addiction to learning from authoritarian science, through books, and through modern-day practises in treatment.

At the end of the meeting, the Elder asked Mason to stick around, as he had some feedback that he would like to share. When everyone was gone, the Elder leaned forward, not looking directly at Mason, shared the following:

"You are not what you think you are. Thinking is your problem. It is not possible for you to become a healer through your 'learning's,' only your actions. Most healers are fakes. As you have said, you have let seeking knowledge override your ability to be aware. As you well know, to participate in healing with genuine caring for others, you must fully explore and understand your own experience with suffering. It is clear that everything you have said in the circle indicates you know what you need to do."

Mason was struck by his bluntness. What the Elder was saying, he had intrinsically known or had been said to him before but had not fully sunk in. "Work on yourself before working on others, and don't make this journey you are on an ordeal." Obviously, he had sidelined this wisdom, choosing instead to forge ahead with his apprenticeship with his head, not his heart.

Mason felt like the curtain had been lifted on the character he had been building for close to three decades. He thanked the Elder for his sharing, gave him tobacco as per the Indigenous custom, and returned home.

The following week, he received a call from Crystal, asking him if he would be interested in offering psychological services to the participants attending the centre. The centre had a two-year contract available. He was taken aback at first, given what he had shared about himself, but he felt honoured. He agreed to offer services for four days a week, which she accepted.

***

Providing psychological services to the residents at the centre was unlike anything he had done before. The residents were eager to engage in dialogue with him but did not want to be counselled. Taking long walks in the park near the centre became his preferred way to engage in individual treatment sessions. Walking alongside a resident felt natural, as did the experience of exploring their issues and concerns. Eye to eye contact seemed to be unnecessary, even invasive and counterproductive at times.

Group sessions happened daily using a talking stick to promote respectful listening. Mason discovered that his Gestalt training many years ago allowed him to interact in the group sessions in natural holistic ways that clearly appealed to the participants. Counselling became an inter-personal experience sharing insights, not about finding out what was wrong and needed to be fixed. What they really seemed to gravitate towards were the role-playing sessions that shed light onto their unconscious patterns and habits without being confrontational or judgemental.

During his time at the centre, he felt that he was seen for whom he was, not what he was. When he interacted with others at the centre, he sensed a natural, spontaneous connection with them. He had not experienced anything like this when he was serving as a professional psychologist anywhere else.

This was the start of him coming out of hiding; stone by stone, he was removing the walls he had built to insulate himself, objectifying both himself and others. It also acknowledged what he felt to be evident—that everyone had a spark of magic within. When he allowed his own spark of magic to show up and join theirs, what transpired was extraordinarily meaningful.

Time went by at the centre, and before he knew it, the two years were up. At the end of the contract, Mason felt an enormous upwelling of gratitude for having had the opportunity to serve others at the centre. Unlike his past experiences in psychological practices, repairing and building relationships was the core foundation of healing at the centre. There was a natural calmness to the centre that promoted and encouraged equanimity and empathy. Participants and service providers alike interacted as a caring community. Different needs, roles, and responsibilities were understood, yet not in any hierarchical way. Respect did not have to be earned; it was unconditionally given.

When it was time for him to leave the centre, an honouring ceremony was conducted on his last day to acknowledge his contribution. Crystal shared that she was sad to see him leave, as he had made an immense difference to the lives of the residents attending the centre, as well as to her and all the staff. Tears started to trickle down her face as she gave him a farewell embrace. Crossing his mind, he remembered the same tearful look she expressed so many years ago when they first parted ways. Now, unlike his past experience, an upwelling of empathy towards Crystal surfaced that also brought tears to his eyes. The feeling of gratefulness for having had the experience of Crystal reappearing in his life was immeasurable.

The ceremony continued with a group of seven drummers with hand drums encircling him and then chanting the centre's healing song. Remarkably, the sounds seem to penetrate him, stimulating his body to vibrate from head to toe in rhythm with the beating drums.

After a traditional feast of Indian food and smoked salmon, Peter, one of the centre's addiction counsellors, approached him, referring to him as "Dr. Roadrunner". This was in reference to a nickname he was given at the centre, as Crystal encouraged residents to use nicknames or Indian given names when interacting with others. The "Roadrunner" reference had been resurrected from his past when he disclosed that in his youth he had been nicknamed "Roadrunner" by other kids. The residents and staff insisted that "Dr." be added, which stuck with him throughout his time at the centre. Peter then offered him a braid of sweet grass as a token of appreciation from the staff. The ceremony concluded with the centre's Elder cleansing him with a sage smudging and then presenting him with a talking stick carved in the fashion of a miniature totem. The Elder encouraged him to use the talking stick with others on his healing journey ahead.

Departing to return to his cabin by the ocean, Mason experienced a twinge of sadness as his experience at the centre had made him realize his aboriginal heritage was distinctively way more important than he ever given it credit for being. This also was the first time in his life he felt rooted.

Shifting his focus, crossing his mind was the realization that he was now at a turning point. The journey ahead had not become clear to him yet.

Chapter Eighteen

❖ Exploring Roots ❖

W ITH NO COMMITMENTS ON the horizon, Mason became pleasantly aware of the impact the West Coast atmosphere was having on him. It was allowing him to settle down and not be so driven to seek answers about the world he lived in. He remained curious, but he engaged his curiosity almost as if he was not connected to his incessant intense questioning ways; it was like the questions were now not from him—they were going through him.

With time on his hands, Mason visited the local provincial museum, which was internationally known for its realistic and lively presentation of natural and human history. A significant portion of the museum was dedicated to Indigenous culture. Walking through the interactive displays, it was easy to become immersed in the portrayed history.

Capturing his interest were the numerous carvings, which included several large masks much like the ones he encountered many years ago at Arnold's clinic. It almost felt like he could pick up the distinct smell of yellow cedar.

They were larger than Arnold's, and the way they were backlit made them much more colourful and provocative. Mason's thoughts went back to Arnold's comment that we all wear masks, but the masks are only a reflection of aspects of ourselves that we want others to see. They are not who we are, and sometimes we hide behind them. Mason remembered wearing the masks, how it made him feel protected, and wondered what feelings and thoughts these masks might stimulate if he tried them on.

The display of mannequins wearing Indigenous clothing and donning various West Coast headdresses was also very intriguing. They left him wondering about the life they led throughout history and how their rich culture developed. It crossed his mind that he knew very little about his own heritage.

Since his encounter with the Carver many years ago, he recognized that he had buried any interest in exploring his roots. The Carver had awakened in him the desire to pursue becoming an apprentice healer and travel the Four-Fold Pathway, which he felt he had done. But he had abandoned his own unique mixed heritage in favour of developing his inanimate identity as a psychologist.

While he had been curious enough to explore Indigenous cultures from an outside perspective, he had never done so from within. Being part Native seemed like it was important, yet there was very little sense that it made much of a difference to him until he had the experience of working at the Healing Centre. Actually, he was aware that he suppressed the inclination for it to make a difference even when he was engaged in Indigenous healing ceremonies. He did so because he felt no sense of having a kindred connection to his roots.

He also bristled at the thought of being identified and categorized as a half-breed. He did not want to think in terms of being attached to a culture with statements of identity such as "my community, my people, and my heritage." In a similar fashion, he rejected the notion of identifying with being a Canadian, as he felt that it separated him from others based on nationality or race. He did have to acknowledge that the salutation "all my relations" resonated with him, as he took that to mean all of humanity, even if others didn't. His understanding of it from an Indigenous perspective suggested that it was meant to acknowledge our relationship to everything.

Now refreshed, he felt ready to take a good, hard look at his underpinnings—his roots. Mason recalled that he often ruminated about possibly visiting his birth father's reserve. It was long overdue, especially from the standpoint that he owed them a debt of gratitude for financially supporting his early education.

He decided that he would make contact with his father's band. The more he thought about it, the more enthusiastic he became, which surprised him. Perhaps he might learn more about Indigenous healing by paying them a visit.

A phone call to his father's band got him in touch with the Band Chief, William Blackwater. Mason introduced himself and shared that his father had been a member of his band. Mason offered a brief overview of his journey over the years as an apprentice healer travelling the Four-Fold Way. What most interested him now was learning more about Indigenous healing practises. He followed up by asking if there were any of his father's relatives still around, and if it were possible for him to make a visit to the reserve.

The Chief warmly responded, saying that only one of his father's blood relatives—a sister named Annie—lived on the reserve. The Chief was aware of some relatives living off the reserve, but none of them had maintained any connection with the reserve for several decades. He suggested that Mason may want to take this opportunity to come to their community to attend an upcoming three-day Powwow. The Powwow and Sun Dance could be a perfect opportunity for him to explore some of the practises of Indigenous healing while getting to know more about his Indigenous background.

Mason had no pressing commitments, and without much thought, accepted the invitation. Chief William, as he liked to be called, indicated that he would connect with him at the Powwow. He also wanted to learn more about his journey on the Four-Fold Pathway.

Mason arrived mid-day on the first day of the Powwow, after a spectacular, crystal-clear flight over the Rockies. He could see the snow-covered tops of mountains in all their awesome majesty for hundreds of miles, as well as the deep valleys and rivers snaking through the mountains below. It struck him how diminutive he felt when viewing nature in her magnificence from far above.

At times, he felt he was in a hypnotic trance. It seemed as if time had slowed down, and everything was in slow motion or not moving at all. Even the sound of the airplane engine seemed to fade away in the majesty of the land and sky scape. He felt connected but not attached. It reminded him of what the "sensei" had said to him at the Buddhist retreat: "When awareness has no agenda, time is irrelevant and everything is experienced as being connected."

The Powwow was situated in a park like setting, and in the centre was an amphitheatre surrounded by numerous kiosks preparing food. Wafting out from one kiosk was the distinct smell of bannock. It brought back fond memories of his mother making bannock prior to his father returning home from the logging camps.

Scanning the area further, Mason noticed a huge circle of large drums much like the one he had experienced at Arnold's clinic. Off on the other side, there were several groups of around six to ten men sitting in a circle sharing stories with one another. On the perimeter of the main area, there were twenty or more tipis spread out over an open field. They all appeared to have native clan markings of animals. One had a large sun imprinted near the top of the Tipi.

As he was continuing to explore the grounds, he could not help wondering the status or reputation his father had in this community. Such a mystery his father was to him.

As he walked around the circle of kiosks, Mason began to feel awkward and disconnected. Then, it was as if a dark cloud enveloped him, as it had when he lost both parents so many years ago. It unnerved him to the extent that he felt an urge to leave. He sat down on a patch of grass and decided that he needed to retreat within himself. He definitely did not feel grounded here in any way. It seemed he was almost invisible as other First Nations people passed by as if he was not even there.

Feeling awkward and uneasy, and not knowing what to do, he decided to just take some deep breaths and allow his curiosity to take over. He began to focus on some children playing with a soccer ball. He noticed how they were smiling and laughing. He had the urge to go over and play with them but decided just to imagine he was doing so.

Jolted by a touch on his shoulder, he abruptly turned around to see a tall, middle-aged man looming over him. At first, he wondered why this was happening. Then it dawned on him that it was Peter; the drug and alcohol counsellor he had worked with at the First Nations Treatment Centre. He was surprised to find out that Peter was a member of his father's band and had returned home for the Powwow and Sun Dance Ceremony.

Peter, in a humble yet awkward way, said that he was sent by Chief William to come and welcome him to the Powwow. It was important that Mason was here, and he thanked him for coming. Not knowing how to respond, Mason asked how he might make contact with Chief William.

Peter responded by saying that he was invited to the Chief's Tipi later that evening. After pointing out the Tipi, Peter said that he would meet him back at the Sun Dance arena after the last dance of the evening. He then took his leave, stating that he was required to assist setting up some of the displays.

For the next hour, Mason watched powerful drumming events that literally exploded with energy that cascaded across the open field. There were six large round drums formed in a larger circle. Drumming and chanting would move from one group of four drummers at each drum to another and then back again. Each group represented different tribes from the western plains. At the beginning of each song a short statement would be made by the lead drummer as to the meaning of the song. All songs were done in native tongue. It was truly spellbinding, reminding him of his first experience with drumming with Arnold so many years ago. From what he understood, they were competing, one group with another for drumming and chanting awards as per their tradition.

Moving on he encountered a group of eight First Nations people, sitting cross-legged in groups of four, playing a stick or bone game as he was told. Mason asked a bystander about how the game was played. He was given a quick rundown on the rules and told that the games would go on for several days, with as many as sixty participants. Mason watched in fascination how simple yet strategic it seemed. He could not help noticing the feeling of camaraderie and respect that emanated from the players.

Taking notice the dancing was under way Mason headed over to the Sun dance arena. Over the course of several hours there were hundreds of dancers; some dances were solo efforts while most were in groups, each with a distinctive theme representing all age groups. It was obvious that the dancers took pride in representing their traditions and their heritage. It was easy to see that countless hours were spent in making their brilliantly coloured multi-faceted costumes. When he casually pointed that out to the aboriginal woman standing next to him in a soft mannered respectful way remarked they were not costumes but rather they were spiritual regalia.

When the last dance of the evening was announced Mason found himself drawn by the hand of this woman toward a large circle of people that was forming in dancing arena. This was a dance that traditionally occurred at the ending each day of Powwow and it was meant to include everyone there attending the dance ceremonies. The circle gradually got bigger and bigger as more and more joined in. Everyone seemed to be smiling and in good spirits. The sound of the rhythmic hand drumming encircling the growing circle combined with the chanting of the drummers was intoxicating. The circle moved clockwise in a circle ever so slowly as the participants gently shuffled their feet to the beat of the drums. It felt almost as if we were all beating our feet together as one heartbeat.

When it gradually came to an end and the participants drifted away Mason's attention was captured by a stunning figure mounted on a horse not 25 feet away just on the outskirts of the dancing arena. At first he thought he was experiencing an illusion and shook his head and looked away. When he returned his gaze the aboriginal man and horse were still there. Only now as he fixed his gaze the image seemed to glow around the edges. The majesty of the scene was breathtaking. "How could this be?" It didn't seem real. Intrigued he moved closer noticing it was an elderly distinguishing looking man sitting tall, bareback on the horse. His bronze face was well weathered, creased with the telling wisdom of his travels. As he got within ten feet he stopped in his tracks. It suddenly felt as if this Elder was looking down at him, embracing him in an envelope of peacefulness and tranquility that flowed over him like a warming blanket. Mason stopped and just gazed for several minutes entranced by the experience. Then without words spoken with a smile of knowingness on his face the Elder turned his horse around and trotted off.

Jolted out of his trance he heard Peter's voice calling out his name at the other end of the arena. Mason crossed over and was warmly embraced by Peter. Mason could not resist inquiring, "Did you see that man on the horse? Who was he?" Oh, Peter said, that is our Heritage Chief. Unlike our elected Chief, William, he is our spiritual leader. Shifting the dialogue Peter went on to suggest it was time for them to head off to the Chief's Tipi now.

Arriving at the Tipi with a Sun design at the top and a Buffalo design on the side they entered inside to an area that was about eighteen feet across and twenty feet high. Peter introduced him to Chief William who seemed to be a bear of a man with a very engaging friendly demeanour. Following this introduction he was introduced to several other Band Council members all sitting in a circle on blankets. He then was taken over by Chief William and introduced to a distinguished-looking Elder named Annie Silvermoon he later learned was his father's sister.

Annie was dressed in a silver shawl and wore her silver hair in long braids. She stared at Mason without saying a word, making him feel uneasy at first, until she broke open a smile and invited Mason to sit on the blanket that was placed next to her.

A smudging ceremony followed, which served to melt away the anxiety he was feeling. Both being in a ceremonial tipi and coming face to face with his father's sister for the first time was unnerving.

After this cleansing ceremony, the Chief welcomed Mason back home to his father's community, as well as to his family tipi. He went on to say that this Powwow most importantly included a Sun Dance, or Okan, ceremony. This ceremony would focus on healing for families and community. He continued, "It was also a time to give thanks to the Creator, Mother Earth and Father Sky, our Elders, and all our relatives."

William pointed to the medicine bundle hanging on a tipi pole directly in front of him. It was cylindrically shaped, wrapped in leather with markings, and looked to be about three feet long and a foot wide. He then shared that Annie Silvermoon was the community's medicine bundle keeper and a member of the honoured Motoki society created for women of high character. The bundle was brought down by one of the band councillors and handed to Annie. The bundle was then smudged and passed from person to person in the circle.

Annie spoke next. "The bundle is brought to Sun Ceremonies to acknowledge the life-giving power of the sun and to release its powers to heal our peoples and bring us all together. The medicine wheel painted on the front in four colors represents the four directions. Yellow is for the east and new life, white is for the north and courage or bravery, black is for the west and mother earth and wisdom that comes with age, and red is for the south for water and nurturing.

Today, we will open the bundle, and it will remain open until the end of the Sun Ceremony Powwow. Inside will be sacred items and healing medicine that have been collected over time by the many medicine women who came before me."

Annie turned to face Mason. She handed him a small leather pouch. She said that the pouch was empty and was given to him to fill with special objects that would acknowledge his healing journey both as a native and a non-native.

It was important, she said, that Mason discover the objects for his healing pouch without looking for them as he continued on his life-long journey. "The objects will have sacred value for healing, and you will find that they will appear to you when you are not looking. Care needs to be taken to not fill the pouch with objects of desire or momentous. That is why it is given to you empty."

She then dipped two fingers into a pot of red paint placed in front of her and painted two stripes on his forehead, and spoke these words: "You now will be known as Striped Calf as you travel the red and white road."

Peter then spoke. He told the group that Mason had achieved significant recognition as a psychologist over many decades. He also said that Mason had also mentioned to him that besides wanting to know more about his heritage, he was seeking information that might allow him to travel the fourth pathway, described to him many decades ago as the pathway of the Visionary Warrior.

Annie responded, "Even though we have healing rituals in our Nation, we do not worship healing or the healer. Healing is nature's gift to all of us in our relationship with each other and the creator. When you allow yourself to be whole again, when healing is not separated from relationship, then your knowledge and experience will serve you and others well.

"In our culture, we have been nomadic travellers, even though this has been discouraged by white civilization by placing us on reserves. I am told that you have also been a nomadic traveller. This allows you to be free without a need to hold onto things.

"To honour your ancestry, there are symbols, like sacred bundles and many ceremonies. These are important to remind us all to not get caught up in the material world, yet to be able to treat everything we receive as a gift, including our existence. No one can guide you to become a healer. You must find the healer within."

The Chief then spoke, saying they were pleased to have him return to his father's birth community, and that there would always be a place for him in their community. "The path of the Visionary Warrior is unknown for us, but The Visionary Warrior is known to exist. We know of this warrior through our storytelling, which is handed down through the generations."

Without saying anything more about healing paths, he suggested that Mason spend the next day just observing the events and participating. It would be a good time for him to become acquainted with his band community members, as well as visiting band members, as he will find that they will be quite receptive to him.

After a long pause, the pipe carrier sitting on the other side of Annie ceremonially lit the pipe and pointed it in all four directions. He then passed it to the person next to him and, in turn, it was passed to all in the circle. At the conclusion of the pipe ceremony, Annie opened the bundle and placed it in the centre of the circle. Chief William thanked everyone for coming to the ceremony and hoped that all would have a meaningful experience at the Powwow.

Peter and Mason then departed. Peter invited Mason to spend the night at his cabin passed on to him by his Uncle that was located on the edge of the reserve community. Both would return the following day to the Powwow.

The cabin was situated along the banks of the meandering Bow River. Both Peter and Mason sat for several hours, spontaneously sharing their experiences during their time together at the First Nations Treatment Centre. Remarkably, Mason found himself opening up and sharing more and more without a sense of being judged. Mason mentioned how troubled he had been over the years, with his excessive analytical thinking and endless questioning, especially about death.

Peter commented in a soft voice, "We humans get so caught up in our ideas, our thinking, and our labeling that we cannot help but judge and condemn ourselves. I am not an educated man like you. My living is simple and very humble. What I do know is this: when I encounter fear, I pay attention to what loss I am currently experiencing—not as an idea but as a fact and nothing more. When I think of the fact, then the fear begins to melt away. When I return here to my place on the river, I just sit and watch the water flow by. Any fears that show up are swept away.

"When I think about death it is the same. It is a certainty, but it is unknown directly. Death is not what we are really afraid of. It is the loss of our attachments to people, to things, to our identity, to our relationships that cause us to fear when death approaches. Accepting our impermanence and gracefully letting go of our attachments allows us to live moment to moment without fear."

Mason felt the humility in his voice and recognized the sincerity in his words. Strangely, he felt a connection with Peter that he had never experienced before when they were

254

both at the treatment centre. It felt as if they were meant to have crossed paths again.

During the following day, Mason discovered that both he and Peter easily engaged with other participants, ate Indigenous food, watched giveaways, observed drumming and dancing competitions displaying amazing costumes, and even got to participate in a community dance. It was like he belonged yet was not beholden to anyone. When the day ended, Chief William approached him and offered him a parting gift of a band blanket, while Peter once again—as he had done at the Treatment Centre—gave him a braid of sweet grass. Mason returned to the West Coast, richer for the experience, with much to contemplate.

Chapter Nineteen

❖ Alchemy ❖

THE END OF SUMMER had arrived, and the bike trails were beckoning him again. It was time to do a tune-up on his mountain bike since he had only occasionally used it during his last year at the centre. Out on his first ride after returning from the Powwow, Mason was approached by a cyclist from behind named Paul who asked if he wanted to have company on his ride. Mason quickly accepted as he was happy to have someone join him. For the next two hours there ride took them along a scenic meandering pathway along the coastline that once served as mining railroad now reclaimed as a bike and hiking path. Mason was thankful for the company learning from Paul about the many trails in the area and how they interconnected.

Near the end of their ride Paul casually mentioned that the next day he was planning a trip up along the West Coast to a gold claim he had staked many years ago, with the intention of doing some gold panning. This triggered Mason's memory of an indelibly imprinted experience of a drowning he had been involved in over two decades ago. At that time, he was deployed as a trauma specialist with a search and rescue team with the local provincial police. They were deployed to a wilde. ness area to find a young boy who had gone missing and had presumably drowned.

"Where exactly is your claim?" Mason asked.

"It's situated in a small valley where the old-growth trees were removed many decades ago. Running through the middle of the valley is a mountain stream that gradually drops off down a slope into a steep ravine. This time of the year, the stream tends to be running about two feet deep, and it's about forty yards across. As the stream disappears into the ravine, it merges with other underground streams, forming a river that cascades down the mountain side. Along its way down the ravine, I have been told, are many waterfalls with the river ending up entering the ocean about two miles away. To get down the ravine is difficult, as the ravine is bordered by vertical rocks walls—some as high as sixty feet. Many have tried to journey down the ravine with climbing gear, but no one has been known to successfully travel down the river to the ocean as far as I know."

Paul's description of the location was remarkably similar to Mason's memory of the area where he had been called for the drowning emergency, leading him to think that it might just be the same site.

Mason shared some historical information about his police trauma team involvement investigating the drowning of a ten-year-old boy, the son of a reclusive miner. "The miner and his wife and son lived in a trailer at his gold claim stake, which fits the description of where your claim is located."

"That's interesting. Why don't you come along with me and my sister to see if it is the same area or somewhere nearby? You also could join us and have some fun gold panning."

Given this potential coincidence, Mason was drawn to find out if he was right. Gold panning also intrigued him, knowing nothing about it except that it was a well-known part of the West Coast gold mining history. Mason enthusiastically accepted the invitation.

"Excellent, it's about a two-hour drive out along old logging roads. We will pick you up at nine in the morning."

The next morning, Mason was introduced to Paul's sister, Isabelle, and then they departed on their journey in Paul's pickup. Isabelle was about his age, yet he thought that she looked much younger. She had a slight accent, which Mason discovered was part of her heritage, as her family came to Canada from Portugal when she was nine years old.

As they made their way west, Mason found Isabelle's cheerfulness to be infectious. Mason let some of the heaviness he was feeling fall away, and he caught himself smiling at her from time to time for no apparent reason. In an inquisitive but respectful way, Isabelle turned and asked, "What was the experience like participating as a trauma specialist in the drowning of a young boy?"

Not quite sure where to start, Mason told the story as best he could remember.

"I remember it being late spring when the call came about a possible drowning. The trauma team was briefed about a reclusive man living with his son and wife in a trailer at his gold claim site near a location referred to as Sombrio Summit. He had reported his ten-year-old son missing. The father's story was that his son was playing with a log in the stream nearby, pretending it was a raft, and then disappeared down the stream. From what we were told, it was likely his son got too close to the edge of the ravine, ended up tumbling down, and got swept away by the river. Our police unit needed to deploy the rappel team to get down the ravine, but after two days of searching, no body was found. Due to a storm that descended upon us, the search had to be discontinued for five days.

By this time, the parents were beside themselves with grief and frantically looking for closure, all the while believing that their son could still be alive—even though that was extremely unlikely. Our dive team was deployed along with a helicopter to take them down the ravine. After two days of perilous searching, the boy's body was found in a cave under a waterfall about a mile down the ravine."

"What was your role in this experience?" Isabelle asked.

"My job was to debrief the body recovery team and provide grief support to the parents. As I recall, the body bag was dropped off and opened. I remember watching both parents stiffen, clutching one another, with overwhelming sadness in their eyes. I also remember standing next to them in silence. No words surfaced for me. I remember feeling a wave of despondency blanket me at the time. When I did find my voice, I said that I was saddened by their loss. I asked them if there was anything they needed, or anything they wanted me to do for them. The father, with an emptiness showing through his eyes, looked up at me and, with a disgusted look on his face, shook his head. Then they walked away, disappearing into their trailer. I did attempt to follow-up with them at the site a week later, only to find them gone along with their trailer. I later learned that the police Trauma Unit had followed up and discovered that they had moved back to Alberta. I know I did not make any difference by being there at least for the parents."

Neither Paul nor Isabelle commented. They remained quiet for most of the rest of the trip, except to point out some landmarks and some historical changes that might have occurred since they were last in this area.

When they arrived, Mason felt a surge of emotion rise as it was obvious to him this was the same claim he had visited with the Trauma Unit years ago. The only difference he noticed was that tree planting had obviously occurred after the area was logged out prior to his initial visit. New growth was now evident everywhere. He found himself wandering over to the stream, almost like he was walking in slow motion and time had stopped. Standing by the stream, as he had so many fateful years ago, he felt mesmerized by the constant flowing water. An eagle flying nearby drew his attention toward the ravine. Images of a waterfall crossed his mind then disappeared. Piercing his awareness were images of a young boy splashing in the stream and then tumbling down into the ravine. It was as if he was watching the images as an observer but not actually feeling anything. In some unknowable way, it was like he had stepped out of time and merged into the landscape as he was part of it. For what seemed like a very long time, no thoughts showed up, just an overriding sense of loss and emptiness.

Mason was brought back from his trance by Paul's voice upstream, asking him if he would like to try his hand at gold panning. Composing himself, Mason stepped away from the edge of the ravine and yelled back "Yes, I will be right over."

Isabelle was as new to gold panning as Mason was, so Paul gave them both a brief lesson in the techniques of gold panning, providing each of them with a tray. Then, with a smile on his face and a spark in his eyes, he departed to the other side of the stream to one of his favourite panning spots, leaving them to fend for themselves.

Taking Paul's suggestion to begin panning in shallow side eddies off the stream, they both started digging. After some trial and error panning, some small specks started to show up, which was both surprising and exciting, if not magical. Mason never imagined that playing in dirt and gravel could be so much fun. It was addictive. Finding one fleck of gold spurred them on to look for another.

Gold panning was like looking for buried treasure. It was all about the hunt. Finding some flecks of gold was a bonus. He found such enjoyment playing with Mother Earth's gems; it was not quite what he expected.

While they were transfixed on looking for traces of gold, Isabelle stated, "I imagine that being here today for you has triggered some memories. I couldn't help but notice that when we arrived, you seemed to be in another dimension."

"Yes, I think so. I have a sense right now that in some incomprehensible way; some part of me is still here from long ago. It's like my footprint is here."

"Interesting, that's what crossed my mind when you walked down the stream when we first arrived."

After a few minutes went by, Mason could not help but notice how peaceful and content she looked. Mason felt as if he was being captured by her aura. In a remarkably similar way, this was much like what he experienced from the Buddhist preceptor several years ago when he attended the Buddhist meditation retreat. It was not an emotional connection, as much as it was an experience of being totally accepted.

The conversation on the journey home after the afternoon of gold panning was spontaneous and free-flowing. Paul and Isabelle both were enthusiastic and upbeat about everything they talked about. The ride back seemed like it was over before it started.

Mason learned that Paul was a geological engineer. His work involved assessing geological stability requirements for building dams and water drainage systems. His interest in gold panning evolved from his research work on aquifers and subterranean water systems. When he was not busy gold panning at the site, he would be looking for soil and rock samples on geological substrates for research purposes.

Without prompting, Isabelle shared her background as a social worker over the years. "My special interest can best be captured by the phrase, 'children of the storm.' These are children who had unsettled or early traumatic development experiences that included loss of parents, family breakdown, and placement in foster homes. Most of my work up to about ten years ago has been with government services. That work was far from being satisfying. I don't do well with bureaucracies."

"Neither do I," Mason commented. "I find them very rigid and lacking in spontaneity."

Isabelle responded, "Yes, I agree. It always seems to be a challenge to accomplish anything meaningful. The system's need to protect itself almost always overrides the best interests of the people it has been mandated to serve."

Mason added, "I couldn't agree more. My own personal experience growing up in foster homes and a group home left me feeling I was a problem for them most of the time. I definitely met some very empathetic caregivers, however, for the most part, they always seemed worried about me not abiding by the rules of the system. When I left social services care I felt I could freely breathe again."

"That was true for me too. I felt suffocated working in the government childcare system," she said. "When I finally decided enough was enough, I struck out on my own, offering my services as private practitioner at a battered women's shelter. After my first year there, they offered me a job as the Director of the Centre, which I have been doing for the past eight years. The centre is one of a number of programs under the umbrella of my Community Services Agency which is a non-profit society. This work is extremely stressful but also very meaningful to me."

"It is a relief for me to hear that women's shelters exist today," Mason responded. "They didn't exist when I was a child. I can clearly remember visions of my mother physically being hurt by my father when he was drinking. Back then she could do nothing about it or go anywhere to be safe."

"It saddens me to hear about your experience growing up," she replied. "A shelter could have saved your mother from a lot of unnecessary pain. Although, a shelter does not solve the problem of domestic violence by itself. More is needed.

"Recently, the society has asked if I would be willing to spearhead the development of a new walk-in Crisis Counselling Clinic. The concept has not been fully developed yet. For some time now, they have wanted to develop a walk-in crisis clinic. They were aware that the community had a long-standing gap in services for families and individuals with a wide range of crises. Traditional government-run mental health clinics or medical-based services have historically not been able to even come close to addressing the need."

"Tell me more," Mason encouraged. "The concept is intriguing to me."

"I would be glad to. As the concept might suggest, the society wants to develop a clinic that does not require an appointment, allowing those in need to seek assistance when they are ready and able. They want the cornerstones of the program to rest on promoting self-awareness, self-sufficiency, and self-healing, and they want it to be compassion-based. They also want the clinic to address client problems in the present and not the past, even though the past may be part of the reason for their present crises.

The challenge that they want me to take on is to find a way to make one session very meaningful, given that no follow-up sessions would be necessarily scheduled. A client could walk in again without an appointment at any time, however. Even more ambitiously, they want the clinic to go beyond just breaking down crises into manageable components and teaching coping skills."

"That's fascinating!" Mason responded. "I have experienced elements of this concept in my work over the years as a trauma specialist and crisis intervention counsellor at various agencies that provided residential-based treatment. My last experience at a First Nations residential healing centre was more past-focused, but still remarkably impactful. My experience before that was at a suicide crisis clinic, which had an outreach component that did its best to address crises as they were happening and without having to be processed before services could be offered. It worked reasonably well but was often hamstrung by medical oversight and government agency interference."

Isabelle continued, "I think they want to break new ground and do something that has never been done before. My experience of their evolutionary thinking has been demonstrated by the free reign they have allowed me in promoting the shelter I am working at now to become more than just a static place to heal. They have asked that I look to find a psychologist who would be a good fit with me in developing the vision of the clinic as well as the underlying services. On the off chance, might I ask, would you be interested in participating in this new program?"

Mason said that he was appreciative of the consideration and wanted to know more. They both agreed to meet next week at the Community Services Agency to see if this could be a good fit for everyone.

Chapter Twenty

❧ In Search of Excellence ❧

A s his two-year commitment to the healing centre had come to an end, Mason had no commitments. It was an ideal time to explore new horizons. Following a number of meetings with Isabelle and the agency board, Mason accepted the position as a co-developer of the Crisis Counselling Clinic Model and Service.

Their partnership began first as collaborators, and then gradually it became more intimate and soulful. For the next three months, working with Isabelle was an extraordinarily productive experience, leaving him feeling privileged to have the opportunity to undertake what was evolving into an exciting new service paradigm. Isabelle was an open book, transparent in all ways, and always focused on working in partnership to accomplish what needed to be done to get the clinic ready.

Since the facility was now close to being finished, they still needed to flesh out the operational guidelines and identify its philosophical underpinnings. The challenge was to clarify how they could instil compassion into the fabric of the clinic. The Community Services Society's operational guidelines clearly outlined the importance of compassion. They wanted it to be a secular, yet foundational, value of the clinic.

To address this unique and intangible task, they engaged in daily dialogues using an expanding question to question format. Starting each session, they presented a question concerning how compassion would be presented. Instead of responding to this question with an opinion, it would be followed-up with another question in a back-and-forth manner between them. This process would unfold with the intention that the answers to their questions would emerge as a collective understanding. They both agreed that, given the esoteric nature of compassion, getting a grasp on how to make it a natural cornerstone for the clinic would indeed be challenging.

Mason recalled starting the questioning by asking, "If compassion is not definable as an idea or a concept, then how do we know we are being compassionate?" Isabelle followed with, "Does compassion show up when we are free from a busy mind?"

From one session to the next, a growing sense of clarity surfaced where they both felt in tune with one another, especially as they were able to resist trying to define compassion.

Mason recalled and shared with Isabelle what he understood about compassion from his Buddhist experiences. Compassion, from this perspective, could best be understood for what it was not. In this oblique way, compassion could be known to be a state of presence that was not past-based or future-focused. One would therefore find its roots firmly planted in the present moment. Compassion rested in the space between the past and the future, therefore it could not be known directly.

Mason followed by asking Isabelle, "If compassion cannot be known, why are we trying to describe or circumscribe it? Are we just playing with words?"

Isabelle responded, "Are you wanting it to mean something? Or is it important for us to simply recognize the thoughts we have about it? And to simply be aware that our thoughts cannot know compassion, cannot measure it or mould it into a recipe? And if we can do that, can we totally and completely end our search for its meaning?"

Mason replied, "When we speak of naked awareness or oneness, which is also not describable, are these just other ways of trying to get a sense of what compassion is? Are they all one and the same?"

"They could well be. I just don't know," she replied. "I remember a quote written by Rumi, the Persian poet, which I took the liberty to personalize: 'Out there, beyond ideas of right and wrong, there is a field. Will I meet you there?' Could this field be naked awareness or the field of compassion? Is it dimensionless? Is this where transformative healing can take place? If so, could our purpose be to simply connect with people who are suffering and join with them, supporting their inherent capacity to self-heal?"

Mason replied, "It seems to me that compassion has its own intelligence beyond that of our minds. Your Rumi quote reminds me of a quote on compassion by Chuang-Tzu, a fourth-century Chinese philosopher, I came across during one of my readings a few years back. He said, 'Compassion arises when one uses their mind as a mirror; grasping nothing; refusing nothing, yet receiving everything without keeping anything.' Can we best serve others in need by being an alert witness without an agenda, simply there to share our energy and wisdom as best we can?"

Isabelle responded, "For me, daily meditation gets me out of my head. When I am able to be clear-minded, it frees me up to be present, alert, but also tranquil. My role or identity as a social worker gets muted to the point that it does not seem to override the importance of staying focused and connected to the needs of others. I wonder what it is like for you as a psychologist and how important that is to you?"

Mason commented "I am pleased that you asked. For quite some time now, I have been quite clear that calling myself a clinical psychologist does not always allow me the freedom to move beyond the role or title. I do not want it to be my primary character any more than it has been. At best, it is a time-limited character pattern. In fact, being a psychologist, a trauma expert, a half-breed, a hypnotherapist, a professor, a meditator, or an apprentice healer—they are all just identifiers or labels. They are useful but superficial and quite limiting. This is evident to me also with mental health labels, which I know we want to avoid using at the clinic.

"These labels have compartmentalized me, and altogether, they do not add up to truly represent who I am. In fact, the identities that underpin these labels oftentimes compete with one another for centre stage. I have allowed them to feed my ego's need to be significant, yet they are never satisfying except for brief moments. They have been detours, redirecting my energy into superficial achievements.

"Letting go of the titles or character labels I have used to describe myself is now called for. For me, this is required if I am to move beyond my accumulated knowledge base and have a transformative impact on both myself and others. On the other hand, I need to be careful not to condemn myself for having been attached to them.

"If we can move away from my identity issues for a moment, let's look at the other foundational principles we have committed to weave into the fabric of the clinic. Can we address what we mean by self-healing and transformation? How do we imagine they can be achieved at the clinic? Shall we start with self-healing before tackling transformation? What is your understanding of how self-healing can be optimized at the clinic?"

Isabelle responded, "From my experience at the shelter, women who are suffering want to tell their story or stories, and of course it is important for them to be heard. More important, though, is for them to *hear* their own story for what it *is* and what the story is *doing* to them. When they tell their story without us adding to it, the pain and suffering they are experiencing subsides. What we have to be careful of is not encouraging them to tell their story over and over again, as this can also cause us to relive that pain and suffering and even make it feel it is worse than it is.

"Can we assist clients in telling their story with the intent to end their story, to finish it so that it no longer has to be told again? That is my primary overriding question. What is in the way of ending or completing their story? We can surmise that they want to be more than the story, to get beyond it. But more often they get trapped in the story. Then they want something or someone to help them escape from the trap they are in."

Mason added. "That I can and do resonate with. On another front, does self-healing get activated when we explore our own understanding of what suffering means to us without judging ourselves? Most people find it difficult to self-explore. I imagine they think that self-exploration exposes them and makes them feel vulnerable and inadequate. They may think, erroneously, that it is self-examination—a dissecting process where they critically analyze themselves. Can we encourage them to experience self-exploration? Can they do this without self-judgement? Can we challenge them to replace constipation with curiosity? Not to fix themselves, but to understand the root cause of their suffering. Can we provide an atmosphere at the clinic that offers clients the opportunity to move beyond their story? Can we assist them end their crises on their own terms?"

Isabelle responded, "When I reflect on self-healing, it is what we are doing all the time, as it is nature's gift. Unfortunately, it gets inhibited when we lose our connection with our true nature and become caught up in our fears of being a victim of life. Our meaning and purpose in life get clouded. We then look for answers to our healing needs from outside of ourselves and seek quick fixes."

She went on to say "I am reminded of Victor Frankl, the holocaust survivor and author of *In Search of Meaning*. He was able to find meaning in his horrifying prison camp experience, which allowed him to stay alert and find a way to move beyond despair and hopelessness. Everyone has meaning as do their experiences. We are there to support them as they use their meaningfulness to find their own way out of their crises."

This hit home for Mason, as it brought to mind his own experience of early childhood abandonment and how he lost perspective and meaning in his life. He recalled appreciatively how Arnold had jolted him out of his despondency, awakening him to find meaning in his life.

"Thanks, Isabelle, for bringing this to my attention. The search for meaning has been a preoccupation for me in my own personal development as well. Also, when I think about the work I have done with others in crisis over the years, finding meaning in a crisis has always been key to any resolution.

"I am curious now about how transformation plays out in one's search for meaning? Does transformation occur when one awakens to their capacity to take their story in the present moment, not tomorrow, and alters it so that it takes on a different form? Can this new form free one to explore with the awareness that they are not just their story or collection of stories?"

Isabelle replied, "For me, transformation is not an idea—it is an action without thought interfering. It cannot be a goal or ultimate end, as transformation is timeless. Suffering gets transformed when we let go of the form of our suffering, face our discontent head on, and accept it for what it is. By letting go, surrendering, we get a glimpse of the falsity in our existence. Fear of surviving, our grasping for acceptance, our endless antagonisms, and our addiction to beliefs bind us to suffering. When we know the false to be the false without trying to fix it, awareness shows up and transformation occurs. Transformation is unbounded energy in action."

Mason added, "Conceptually, I get what you are saying. But looking at it critically from my experience working in many different treatment venues over the years, I am not sure transformation is a concept that can be easily achieved by those in crises. Are we being too esoteric? All the sages, mystics, religious icons, philosophers, and self-acknowledged healers over the centuries have apparently not made transformation any easier to accomplish. Is it possible that human beings may want to transform but generally don't trust the unknown aspects that it could manifest?"

Isabelle responded, "As far as I am aware, transformation can be contagious. Is it possible when one transforms one's experience with suffering, the focus is no longer inward on suffering; it is outward on healing? Is it like a ripple a stone makes in a pond that can amplify our capacity to broaden our range of healing? Can it also embrace others in relationship ways to achieve the same?"

Mason replied, "I think I get some of which you might be suggesting at least the inward part. When I reflect on my relationship with suffering, I am aware that, at times, I indulge in my suffering, ruminate about it, and become resistant to letting it go. Sometimes when I realize what I am doing, I start condemning myself, which just produces more unnecessary suffering. When I just notice doing this without making it wrong, the suffering subsides, and I begin to move away from it. Being at arms-length from my suffering allowing me to see how suffering can be a catalyst for me to learn how to be in tune with my own self-healing capabilities."

Isabelle added, "On a cautionary note, will it be important for us to be mindful that the client may only want a quick fix to their crises, practically and not psychologically? They may even not want to end their crisis completely, as it may have both conscious and unconscious value for them to maintain it."

Responding, Mason said, "If they are not seeking transformation, but only temporary relief, do we need to just respect where they are and not confuse them with the complexity that transformation could present to them? It also can be a problem if they think their mind is their enemy rather than a resource. Our efforts to explore the workings of their mind, however simple, could create more resistance to self-explore rather than less."

Stepping back from their intense dialogue for a moment, they both agreed that their ideas and thoughts were being threaded together in ways that offered a beginning platform to build on. The felt sense was that they were both on the same page but there was much more to process.

It was obvious to them both that clarifying these concepts and understandings would continue to be a challenge that would need to unfold over many more such conversations. Beyond dialogue, the crucible of day-to-day service delivery would allow them to refine and operationalize these concepts.

As they got underway, the initial results were very promising. Besides client feedback, which was remarkably supportive, they both became more aware of how their relationship alchemy would be what would make the difference at the clinic. Both committed to practicing their own unique ways of meditative self-exploration as a natural daily experience. They reminded themselves to be mindful and not make meditation an ordeal, but rather a simple way to allow calmness and self-acceptance to be a grounding experience.

Chapter Twenty-One

⊰⊱ Fine Tuning ⊰⊱

MASON WAS IMPRESSED BY how Isabelle was naturally at ease with clients. She exuded confidence without any hint of being self-absorbed. She was never in a hurry, yet never kept anyone waiting. Time was not a problem for her. She radiated openness and acceptance of others; she had a refreshing curiosity and an intense desire to ensure that everyone lived their lives fully without hesitation. She had a fluidness about her that was gracefully laced with an attitude of gratitude for just being available and able to contribute to others. Compassion, as he now understood it, seemed to flow from her effortlessly.

Experiencing Isabelle in these ways had a powerful impact on him as it encouraged him to explore who he was, both to himself and others. *How remarkable,* he thought. How was she able to do this without apparent effort? Or, perhaps more accurately, he should ask himself why it was more of a challenge for him to do so. Had his journey of being a psychologist over the years obscured him in ways that he was still not clear about? Why did he have to work at being compassionate as if it were a skill to be learned and not an attribute to be naturally expressed?

On a more pleasing note, the more he engaged in single sessions at the clinic, the more at ease he felt. His identification as a psychologist had almost completely melted into the background, and a sense of simple awareness prevailed. This awareness seemed to flow, as there was no pressing need to figure out what to do or how to intervene. He sensed that he was more connected to the clients and the suffering they were experiencing, while at the same time not a co-sufferer. Increasingly, he experienced being a witness, observing, inquiring, questioning in ways that were more transparent and freeing. In a way difficult to describe, the sense of caring *with* the client in contrast to caring *for* them prevailed as they revealed their vulnerabilities and sought ways to discover their strengths.

Additionally, he discovered that, from time to time, he imagined that he could fashion a raft with the client and be of service to ferry them across the river of suffering. He took care not to make the raft or strategy more important than the journey—something he noted he had not fully done for himself.

Being more aware of his own self-healing needs through weekly meditation and dialogue sessions with Isabelle allowed him to see much more clearly how his own issues in life were interfering with being clear-minded and fully available to be of service to others. The power in being present was exciting and, at the same time, humbling to experience.

Now, he was discovering that the suffering of others, no matter how minor, had deeper meaning that warranted unconditional acknowledgement. When they experienced unconditional acceptance from him, their confidence to take action for themselves seemed to increase. At times, it was almost magical to watch them using their untapped resources to address their own healing needs.

This transformation in his service experience was refreshing and revitalizing. He now experienced that his service to others was more synergistically impactful than at any other time in his professional career. Mason was clear that he need not be defensive or regretful about how he had served others in the past. It was not that what he had done was not valued and useful. Simply, it had not been useful or impactful enough.

If compassion was the doorway to transcending human suffering, of which he was more and more convinced, meditation on compassion could open the doorway for compassion to become activated. He decided to revisit compassion from a Buddhist perspective.

In this review experience, he was reminded that compassion could be facilitated by a number of practices besides meditating on it. One such practise was to pattern one's behaviour after someone who was known to be transparently compassionate towards others like he felt Isabelle was.

Buddhism also suggested practise in taking on other people's suffering as if it were one's own. It even suggested that one should exchange oneself for another. It was like being in the other person's shoes and having their problems.

Mason could not find a way to experience being in the other person's shoes. It was difficult to get his rational mind to understand that if the ego was the source of suffering and the ego was an illusion, then suffering, by default, also was an illusion. There was no clear way that he could find to accept taking on the suffering of others if it were truly an illusion.

Mason took relief from this entanglement by connecting compassion with being a witness. Not a witness on the sidelines, but a witness that was truly there, fully without an agenda—not even an agenda to show compassion.

Actually, compassion did not need an agenda. It simply existed when we got out of the way of having to make it happen. When he let go of needing to be compassionate, it showed up as Mother Teresa had suggested. No mind games were necessary.

Six months into the clinic's operations, Mason and Isabelle decided that it would be an opportune time to review some of their notable findings from clients presenting at the clinic. By far, clients' most mentioned concern was the issue of depression. What they were depressed about was all over the human suffering map. There were many faces to their grief, all related in some form or another to breakdown in the domain of relationships. Loss of power was pronounced and wide-ranging.

The domain of relationship loss included areas such as loss of physical integrity due to injury or illness, loss of family relationship integrity, loss morality, and loss of social or cultural acceptance, loss of meaningful employment, loss of mental acuity, and loss of self-acceptance.

Most often, clients presented as victims of their life circumstances, and they were feeling stressed, trapped, confused, and wanting relief from feeling down and deflated. They wanted their relationship problems to go away and very little they had done up to the point of attending the clinic, including past counselling efforts, had made much of a difference. These clients had almost always tried many medications, which had minimal effect. Both Mason and Isabelle chose to attend to their concerns not through the lens of depression, but rather as a human condition perpetrated by clients struggling with a limiting mindset that was not user-friendly, resulting in a stuck state of being. This "stuckness" was almost always accompanied by a deflated sense of self-worth and a lack of confidence in being able to do anything about their struggles.

This was enormously challenging for Mason and Isabelle, as most often the clients were very sensitive to any form of self-exploration. Most wanted temporary relief, not convinced that anything could really fix their situation.

They felt their primary challenge was to "unmask" their clients and encourage them to let go of what they were holding on to and come out of their mental caves. The goal was to assist them in becoming aware that depression was primarily related to their beliefs about their experiences and their sense of impotence. Unmasking—if it could be accomplished—needed to be done very delicately without any hint of judgement.

Compassion was critically important. Quite often, when the client was invited to tell their story, they would hear them say no one understands their situation. Understanding needed to be a gateway for relief, and it needed to be self-understanding first and foremost. Some clients would courageously rise to the occasion, experiencing self-understanding as worthy of exploring. In these circumstances, the single sessions tended to be very focused on promoting self-understanding with the aim of achieving self-awareness.

Many clients, however, did not want to seek self-understanding, so unmasking was not a possibility. In these situations, the clients were encouraged to engage in self-healing energy raising activities that would allow them to better address their relationship struggles.

So, in retrospect, they both felt that depression or "stuckness" could be modestly but meaningfully addressed in a single session. When the session was compassion-based and self-knowledge focused, transformative outcomes with relationship issues seemed possible. Whenever the sessions drifted into exploring coping strategies, the outcomes were marginally valuable, if at all.

Besides depression, there were many other issues that could easily be labeled if they were inclined to do so. Both agreed, though, that relationship breakdown for almost all clients was the underlying core issue, whether it was with the self, others, or with anything meaningful in one's life.

Isabelle shared with Mason, "When I do not label someone, I am drawn to connect with them as they are. My interaction with them becomes curiosity-based rather than assessment of need based. What almost always unfolds is the client moves away from their problem far enough to become curious about what resources they may have overlooked both externally and internally. I do my best to be a clarifier for them as they increasingly become confident that they can move beyond their issues."

Mason responded, "This suggests to me that mental health diagnoses and focusing on the past might be meaningful but not essential. To label someone as mentally ill indulges the expert's view that mental wellness is taken to be the absence of mental illness. The diagnosing of mental illness does not mean we know what mental wellness is. What troubles me deeply is how labeling someone with a mental disease can lead to them being more imbalanced and discredited as a human being. Imprinting human beings with labels—besides being degrading—is morally wrong."

Over the years of searching for meaning in human suffering, on many occasions I have reminded myself of what my mother said to me when I was bullied and labeled by other kids as a 'stupid Indian.' She said to me, 'Bad things happen to good people. It's not your fault.' I can understand and accept that natural disasters can wreak havoc on our existence and that is just nature's way. I can even accept that accidents or illnesses happen that can be fatal to us due to no fault of our own. What seriously troubles me, though, is when bad things happen *to others by others* with an intention to do harm. I have looked at this phenomenon from my forensic work over the years, only to reach the conclusion some people become addicted or predisposed to being evil. 'But what is evil?' I ask myself. Conceptually, it can be so broad banded and extremely difficult to reach agreement on with others. One person's evil can be another person's good. For me evil is best characterized as ignorance of the true nature of being human.

This brings to my attention how immorality has been historically intractable in the human domain. Is evil only the absence of good, given what we know to be true about the human condition and our character development? Encounters with those who seek power by aggressive control of others have been incredibly disconcerting to me. I see evildoers wearing masks that disconnect them from the humanity of others and even themselves. It's difficult to accept that the evil of others can be justified on the basis of their privileged position, their addiction to deception, or their self-aggrandizing beliefs. To unmask them, I have discovered, cannot be accomplished by showing them alternative realities. They simply are not interested.

My intentions when encountering the impact of evil actions perpetrated on others is to assist them minimize their suffering and find ways to erase the indelible impact it has had on them. Even then, I know this not to be enough."

Isabelle responded, "Evil from my view is the Dark side of God. When we gravitate to living in our shadow, we lose our ability to be enlightened. We have much more to clarify about this and I am sure we will do so over time."

Mason and Isabelle continued their dialogue, noting that they needed to be very careful not to highlight concepts they had considered in the past to be too idealistic. They did not want to mislead themselves or others that the clinic could achieve magical results.

Transformation was one transpersonal buzzword that they were already clear on. Another was *self-actualization*. Both agreed that self-actualization was nothing more than to reside in the power of the moment. It was a fancy word for self-awareness.

Enlightenment was yet another concept that did not fit for the clinic in terms of outcomes. While *enlightenment* was considered invaluable as an aspiration it existed in a domain well beyond the clientele they served.

After this intensive dialogue, they both agreed it was time to step back and give this experience time to be integrated into their unfolding philosophy of the clinic. They felt confident they had made good progress towards being clear with one another and they were excited about moving forward.

Chapter Twenty-Two

⟡ Sun Setting the Apprentice Healer ⟡

Mason's relationship with Isabelle blossomed over their first year working at the clinic together. They found themselves ending their challenging days by taking long walks along the ocean trails near Mason's cabin. After debriefing the day's experiences, they would often walk side by side in silence, just absorbing the aliveness of the natural surroundings.

Several weeks into making this their routine, on one of their walks Mason was taken off guard as he felt Isabelle's hand slip into his. At first he had the urge to pull back but, unlike what he might have done in the past, he found himself accepting this act of intimacy. Within a few minutes, he surprisingly became quite comfortable with it. Thereafter it became a practice for them to hold hands on their walks, which he quite looked forward to doing.

Feeling the growing urge welling up inside to be even more intimate with Isabelle, on one of their walks Mason got courageous enough to ask her back to his cabin to stay the night. She accepted with a warm smile and a hug. Very soon this became a regular experience. All his inhibitions seemed to melt away the more time they spent together. It felt like his way of being was transformed by the power of their growing connectedness. Mason's relationship with Isabelle was so natural and free flowing that he felt confident he could open himself up to her and reveal his innermost thoughts. Her wisdom was simple yet powerful. Her caring curiosity drew him closer and closer to her.

The desire to more fully share his apprentice healer story surfaced as he felt, without any hesitancy, she would be a mirror for him. The opportunity occurred when they both were having dinner together at his cabin and talking about how their experiences in life had impacted their career paths. Mason asked Isabelle if she would consider being a sounding board for him, as he felt that he was approaching an end point in his long, challenging journey as an apprentice healer. Isabelle announced her pleasure in being asked, stating she would be delighted to assist him gain clarity about his journey if she could.

So, he began. "I sense that I am at a tipping point. I have come full circle. In my developmental years, my operating foundation was constructed on a platform of scarcity and doubt about my abilities and overall self-worth. Being part native has been confusing and difficult to make sense of. It has imprinted in me—from the very beginning—that I was less than others. I learned to escape from the felt sense of inadequacy and doubt about my capacity by choosing to isolate myself, to live in my own bubble, and only participate with others on my own terms. In this way, I discovered that I could get by without being noticed or being the subject of criticism from others.

I also discovered that I could trade loneliness for aloneness. Being alone became a sanctuary, certainly not an oasis. Fear drove me. Although I denied it, I was afraid of becoming that 'dirty, stupid half-breed' that school bullies labelled me as so many years ago. I was fearful that I would end up being an insignificant and unworthy nobody. Even today, this aloneness still overshadows who I am.

During my earlier years, I learned to be friends with nature and hone my observation skills. I avoided or side-tracked my inner sense of unease by studying the problems others were having in life. This led me to becoming more and more curious about human suffering. That spurred me on a pathway of seeking to become a healer. I saw the road ahead as a healing apprenticeship. I then did what I thought was best: to travel what was revealed to me by Indigenous Elders many decades ago as the Four-Fold Pathway."

"This is very intriguing. Tell me more." Isabelle asked.

"Before becoming a psychologist, my original focus was on interacting with nature as an ally, keeping my senses tuned into the rhythm of healing. Elders told me that this was the Pathway of the Peaceful Warrior. I did my best to honour the extraordinary power of nature, recognizing that nature was in charge. In the beginning, I was an amateur warrior. I was driven to find out as much as I could about how humans interfaced with nature. I did whatever I could to challenge myself to be in in step with nature through my wilderness experiences as an outward-bound counsellor. On countless occasions, I was reminded of how powerful and continuously transforming nature was, and how just being in rhythm with nature was all that was necessary to allow healing to unfold. Nature revealed itself as the ground of goodness to me.

As my experience matured, I became more a part of nature and not separate from it. I developed a felt sense of being privileged to be one with nature, even if only for brief moments. It was not like I, along with other travellers, was in nature; nature was within us. The interconnectedness of everything became apparent in an evolving, yet timeless manner. The peaceful part of the Peaceful Warrior pathway revealed itself to me, and I no longer viewed the outward-bound experience as a challenge of human against nature."

Isabelle responded, "I have observed this firsthand and I can clearly see how connected you are to nature and how this has grounded you."

Mason replied, "Thanks for noticing, Isabelle. It is reassuring to know that the impact of nature has not been completely overshadowed by the pathway I took next. With nature as my foundation, I began my second leg of the Four-Fold Pathway by learning about healing in as many ways as I could. I took a deep dive into learning about healing—biologically, socially, mentally, and spiritually—even though I doubted that I could ever become a full-fledged healer. Learning became all-consuming. Knowledge became an addiction. I could never quite get enough of it. Yet, this journey was bottomless and never completely satisfying, leaving me hungry for more.

Unfortunately, this addictive focus on learning moved me away from nature and toward being more information-focused. I was unrelenting in my search to find new ways to use knowledge to heal.

On many occasions, I had the opportunity to gain self-awareness and self-understanding. However, this was not a primary focus for me. Becoming qualified as a psychologist was the driving force in my life. When I actually achieved this qualification, it felt surreal, as deep down I did not believe that it was possible or appropriate for me."

Isabelle asked, "How was it that you doubted your capability when the results of your efforts suggested otherwise? Is this what psychologists refer to as cognitive dissonance? Were you struggling with two conflicting viewpoints about yourself?"

Mason replied. "Yes, I believe so. Despite my knowing this, it was almost as if I wanted my self-doubt to be a security blanket that would protect me from my fear of failure. I know how ridiculous this sounds, yet the monkey of self-doubt prevailed and, in some ways, still hangs around me today."

Mason went on, "Following this milestone, my next steps on my apprentice healing journey—and one that continues to this day—was to learn through practicing; the third path of the Four-Fold Pathway."

Isabelle responded, "Did you see yourself as an apprentice healer in action? What drove you to focus on trauma and crisis intervention?"

Mason replied, "When I was in the care of Social Services as a youth, I had an extraordinary experience with an aboriginal child psychologist named Arnold. He quoted an ancient Chinese proverb back then that has guided me ever since. What he said was, 'A crisis was an opportunity riding on a dangerous wind.' When I ended my contact with him, he gave me a small wooden brass plaque with those words stamped in the brass. Ever since then, those words have driven me to look for those opportunities that were not easily seen under very challenging mental health circumstances. Doing this, I felt I could play a role in reducing needless suffering in the lives of others."

"How has this worked for you?" Isabelle asked.

"It has so far been an incredible journey, though it hasn't been seamless. It has been extraordinary, in the sense that in a privileged way, it has allowed me to probe into the healing needs of others. On the downside, this journey of being a practicing healer has led me to the conclusion that suffering is largely a human driven phenomenon."

"Yes, I agree. That appears to be the case." Isabelle replied, "As creatures of habit; we have given in to allowing our conditioned, fear-based mind to run us. Fear of loss keeps us on a never-ending journey of grasping for more and craving after certainty in an uncertain, ever-changing world. It's as if we are stuck thinking that our identity or identities are all important, and the quality of our lives is based on who we think we are and not who we really are."

"I couldn't agree more," Mason responded. "When I examine my past even further, it is evident that I have carved out a journey developing numerous identities or selves, all in search of seeking significance and self-acceptance. I have sought to be a masterful crisis intervener, a person of knowledge, an outdoorsman, an amateur athlete, a healer, a psychologist, a leader, an adventurer, and a meditator, not to mention a self- doubter and a sceptic.

"All of these roles, and perhaps others I am not fully aware of, have carved up my life into compartments each compartment seeking acknowledgement, and with none actually being completely fulfilled. It has been very frustrating at times, not knowing how to satisfy these characters or roles craving for my attention.

In a nutshell, my life has mostly been a struggle trying to become a 'somebody,' most notably seeking to become a masterful healer. I have been driven by the desire to acquire credibility in the eyes of others, all the while minimizing my own view of self-acceptance. It may be that, from time to time, I have lived in other people's shadows as a voyeur, seeking to understand how the suffering of others applied to my life."

Isabelle added, "I don't get a picture of you struggling. I get a picture of you probing, being a deep thinker, and challenging the world you live in."

"For sure that is the case now," Mason responded. "Gradually over the last decade, I have become more aware of my origins and the impact that my experiences and accumulated knowledge have had on my character development. My intent has been to understand the tapestry of my past, not as a blueprint but rather a launching platform to move forward on.

I now do no longer want to travel the path of learning how to be a better healer with the aim of making a better world. It is time for me to sunset this way of being and to allow self-awareness and self-understanding to be my primary focus, along with an intention to be contributory to others."

Isabelle interjected, "From what you are sharing, it sounds as if you have come to the end of the road of being seen or known as a practicing healer, or psychologist, and maybe some of the other identities you have adopted over the years. The image of wearing masks comes to mind for me. Do you want to be 'mask less,' without having to be run by one of your identities? Do you want to eliminate them or just not let them run you anymore?"

Replying, Mason said, "I don't think it is possible to be 'mask less.' Not wearing a mask is just another mask. What I am seeking is to not be attached to my masks. As you put it, I don't want them to run me. It is okay for me that these selves I have adopted over the years visit me for a while from time to time. But I do not want them to dominate my existence. I know they mask my true nature; they are not to be totally discounted, as that would be discounting aspects of who I am.

What excites me now is the sense of being freer to choose and to not get caught up in taking my various selves or characters so personally. I am also excited, in a more esoteric way, that I will now have a more transparent way to use my masks. I can see myself using them to plumb the depths of my ordinary mind in search of a connection with what some consider being a more universal mind."

Isabelle added, "It is quite revealing to me how you feel about masks. The masks I wear are challenging for me as well. I know I predominantly wear the mask of being the 'rescuer.' This ingrained character pattern always wants to help others, sometimes even when they don't want help. It seems, rather ironically, that I can't help myself doing this. When I do catch myself rescuing when it is unnecessary and step back, I get drawn to put on another mask, which I really don't like. I become a rebel who wants to get people to challenge the wrongs in their world like I do when I rebel against rigid authority."

Mason replied, "I too wear the rebel mask. In an overall sense when I am engaged in one of my character patterns such as being a rebel it feels incomplete and lacking in integrity. On a sombre note, it is my view that our attachments, roles, and cherished beliefs, which get profiled as masks, are the root cause of suffering."

"That I agree with," Isabelle replied. "Can it be that all of humanity is limited in its ability to escape wearing masks? Are we all just trading one mask for another caught in the web of self-deception? More interesting to me is do we use our masks unwittingly, resulting in them suffocating our aliveness? Can it be that our true nature and natural intelligence lie dormant as we give priority to our character patterns? Our addiction to our attachments and our focus on disease undermines our well-being. In today's human world it is abundantly evident we are on a path to our own self-destruction. Humanity is on a suicide course, although almost everyone lives in denial of it, being deluded into thinking science will save us as we go about wearing our masks and continuing to make the assumption tomorrow will take care of the ills of today."

Mason replied, "As you point out, I agree that our addictions, our cravings, our attachments are what craft our masks. These then become the masks of insanity. Masks do not honour who we are. They diminish our lightness of being, making us heavy with thought and fearful that we might lose and become a victim of the very world we are creating."

With that comment, they both sat back and remained silent for several minutes. Then Isabelle continued, "Mason, I find your journey to be fascinating and enlightening. It also leaves me with the impression that you have come full circle. Now, it seems evident that you are merging your inner journey with your outer journey, seeking for them to become one. I also get from what you have shared that you have come to terms with your historical conditioning and that both doubt and inadequacy have been revealed to be illusionary. It now seems that you recognize them for what they are. I can't help wondering, though, whether you will choose to use this freedom from the tyranny of your 'selves' or identities in a way that will allow you to lighten up, to be free, to transform your aliveness—naturally, creatively, and maybe even magically."

Mason responded, "Yes, letting go and unmasking is unfolding for me. The transformation that I feel is about to happen can only be imagined at this point."

Isabelle commented, "I also find it remarkable how adventurous you have been! Your openness is refreshing, and it is encouraging me to move beyond my own identity comfort zones."

"Thanks for the acknowledgement, Isabelle. If I may, let me continue by sharing what I know about the Fourth Pathway. The Pathway of the Visionary Warrior, sometimes referred to as the Sacred Warrior, was originally mentioned to me by Elders. They mentioned that it exists in another dimension beyond human consciousness—perhaps the 4th dimension, if you will.

"It is a mysterious pathway, and it is unclear what transformation it takes to travel it. Perhaps it is really an oxymoron to think that there is a real pathway. Some Buddhists say that this pathway is really the pathless domain of primordial or naked awareness. To seek it is to not find it. It is a state of pure, unadulterated awareness."

Isabelle commented, "Mason, it also has been my sense that there are other dimensions that humans have not encountered. To discover or uncover this or other dimensions is quite a challenge. I personally resonate with the notion that natural, unadorned awareness can allow one to connect with the realm of universal intelligence. It is the doorway opening us to the potential of exercising our natural creativity."

"This resonates with me also," Mason replied. "I have, on occasion, experienced glimpses of naked awareness through meditating on having an empty mind and being one with everything. Also, on rare occasions, visionary blips of energy have surfaced, only to quickly vanish when I have tried to make sense out of them. So, as I have been told, the Visionary Warrior's Pathway unfolds when you are not looking for it. Thus, my primary question is: how can I release the genie from the bottle?"

Isabelle responded, "Outside of the occasional insights that you have had on the Visionary Pathway, what do you know about this genie, or Visionary Warrior as you call him?"

Mason replied, "Shared to me by Elders, the Visionary Warrior does not entertain distractions or indulge in the material, self-grasping world. He or she has no need for props of any kind. Additionally, respect of everyone and everything becomes the ground they walk on. Ideologies are of interest but do not corral his or her attention. The Visionary Warrior avoids self-deception and being thrown off balance by engaging in the discipline of daily meditation.

"Meditation allows the Warrior to take his or her seat in the warrior's world, thereby rebalancing when the inevitability of life's circumstances generates imbalances. This is what returns the Warrior to Mother Earth to be grounded, and it frees Father Sky to open up visions of freedom and possibility.

Perception wise, the Visionary Warrior is wary of thoughts that show up and distract his or her purpose. There is no attraction or need to practise a discipline or a visionary technique in order to become better at being a Warrior. The Warrior trusts in the phenomenal world, which is a rich reservoir of resources. These resources are available to be tapped into as naturally occurring. When acting out of a selfless intention to contribute to the well-being of others and the planet that we all live on, resources automatically show up.

The Visionary Warrior knows that there is no perfect discipline, just perfect action. The Visionary Warrior knows that visions run through them but do not originate from within. In other words, they are not visionary; they simply are a conduit for visions to manifest."

"What a fascinating overview, Mason! What is the Visionary Warrior's core purpose? How does this Warrior have anything to do with healing?"

"The Visionary Warrior, as I understand him or her to be, draws on the vastness of healing into evolving visions. Magic then shows up, spirit flows, and healing unfolds. It is not a supernatural magic; rather, it is a natural flowing magic that exudes the wisdom and elegance of all that is living. The wisdom of the visionary warrior and the wisdom of nature merge as one, promoting optimal healing pathways. The Visionary Warrior is healing personified.

"The fundamental vastness of the healing domain is not experienced in a single perception or vision. Thus, the visions are explications or windows of perception revealing ever-flowing interwoven patterns that magically reveal healing as simply spirit engaging its own natural expression. Healing for the Warrior cannot be grasped; rather, it can only be acknowledged as existing within the field of its own magic.

Healing, as suggested, is really magical, as it happens beyond our ability to comprehend. Healing cannot be mastered, as we are not meant to be masters of healing; it occurs deep within the core of nature. Its non-local attributes are powerful beyond imagination. It is the natural order of existence itself. It ebbs and flows, depending on our alignment with it. Much as the sun gives off light and promotes healing, it does so naturally, without emotion. The energy of our daily life is the source of our magic. More often than not, however, it succumbs to humankind's collective consciousness, which rigidifies our awareness to perceive life as an ordeal, from birth to illness to death, and repeated again and again as we become encapsulated on the wheel of endless suffering."

Isabelle commented, "So, Mason, what you seem to be alluding to is that we all have the capacity to be a Visionary Warrior if we let go of trying to become one. Letting go of our attachment to being a healer may, paradoxically, promote our potency and allow us to be much more an integral part of healing. Is this what you are getting at when you say that it is now necessary for you to let go of your attachment to being a psychologist, a trauma expert, a wisdom seeker, and an expert on human suffering? What is in the way for you to allow this to happen for yourself?"

"Yes, I am suggesting that is the possibility. What is in the way for me to move beyond my conditioning? Fear, scepticism, and doubt are what restrain me. This leads to many questions. Why is there fear in the first place? Why is the human being so riddled with fear? In all my exploration through analyzing, dissecting, partitioning experiences, and life itself, clarity has not been the outcome; I have just found continued obfuscation, confusion, and, of course, more fear.

"Can I observe my fear and the fear of others without analyzing? As a pioneering psychologist, I have examined the fears of others like branches on a tree, offering suggestions for alleviating fear. Getting at the root of fear; that was never my focus.

"Can I now simply observe my own fear without thought, completely without a mission to change or avoid it? Can I go into fear? I know fear to be very complex. I know that it involves time—yesterday and tomorrow. I remember from my beginnings how rejected, abandoned, and empty I felt. I have carried these feelings throughout my life, doing whatever I could to camouflage them, fearing that they would annihilate me. Inwardly, psychologically, I have ignored them, determined instead to learn about them as external effects on myself and others. More information and evidence was the focus, and this took more and more time."

Isabelle responded, "Mason, my head is spinning with all your deep probing questions. Sometimes I get the feeling you think too much, and it leaves me confused. Can you share with me how you plan to move forward now without being fearful?"

"As I have said, I have not rallied the courage to totally break free yet, although this is what I tell myself repeatedly to do. My thinking mind has a hundred reasons for staying stuck in my conditioned state of being. Though I like to think I can harness my resistance and face my fears head on."

Isabelle responded "Wow, what a lot to think about and digest! From what I know of you, Mason, courage—even fear—may not be your problem, unless you consider fear to be another word for doubt. In so many ways throughout your life, you have demonstrated ample amounts of courage, such that who you are today reflects your willingness to take risks and to not give up on yourself or others. However, as you have said in your own words, doubt is your enemy. Some have said that doubt is the enemy of the soul, which makes sense to me in your case. It is clear you doubt the existence of the Fourth Pathway; you doubt that you really can make a difference; you doubt that there is a soul, and you are even sceptical about your life having any meaning at all! In many ways, you still reside in your own homemade bubble or cocoon of doubt. If anything, doubt seems to be reconfigured as scepticism, as you tend to use your well-honed reasoning skills—both scientifically and personally—to remain aloof and independent. Perhaps in this way you avoid becoming vulnerable to criticism and rejection. My intuition tells me that you are very close to fully coming out from behind your shadow. I see your lightness of being surfacing all the time, especially when you are not seeking ways to transform yourself."

Mason completed their intense discussion by responding, "Isabelle, your willingness to listen to me speak aloud has been invaluable. Just sharing has given me an immense sense of relief from the stress of carrying these thoughts, which have constipated me to no end. I cannot be more appreciative for the opportunity you have given me to share today. It is clear to me that your clarifying comments have immeasurable value for me and perhaps for both of us moving forward in our relationship and our work together. I feel refreshed and ready to take the next steps, perhaps with you as a soul mate as you are willing."

Chapter Twenty-Three

✦ The Journey Ahead ✦

THE FOLLOWING DAY AFTER their intense dialogue, Mason jumped on his mountain bike and took a long ride out along the coast until he arrived at a bluff overlooking the ocean. Stopping, he sat down and reflected on the day's previous experience with Isabelle. He again felt immensely grateful for her feedback. She truly was a mirror for him. She saw right through his masks. Her tranquil, yet intensely curious ways were contagious. In innumerable ways, she was a kindred spirit, always promoting the best of him. At the end of their many meetings, he always felt an overall sense of being more whole and complete. He was privileged to be a partner at the clinic with her, and he was blessed to have her as an intimate friend. He could envision himself spending more quality time with her as they continued to find effective ways to serve others at the clinic.

Running in the backdrop of his mindscape was the urge to revisit her perspective on how self-doubt had played a significant part in his apprentice healer journey. Isabelle had been quite blunt—yet in a very caring way—in pointing out his habitual pattern of self-doubt, which he fully appreciated. Doubt had drawn him back into his past countless times. Living in the shadow of his potential had become his modus operandi. It was the way he protected himself from the unknowns in the world, at the expense of not being courageous and taking total responsibility for his aliveness moment to moment. In fact, he often used doubt as an excuse to not perform to his fullest capacity moment to moment, relying primarily on curiosity to push him forward.

In an interesting way, he was now aware that he had attempted to sideline self-doubt by continuously moving from one adventure to another. Essentially, he recognized that his pattern was to always be "on the road again." Experiencing the full impact of the end of anything was aborted or side-tracked by his movement on to the next adventure and then the next.

So, letting go was never a problem when it came to relationships, professional careers, philosophical beliefs, and a host of activities, such as running, writing, and personal growth. Ironically, he did not have to let go of what he was never fully attached to. Nonetheless, he felt he had a built in program to repeatedly and inexorably slip back into the envelope of doubt despite his adventurous nature.

Perhaps these two opposite patterns were actually interconnected. The more he "cycled" these two patterns, the less he had to address his underlying sense of inadequacy and insufficiency. Mason was fully aware that he held back on going all in on the journey to discover and fully participate in what he knew to be the magic of healing.

He also was acutely aware that his potential for being light-hearted had been shrouded by the seduction of taking life too seriously; by being consumed by incessant inner mental probing. The journey ahead, without being hinged to doubt, would be interesting.

It was transparent to Mason that he could not simply pursue the unknown. How could one find the unknown through the known? Was it even possible? Pursuit was not the way. The unknown showed up when we were not searching for it. Fear was always about the known—what we might lose. One really could not be fearful of the unknown, as it was not manifest. It had no form.

Again, he reminded himself, as so many along his path had mentioned, this would need to be an individual journey. No teachers, no gurus, no books required. There is no pathway that had been clearly delineated by others. If there was, many would be on it.

Also, recognizing that he had used psychology, philosophy, Buddhism, Taoism, and Indigenous teachings as stepping stones in his apprentice healer journey, it brought to question what resources he needed to move forward.

The pathways he had travelled so far were all well-crafted from his ordinary mind, and they were characterized by dimensions of time and space. Visionaries, on the other hand, were not personhoods, and they travelled outside of time and space. Intuitively, he sensed that this way of being would show up when he was ready and fully committed.

Consistent with this perspective, he was convinced that visions surfaced from the unconscious. They manifested out of the natural or primordial mind field that has incalculable intelligence.

Tell tales of this state occurred for him when his consciousness rested in that infinitesimal timeless space between thoughts. This was when a tranquil state of naked awareness presented itself albeit only very briefly and unpredictably. It was experienced as a meditative state. It was choice less awareness, unfettered, not driven by a desire or a goal to become more aware. In this state of grace, there existed the capacity to be sensitive and receptive to the intimations of the universal mind.

Deep down, he knew that life really was a challenge, not necessarily an ordeal to suffer or shrink away from. It was a gift that need not be analyzed as if it were a problem of immense proportions.

Mason decided that right now was the time to make a courageous leap of faith. To move beyond his current state of treading water between two dimensions—his conscious conditioned knowledge-based world and into the world of transformative healing— courage would now be his ally allowing him to act fearlessly, in overcoming his habitual need to be somebody, as there would be no selves or identities in charge. With no pressing identity running him, living moment to moment could now be fully experienced without being discoloured by doubt.

The masks he had worn throughout his life could now be cast aside as transparency would prevail. Trusting all of his senses as well as his intuition, they would now guide him forward accompanied by the intention to contribute and powered by the energy of compassion.

Daily meditation would be called upon to continue to burn away the layers of buried unconscious memories, any lingering prejudices, resentments unhealed wounds and fears freeing them to flow away down the river of life. He now would be open to the full spectrum of consciousness of which the conditioned mind would only be a very small part.

Now also there would be no need for an agenda, no goal to attain anything, no healing to be accomplished. He would be free to exercise thoughts without getting attached to them. He no longer would allow himself to be tortured by an information overload. Simple, profound, naked awareness would be all that was necessary. He was free to be one with healing and not an architect of healing.

As he gazed out at the ocean images started to flood his awareness in a magical way. At first, he imagined seeing himself exiting a cave and walking out into a forest blanketed by old-growth trees. The he saw himself holding an eagle feather as his mother did when he found her no longer alive. Exquisitely, everything around him seemed to be luminous. This energy field reminded him of seeing the luminescence of the Heritage Chief at the Sun Dance Ceremony on his father's reserve as he sat tall and stately on his horse overlooking him. It was embracing then as it was now.

It felt like he was in another dimension as he imagined walking along a path as it coursed through a meadow, arriving at a cliff overlooking the Straits of Juan De Fuca. At the cliff's edge, he descended a path that led to the beach below. He then saw himself striding along the water's edge, allowing the cool ocean water to lap at his feet. A profound sense of stillness and unimaginable peace flooded his being. He sensed intimately the interconnectedness of everything. No longer a "me "was there separated and distinct from everything else. He was now the "Observer being the Observed."

Wandering down the beach, he felt the wind as it blew salt spray across his face. The power and gentleness of nature was undeniable. Every cell in his body appeared to resonate with this power.

Catching his eye he stopped and picked up a shiny, burgundy oblong stone about the size of a large marble streaked with quartz-like veins. He opened the leather pouch hanging around his neck; the one that Annie Silvermoon had given him at his father's Reserve. He dropped it in intuitively sensing this stone would assist him facilitate ripples of healing in the ocean of human suffering. How empowering all this was!

His purpose was now crystal clear. There would be no more striving along an endless pathway. He had arrived home and now his journey ahead was to be a beacon for others shedding clues for them to discover their own unique transformation of spirit, body and mind.

Down at the end of the beach, Isabelle was perched on a rock outcropping. She turned her lightness of being toward him and waved. Nothing but reverence, gratefulness and a deep sense of connectedness flowed through him, sensing her presence as if they were one. The experience of oneness, with no masks, was truly transformational. Mason was now on the path less travelled. The "Observer" would be his guide.

About the Author

PHILIP PERRY has been a practising psychologist for four decades. He has explored psychology from an academic perspective, both in his doctoral studies and his subsequent work as a university professor. While working in private practices, his focus has been on suicide prevention and significant loss. He has been involved with developing and directing treatment centres for troubled youths and their families across Canada. He is a trauma specialist with First Nations residential treatment programs, and he has professional interests in forensic psychology and hypnotherapy.

Philip wrote Unmasking: A Journey of Awakening to examine the discipline-specific difficulties that face psychologists, particularly the tension between the professional pressure to improve oneself and the healer's call to attend to the needs of others. Perry has published one other book, Beyond Content: Uncommon Interventions with People in Crisis (1990).

In his spare time, Philip enjoys mountain biking, flying, marathon running, wilderness hiking, and daily mindfulness meditation. Philip and his spouse, Nancy, reside in Nanoose Bay, on Vancouver Island, B.C.

Printed in Canada